My Name Is Lucia

By

Susan M. Khalil

Copyright 2023 by Susan M. Khalil
Front Cover Illustrated by Stephen J. Mraz III
ll rights reserved. No part of this book may be reproduced, or transmitted in any form or by any means, electronic or mechanical, including photocopying, recording or by any information storage and retrieval system without written permission from the author.

Prologue

On October 13, 1884, Pope Leo XIII had a vision after holding mass in his private Vatican Chapel. As he stepped down from the altar, he was paralyzed by a vision that left him in awe. As his body came back under control, the few in his presence noted his face was ashen white. He staggered a few steps to gain his balance and immediately fled to his office. His vision was so powerful, so real, that he composed the St. Michael prayer in that instance. He knew what was coming, and instructed those faithful to recite it at every mass and to share it with those that would listen.

When one in that group dared asked what happened, he revealed his vision to them. In a weak voice, he recounted that he heard two distinct voices coming from the tabernacle, one kind and gentle and one guttural and harsh. Their conversation was as follows:

> The guttural voice, the voice of Satan in his pride, boasted to Our Lord:
> "I can destroy your Church."
>
> The gentle voice of Our Lord:
> "You can? Then go ahead and do so."
>
> Satan:
> "To do so, I need more time and more power."
>
> Our Lord:
> "How much time? How much power?"
>
> Satan:
> "75 to 100 years, and a greater power over those who will give themselves over to my service."
>
> Our Lord:
> "You have the time; you will have the power. Do with them what you will."

The 100 years is over.

Reference
UCatholic, The Terrifying Vision That Led Pope Leo XIII to Write the Saint Michael Prayer

Chapter I

    Lulu sat in a frayed and soiled dark green armchair with only the light from a small table lamp beside her. She waited patiently for the doorbell to ring. Her daughter promised she would come visit her tonight - one of many promises she had made to her in the past eight months. In her hands lay her Rosary as she said her nightly prayers. Some evenings, like tonight, it was hard for her to be kind and loving as Our Lord had preached, and instead her thoughts turned to the betrayal that led her to these dark and desperate times. Sitting alone in her chair, she relived it over again. Silent tears fell down her cheeks each time she thought about it; her stomach would churn painfully and her heart would ache terribly whenever those memories replayed in her mind.

    Lulu was a small woman in stature and presence. The lines on her face made her look older than her forty-nine years. You pass people like her walking down the street and they would not entertain a second glance. She had soft curly brown hair peppered with gray coarse strands. Her sad brown eyes and the darkened bags below them reflected the sorrow and defeat she had endured. Deep worry lines marred the flawless olive skin that used to shine in boundless love and happiness. Her lips had adapted a tight frown from several years of ugly dishonesty from those she thought loved her. All her clothes were second hand from Goodwill since that was all she could afford now, and fit just as well. The small pittance she was able to save went on little luxuries, like decent sneakers since she spent the day running around on her feet. She had worked at her job for a few years, yet, only a handful of people knew her name. She had lived in her apartment for over a year and kept mostly to herself. It was a rare moment when someone passed her by and acknowledged her with even a smile. Was it really only three years ago that her world had collapsed?

Lulu had married her high school sweetheart soon after he had graduated college with his pharmacy degree. They had rented a small apartment in the city and had established a comfortable schedule of meeting up after work at one of the local restaurants for dinner. He worked full time in a pharmacy several towns away and she worked as a receptionist in a nearby clinic. Even after graduation, he would study his journals and other pharmaceutical magazines late into the night. He could be so focused at times! She was happy then and he would often tell her that he would always take care of her. Shortly after the wedding, Lulu got pregnant and her son was born nine months later. The couple was overjoyed with the birth. Both of them were only children and had agreed that they wanted their child to have at least one sibling down the road. Lulu continued to work at the local clinic, but was able to structure her hours around the baby's needs. They bought a three-bedroom ranch out in the suburbs where they had both agreed was a good place to raise a family. She felt her husband was always busy working or in his home office behind a closed door. Even though the spark of attraction they first shared waned, Lulu still thought the marriage was going well.

Two years later, her daughter came into the world and Lulu could not have been happier. She had two babies that kept her very busy and the wonder of them filled her with contentment. Once her daughter was born, Lulu quit her job to stay home since daycare proved to be more than she was making at the time. This loss of income upset her husband but when Lulu showed him the numbers, he reluctantly acquiesced.

Lulu and her husband had a beautiful home and she was very active in her community. Even though her husband was always busy, she still felt that their family was a strong unit. He made good money or so Lulu surmised, but he discouraged any extravagant spending. Her husband handled all the finances and reprimanded her when she asked any questions about the money. In fact, when she started asking questions, he began locking up his ledger and the check book in his office. He even stopped the bank statements from coming to the house and sent them to a post office box. Lulu knew this because she found an envelope with the bank's logo on it in the car one day made out to her husband with a P.O. Box number for his address. Not wanting to make him angry, she kept her questions to herself. He was so mean to her when he was angry. He allocated Lulu a tight budget that she managed efficiently, spending money on the children rather than on herself.

Their annual vacations were limited to camping for two to three days or visiting distant family two states away. However, the most significant expense was her husband's mandatory continuing education conferences he attended several times a year. Over the years, it had worried Lulu that she and her husband had not shared many intimate moments after the kids were born, but Lulu thought that the stress on her husband from working at a busy pharmacy and the necessity of his frequent conference trips was the cause. She often thought it would have been nice if he had asked her to join him since the conferences were always in popular southern resorts and shared her concerns with him, but he dismissed her saying she would be bored while he attended his conference and met with colleagues. His attendance was necessary to maintain their lifestyle, he told her. He also gave her the excuse that they had no one to watch the children since Lulu's parents and his father had passed and his mother always refused to watch them when he asked. It was obvious that her mother-in-law disliked Lulu and did not think she was worthy of her son. In order to keep the peace, she left well enough alone and continued her daily routine. She kept the house clean and organized, took care of the kids and prepared a healthy dinner every night as requested by her husband. The routine was monotonous at times, only deviating when her husband was away.

    Overall, Lulu could honestly say she was happy and other than her limited access to their finances, she did not spot any other "red flags" from her husband. So it came as quite a shock when, after twenty years of marriage, on a cold and rainy night, her husband did not come home from work as usual. She was out of her mind with worry calling everyone she knew to no avail. Later that night, he finally called and said he was at his mother's house. His voice, flat on the phone, told her that he was depressed and had been feeling like this for some time. He said he had a nervous breakdown and went straight to his doctor; he then informed his wife that he just couldn't go back home for fear of triggering his already fragile state. He had quit his job that morning and on the advice of his doctor he had made an appointment with a therapist the next day. He told her that it would be best for him right now to stay at his mother's house for the time being, but he would keep her updated after he met with the therapist. Lulu pleaded to come see him - she wanted to help him, to care for him, to be with him at this time, she was his wife after all - but his voice immediately switched tones and called her selfish and uncaring. He did not want to see her --- or go home. He finished the call with some choice words, accusing her of contributing to his state of mind and need to "get away." So, she could only let it be.

    Lulu stood in the kitchen holding the phone in her hand for some time. After the shock wore off, she shook her head to clear her thoughts and went back into the supportive wife and mother mode. She respected his wishes and waited each night for him to call, hoping that each call would be the one to tell her he was coming home. However, when the bills started piling up, Lulu timidly asked if he was able to help or if she could have access to their bank account so that she could pay what was outstanding. Apparently, that was the wrong thing to say. He became irate and after a short tirade told her that if she was so worried about money, then she should get a real job for once in her life. He flat out refused to give her any access to their account. He said he needed it all for his therapist. Before ending the call, he called her a selfish bitch and hung up. Lulu was left shocked. Was she the one being selfish and uncaring? That thought kept her up until late into the night. All this time she had tried to keep her house in order and her children with some semblance of normalcy, but her other half was turning into someone she didn't even know.

"What happened? Was there something else? Was there someone else? Were there other forces in play? What is happening to my life?" she thought.

It wasn't until around 3 am that she fell into an uneasy sleep.

She woke up a little later than usual the next morning and with a sense of nervous determination, Lulu started to look for a job. She lucked out in her second interview with the local hospital. They needed someone to help with the morning shift at the hospital cafeteria. It wasn't much, but the flexibility allowed her to work while her daughter was in school, and get out just in time to pick her up. She was seventeen years old but Lucia recognized that her daughter was having trouble coping with her father's absence and the mother felt it best if she was home with her as much as possible. Her son came and went as he pleased, feeling he no longer had to answer to his mother.

Weeks turned into months and her husband's communication with her grew less and less. Her frantic inquiries of his condition were answered with his accusations that she had caused his breakdown. As a result of her frustration and exhaustion from trying to maintain their house and family expenses, she threatened to seek legal advice. He quickly and adamantly discouraged her and thereafter always ended his calls saying he hoped to return to their family and envisioned their reconciliation in the near future. He even promised her a family dinner if his therapist approved, however this never came to fruition. During this time, her son who was nineteen and her daughter who was seventeen, would visit him every two weeks at his mother's. He asked that Lulu not attend and respect his wishes. Her son refused to give any feedback on his bimonthly visits; however, her daughter came home after each visit, unable to make any eye contact with her, saying only that Dad was getting better slowly. Her daughter would then retreat for the next few days to her room, coming out only for meals but refusing to talk to Lucia.

On the eve of her daughter's 18th birthday, Lulu was served legal documents from a sheriff. Her husband had filed for a divorce and was demanding half the worth of the house. There was no savings as he had exhausted all they had in the bank on his "supposed" medical care and he had closed their joint charge card at the start of his "breakdown," forcing her to open one in her name only which she did in order to survive. The biggest shock came when she later found out that he had never quit his job and was living with his girlfriend in an exclusive upscale community 15 miles away. Lulu felt totally betrayed and her heart was shattered. She found it impossible to believe that the man she married had lied and cheated on her in such a cruel and malicious manner. As if that wasn't enough, she then discovered both of her children were complicit in the deception. She was totally destroyed mentally, physically and emotionally. It was truly a miracle that she was able to function at her job, however, she became a total recluse in her home. She finally hired a legal team.

It seemed that there was no end to the utter devastation she was going through when her lawyers insisted that the house be sold immediately and divided equally between them. Lulu was forced to move from her spacious house in the suburbs to the inner city and live in low-income housing. It did not matter that her husband made a lot of money and had lied to her for over one year. She was numb and her mind refused to function. Her lawyer took full advantage of her ignorance and catatonic like state by failing to protect her interests and had her sign paper after paper. Unfortunately, her share after paying the lawyer, credit cards and her car was a pittance. It came as no surprise that her son left home shortly after the divorce to live with his father. His parting words were that she was a stupid and gullible bitch and he had lost all respect for her. He was truly his father's son. Her daughter said nothing but found any excuse to escape their small rundown apartment.

    Lulu asked herself over and over how a husband could do this to his wife. This was the question that haunted her in the silence of her tiny apartment. His mother knew and was complicit in the charade her husband had devised. Her children also knew and they too stayed silent. Lulu had no siblings or cousins as her parents were only children themselves. She had many acquaintances, especially from the time she volunteered at the school and church, but embarrassment kept her from seeking support during this trying time. She did have Sister Margaret or Maggie as she asked Lulu to call her who was the principal at her daughter's school. Lulu had been a frequent volunteer at the school office before she was forced to get a job, and often shared lunch with Maggie. The Sister was always so kind and friendly that Lulu found great joy working with her. Hearing of her trials, Maggie had reached out on multiple occasions offering to help Lulu anyway she needed, but Lulu was too humiliated by her husband's betrayal to accept any offers of help.

It was extremely difficult, but Lulu continued working at the local hospital serving meals in the cafeteria making little over minimum wage. In addition, she always worked as much overtime as she could get just to pay her bills. What little money she had left after paying her rent and utilities was used for food and gas to get to and from work each day. Thankfully, her work at the cafeteria provided breakfast and lunch, so only a very small portion of her wages went on food. Her life had become a monotonous cycle of work and sleep. She rarely left her small apartment except to go to work and weekly Sunday Mass.

Lulu's son married soon after his parent's divorce; and it came as no surprise that she was not invited to the wedding. This only confirmed to Lulu that her son truly held contempt and loathing for her and felt an unhealthy admiration for his father and his father's girlfriend. But Lulu's daughter continued to struggle with her feelings and could not alienate herself from her mother entirely. Even though she chose to stay at her brother's condo (financed by their father), voicing her disdain for her mother's small cramped apartment with hand-me-down furniture from the Goodwill, she still called every couple of weeks to make sure her mother was okay. She frequently said she would visit but always found a reason for not coming. It seemed this was one of those nights. And so Lulu sat in silence, alone and lonely with her Rosary wrapped in her hands, praying to God that things would get better and that her heart would not carry such a dark, heavy burden.

Chapter II

Lulu was so tired and drained from thoughts of her broken family that she must have dozed into a restless sleep while waiting for her daughter. She woke up disoriented and startled to a blinding light in the corner of the living room. She leaned forward in the chair trying desperately to adjust her eyes and her senses to what woke her. At first she thought it might be a fire, but there was no smell of smoke. It took several seconds for her eyes to gain clarity and then stood frozen and mute to the absolute miraculous wonder standing not ten feet in front of her. There was a man with curly black hair, large soulful blue eyes with dark long lashes, and a magnificent body of powerful muscles hovering just above the floor in her living room. A soft white linen cloth was draped comfortably over one shoulder, covering most of his torso down to his knees with a gold braided cord around his waist. He had large gray-feathered wings nestled along the sides of his back that fluttered ever so slightly around him. She now saw that the light surrounding him was like a white cloud but had puffs of lavender, blue, green and pink floating gently through the white aura.

A soft melodic voice gently called from the light saying, "My dear sweet Sister Lucia, Our Lord has heard your prayers and wants you to know He loves you very much. You have been faced with fierce adversity and have not lost faith in your God. Please do not think Him selfish as He asks more from you. He has sent me, the Archangel Gabriel to deliver his message."

Lulu jumped up and held herself against the wall, her eyes and mouth wide open and unable to respond. She pinched her arm hard to confirm that yes, she was awake and yes, an angel was, indeed, in her living room. He was beautiful and emitted a loving and peaceful aura around him.

It was with disbelief and fright that she responded to the messenger in front of her. "What would Our Lord want from me? He must know that I am broken and weak. It has been very difficult for me just to get through each day. I think you have the wrong woman. There is no way the Lord has picked me. Would not a stronger person be better to serve?"

The Archangel replied, "You are perfect for this mission as you will understand the desperation and despair of those who have lost their way. For too long, Satan has coveted the earth and spread his evil intentions through laziness, immorality, pleasure seeking, anger, greed, selfishness and envy. He has worked diligently to turn good men and women away from Christ and his teachings. The Lord asks that you be an instrument of his mercy and affection to help those lost sheep find their way back home to their loving Shepherd. You will heal their bodies and their souls with God's abundant grace so that they may find everlasting life in Heaven. Find those that are sick and lost and show them God is loving and forgiving. Our Lord will guide you in this quest."

Lulu barely acknowledged the angel's request with a nod and found herself falling back into the chair where she immediately fell into a deep slumber as an overwhelming cascade of love and peace filled every molecule of her soul. And for the first time in a very long time, the profound bitterness and anger she had carried inside her dissolved from her body and mind, and found the constant heaviness of her heart was lifted, allowing her to breathe easily. Lulu slept the night away, free of the usual nightmares that haunted her sleep.

The Archangel Gabriel watched as the woman fell into a dreamless sleep, her body healing and preparing for what was to come. He looked around the room and shook his head. The paint on the walls was peeling and the carpet below his feet was worn and frayed. A small television sat on a cheap metal stand across from the old chair the woman was sleeping in. The sun faded the curtains hanging on the window. He could see a small kitchen off to the side. The appliances were severely outdated and he could see the linoleum had broken pieces throughout the flooring and the corners had curled up with age. He was glad that the Lord had chosen her; she deserved so much better than this. He could hear yelling and gunshots outside the building Lulu lived in. Not only was it not maintained within, but the streets were unsafe with gangs and thieves.

Gabriel smiled softly at the woman in deep slumber before him. She was the first of many that he would enlist, and she had been so humble to think that she was not good enough for this task the Lord has called on her for. He also thought of the others he had visited that would help her in her journey. Gabriel assessed the small curly haired woman before him.

"She may be small and weak now, but with the Lord's help, she will be strong and mighty. She will have to be in order to counter Satan's one hundred years of infecting souls with evil," thought Gabriel.

The angel covered her with a plaid blanket he found in the bedroom closet after a short search. It was clear that she had been thrown into poverty and despair, with few possessions and fewer clothes. He had been told that her husband had taken everything from her and abandoned her, but what kind of man leaves a wife like this; to live in poverty and alone? Certainly the man would burn in hell for eternity. The Bible warned humans that this earthly realm was temporary.

Her husband was another example of the effects of Lucifer's influence and manipulation.

      He knew she would not be awake any time soon with the healing taking place within her. Sister Lucia was to be the first Healer the Lord recruited in order to demonstrate to the human race not only His omnipotence but also His great mercy and love for His people. For as all of heaven and hell are aware, Satan's time was over on this earth and, unfortunately, he was quite successful in his quest to spread wickedness and ensnare humans. So many people have been corrupted and have turned their backs on God, although Gabriel was sure it was a result of the large number of evil spirits that roamed the earth unimpeded. Governments had forced its citizens to replace religion with allegiance to the state; people were discouraged from church attendance because of laziness and disregard for the Sabbath; prayer was abolished from the schools leaving children to believe in the power of drugs, alcohol and gangs in the void created. Heads of state passed laws that diminished religion and instead glorified the evils of greed, lust and idolatry. So much of this evil constantly surrounding good faithful people had its effect and infiltrated their souls, turning them into a species that were self-centered and self- absorbed with little respect for human life except their own. Yes, Satan had been quite busy diminishing our Lord throughout the lands. Many of my fellow soldiers thought the people should reap what they had sowed, but the Lord was determined. He wanted His flock back.

Gabriel stared at her small frame and tired face and cast away his reservations of whether she would be up to the task before her. Much strength would be required in order to stand up to those who were filled with bitterness, distrust and hate. The angel knew she was unaware of the hardship she would face once she began her mission. There were still many demons around who would plant seeds of doubt throughout the faithless population causing them to question the origin of her powers. They would constantly discredit her and defile her work in the name of our Lord. There was no need to warn her as Sister Lucia did not know it yet but there was an army of soldiers waiting for her to command and many others to protect her from the evil onslaught she would encounter when fulfilling the promise, she made to the Lord when she nodded her head. The chess pieces were all in play now, the game had begun.

Gabriel reached to his side and pulled the black shawl that was attached to the cord wrapped around his waist. St. Mary had instructed him to deliver it to Sister Lucia. It was made from the finest linen in Heaven and had been worn by St. Mary herself on her visits to purgatory to save souls. The shawl smelled of fragrant roses favored by St. Mary and a sign of her purity. St. Mary told him it would give the Healer strength, comfort and confidence to carry out her mission. Gabriel left it on the table beside the front door. It was the only evidence of his midnight visit to Lucia and a reminder of the consent she had given to accept the task our Lord had solicited her for.

It was time to leave her. Gabriel pulled out a small vial of oil from his side pocket and dipped his finger in the bottle.

He then marked the sign of the cross over her forehead, her mouth and her heart, and spoke the following, "May your thoughts be free of impurity, may your words be filled with kindness; may your heart be overflowed with love." The cloud of light enfolded him and slowly evaporated as he returned to the heavens.

Two Angels from the 2nd Triad of Choirs were assigned to Sister Lucia to guard her and keep her safe from the wickedness and evil debauchery outside her apartment. Any remaining demons on earth would target the Sister once she began healing the sick. The warrior angels were assigned to protect the small Sister until she moved away to a much safer place. Then, faithful soldiers who were recruited decades ago would take over. Gabriel had assured them earlier that the Sister's relocation was expected in the very near future.

Chapter III

Lulu woke in the morning to the sound of the alarm in the next room. She was still in the chair and wearing the same dress from the evening before. She looked down and saw that she was covered with a blanket, but had no memory of covering herself. With her hand, she wiped what felt like oil from her lips, although she could not remember eating anything that would leave the residue. Somewhat disoriented, she looked quickly around, but nothing in the room seemed amiss. She must have fallen asleep while waiting for her daughter who again was a no-show. The sun was just rising over the horizon and she took a moment to watch it. The sun came blazing into the world every morning and she smiled at the wonder of it. Shaking her head, she reprimanded herself, there was no time to contemplate the sun rising this morning because she had to get washed and dressed for work.

As she hurried off to her bedroom to shut the alarm, Lulu remembered the dream she had last night. She looked around the room again, almost expecting to find the beautiful angel standing in the corner, and then laughed to herself. "I'm sure it was just a dream."

As she moved silently through her small apartment, she acknowledged that something was very different about herself. For one thing, she was smiling. She could not remember ever wakening with a smile on her face, and the heaviness that usually surrounded her heart was gone. She felt good. She felt happy. She felt blessed. She didn't know what to make of this new-found serenity that seemed to engulf her but she gave a quick thanks to God for she was so, so tired of feeling angry and bitter.

Once dressed, she went to the bedroom closet to get her coat. Lulu looked at the closet door that was open wide.

"That's weird," she thought, "I don't remember getting the blanket and I certainly don't remember leaving my closet door wide open." Shrugging her shoulders, she contributed her confusion to an overworked mind and body; but leaving the closet door ajar was so unlike her. She glanced at the white clock on the wall and saw that she was running late. She would have to rush to work now. As she walked to the front door to leave, she saw something on the small table she had bought at a tag sale a couple of months ago. Lying on that table was a black scarf. She did not recognize it and thought maybe Becky had come and dropped it off while she was sleeping. Lulu reached down to pick it up; it was so soft to touch, definitely a pricey piece that she could no longer afford, and she felt a warmth that radiated off the fabric. She brought it to her face and smelled the aroma of fragrant roses and thought it was one of the most beautiful shawls she had ever seen, but as to where it came from was a mystery she had no time to solve today. Placing it carefully back on the table, she ran out the door to her car to begin another day at work.

Lulu owned a small black Toyota that was overdue for every type of maintenance check. The last oil change was over eight months ago, so she always prayed that her little compact car would not break down. She only had to drive less than fifteen minutes to work, which was the exact time it took for her to say her Rosary. Since the radio did not work, this filled the tedious daily drive and brought her hope that her life would one day have meaning and a better purpose than cooking and serving meals every day. Again, she found herself smiling and feeling weightless. She couldn't wait to tell her friend Bea about her dream and get her feedback on what it could possibly mean.

Bea was her best friend, really her only friend, who had started work at the cafeteria shortly after Lulu's divorce. She had been the lifeline that Lulu needed. She was a good Christian woman like Lulu, but Bea seemed to inject humor and humility into every scenario.

When one of the cooks burned himself, Bea would stop what she was doing and make Lulu say a prayer with her, which she always ended with, "Maybe now he'll pay more attention to his work instead of the girls with their tight shirts." Yes, Bea always managed to get Lulu to smile no matter how dismal her days were.

Her job at the hospital cafeteria began in the early morning hours at 6:00 am, and lasted until food preparation for dinner was finished which was supposed to be 3:00 pm, but was usually closer to 3:30 pm. She enjoyed the work, especially with Bea by her side, as it was very demanding and had taken her mind off of her problems. Bea had helped her find the strength to get through each day. Lulu had often thought that maybe God did hear her prayers and sent her Bea. At times, her friend could even make her laugh until she cried. Bea was the only one she told about her divorce and the events leading up to it. Bea offered to have someone rough up her ex-husband but Lulu stopped her. She would not let Bea get mixed up in her own family drama. And so, Lulu rarely missed work or any chance to spend time with her only friend, her only sunlight in the very dark world Lulu was thrust in, certainly, by no fault of her own.

Upon her arrival at the hospital, Lulu, who usually arrived before her friend, found Bea in the break room, applying her red lipstick. Bea always wore makeup over her caramel colored skin with shimmery green eyeliner. Her hair was cut close to her scalp, which allowed others to focus on the large round gold earrings she always wore. Lulu had never seen Bea without her makeup and perfume, which her friend said was to keep her husband interested after fifteen years of marriage; but Lulu had met Bea's husband and found him to be very much in love and dedicated to his wife's happiness. They had a small home close to the hospital where she, her husband, several children and her parents lived. Bea invited Lulu frequently for dinner, but she did not want to impose on Bea's full and busy household.

Lulu rushed over to Bea and excitedly told her about her angelic dream. However, she omitted the part about being chosen by God to heal the sick. Lulu thought that was a bit too much for shared friendly conversation. They did not have much time as their supervisor was always watching them and admonishing them for talking while they worked. This happened because Bea could not be quiet or hushed in her commentary about the doctors, nurses and administrative staff that came for a meal. There was always a rumor about one of them and Bea just could not help herself from whispering a comment in Lulu's ear when they showed up in the cafeteria line. This was the highlight of Lulu's day. Bea always made her laugh with her sarcastic remarks.

After telling Bea about her dream, Bea became quiet and thoughtful. Bea knew how deeply religious Lulu was and told her that maybe this was a sign from God that he heard her prayers and was ready to step in and bring the full weight of heaven and earth on Lulu's SOB of an ex-husband. Lulu silently thought that she should agree with Bea, however, she found that she truly did not care one way or another about what happened to her ex-husband. She realized that his past actions no longer had the power to hurt or anger her. In fact, she laughed at Bea's response and redirected her attention to the work at hand. The cafeteria line was getting long and the last thing she wanted was her supervisor criticizing her in front of the hospital staff, despite the fact that, in reality, none of them showed any concern at all for the lowly staff that worked the food line. It truly was a thankless job as the providers and nurses paraded down the line pointing to their food choices as they discussed their work or leisure activities. There was one provider who always made eye contact with the servers and thanked each worker for their help. The food line was always anxious to help him because he was so well mannered and was one of the few who treated them with respect. He was a young handsome doctor, not more than thirty years old, who Lulu noticed never spent long in the cafeteria. He would eat fast and bolt out the door to return to his patients. Bea had told her his name was Dr. David Woods and he was a Pediatrician.

"So handsome, isn't he?" Bea asked.

That night at home, Lulu went to sit on her old soiled and frayed chair to pray the Rosary. Becky had called earlier to apologize for not coming over. Artie, her loser boyfriend, had borrowed her car and he did not get home until late. Lulu forgave her as usual and Becky asked how she was; after Lulu assured her she was fine; Becky promised she would try to visit soon and hung up. As

Lulu prayed her thoughts wandered. Well, I guess she did not leave the black scarf. Her eyes traveled to the blanket that was covering her last night. She had thrown it aside this morning so that it was still lying on the arm of the chair. The blanket was always stored in the bedroom closet with her clothes. Was she so tired that she did not remember getting up to get the blanket? And why did she not just change into her nightgown and go to bed. Lulu just shook her head. She went to the small wooden table by the front door and lifted the black scarf to her face, again. It still smelled of roses and again Lulu thought it was the softest wool she had ever touched. It was absolutely beautiful. In her mind, she relived the dream of the angel's visit, but was it a dream? Did God really have a mission for her? How was she expected to carry out God's work? She was poor, afraid and all alone. The Lord couldn't choose someone like her.

Suddenly, an inner voice spoke inside her head, "Sister Lucia, you must be strong and unafraid. I need you to visit the sick and lost. Please do not fail Me."

Lulu paced around her small apartment for over an hour thinking that she must be going crazy. Did she really just hear a voice in her head? Did an angel really come to her living room last night? She fell to her knees and began to ask the Lord for just one more message that this was not a dream or that the voices she heard were real. Could she do this? Could she actually go up to the sick and say the Lord sent me to pray over you? Suddenly, Lulu felt an overwhelming feeling of warmth spread throughout her body leaving her feeling calm, confident and clear. She looked at the clock and it read 8:00 pm. Now was the time. Visiting hours would be over. She placed the scarf over her short curly brown hair and draped one side of it over her shoulder. She walked slowly over to the mirror. At once she noticed how the scarf softened her eyes and added a slight pink hue to her skin. The soft brown curls slipped from under the veil to frame her face. She smiled and just knew that this scarf was sent from heaven to give her strength to carry out her divine mission. Taking a deep breath, she grabbed her keys and walked out the door. Now, if only my old car doesn't break down, she thought with a grimace, but something told her not to worry, God had her back.

    Lulu walked over to her car that was parked across the street from her building. She knew there were several gangs that hung out in a building next door, so she never carried a pocketbook. Unfortunately, that did not deter the two young males walking quickly down the block toward her. They were asking her for money but she told them she had none, then they asked for a cigarette; all the while getting closer and closer. Lulu never left her apartment after dark and this confirmed that she was right in staying in her home. She tried to hurry to her car, but became so nervous; she dropped her keys and struggled to pick them up.

    Lulu knew they had to be very close by now and hoped they would not hurt her. She had nothing on her. She stayed down close to the ground with her arms over her head protecting it from any blows the two boys might give her. She had heard how the gang had beaten other tenants, but after a few minutes, nothing happened. She peeked between her fingers and saw that the coast was clear. She did not know what happened to the two gang members but they were gone and no one else was on the street. She picked up her keys and jumped in the car. Looking around once more, she saw the street was still clear and gave a huge sigh of relief. She started the car and decided that she would drive to the hospital where she worked and hoped no one would recognize her. Unseen by her were two angels standing guard in front of her building, both giving each other a victorious smile. The two gang members lay unconscious in a nearby alley.

Chapter IV

Lulu parked on the ground floor of the almost empty hospital parking lot. Visiting hours had just ended. She adjusted the scarf surrounding her and exited her vehicle. She walked through the front doors and was greeted by security with a nod. She entered the elevator and pushed the button for the sixth floor – Pediatrics. She almost lost her nerve as she got off the elevator but clinging tightly to the edge of the scarf, she did not stop.

Praying for direction and divine intervention Lucia kept walking until she got to the first room on the floor. The nameplate on the outside of the door said Rose Stevens. She could see a mother and father sitting quietly by the bedside. She could also see many tubes and medication administration units set up around the bed. Lucia softly knocked on the door and was acknowledged by both parents. She had practiced her introduction and what she would say to the families while in the car, however, here in the room; the environment was just too solemn, too painful, for a long speech. Lulu walked over and stood between the parents and the bed. She introduced herself as Sister Lucia, and as quiet as a whisper, asked if they would mind if she prayed to Our Lord to heal their daughter. The mother's face was tearstained and the father's tense and strained.

"Certainly," they said, "Our daughter needs all the prayers she could get."

Lucia turned and stared at the small body lying on her side. The little girl was unresponsive and her breathing was shallow. Her face was pasty white and her lips had a faint bluish tinge. The poor girl's head was hairless and Lucia could see her bones prominently along her spine where the hospital gown was open. Lulu's heart broke and she held her breath for several seconds before making her way to the side of the bed. She was unsure the child was still alive but closed her eyes and held her hands over the child's torso. She quietly said several prayers and then asked God to heal this small diseased little girl with His light and grace.

Lucia kept her eyes closed the whole time so she did not see the stream of white sparkly light seeming to ooze slowly from her fingers as they covered the girl's chest. She did feel what could be described as a strong current of electricity traveling down her arms and transforming to a steady prickly sensation filling every nerve ending in her hands. The new Healer was scared of this new feeling and her hands started to shake. After a few shakes, she suddenly felt the tingling heat of the energy being released through her fingertips. So afraid to open her eyes, Lucia could feel and hear the outpouring of tiny sparks snapping as the energy flowed from her fingertips.

Still frightened by the sensations traveling through her body, Lucia squeezed her eyes shut more tightly and continued to pray over the child until the feeling stopped. She slowly opened her eyes. She looked at the bed expecting to see some trace of the sparks leaving her hands, but the sheets were still white and undisturbed, which made Lucia question whether there were sparks at all. Nothing seemed to have changed. The little girl still lay unresponsive on her side. Her face was still pasty white; however, her lips seemed to take on a pinkish glow that was definitely not there before. Lucia stepped away from the bed and turned toward the parents.

She shook their hands and said, "Hopefully, God has heard our prayers."
Then, she left the room as silently as she had come. Taking another very deep breath, she glided to the next room.

Again, she softly knocked on the outside door. A middle-aged woman looked up from her chair. Lucia walked in and introduced herself. There lying on the bed was another young girl, maybe age ten or eleven, without hair or eyebrows. Her face was as white as the sheets that covered her and her breathing was erratic. The woman just stared as Lucia asked if she could pray to God to lessen the suffering of the woman's daughter. The woman returned Lucia's request with empty glazed eyes, so Lucia, finding no resistance, proceeded to walk to the bed. As she leaned over the girl, the women grabbed Lucia's hand tightly and began to pray with her. The woman's eyes were closed as tears slid down her face. Lucia extended her hands, which were still connected to the mother's, over the girl's body, closed her eyes and began quietly praying. Halfway through her prayer, Lucia could feel the strange and foreign sensation filling her arms and hands again. This time, Lucia bravely opened her eyes and noticed that though she heard no other voice other than her own praying, the mother's lips were moving in rhythm with her own. Glancing down at the girl, Lucia noticed the white light streaming from her fingertips with only a few occasional sparks snapping as they met the air. Her chapped and worn hands appeared to glow with an ethereal pearly aura surrounding them. The white energy flowed down toward the bed and was absorbed into the little girl's body. She was utterly amazed at this happening but continued to pray. Unlike the mother, Lucia kept her eyes open, watching the soft white light being emitted from her fingertips.

Once the flow stopped, she noticed the little girl opened her eyes and weakly mouthed the words, "God Bless you, too, Sister."

Lucia smiled, untangled her hands from the mother's and guided her back to the chair Lucia first found her in. She hugged the mother, hoping some of the white light would help this woman, too.

As Lucia entered the next room, she found a young father holding his three-year-old son. The father was holding him tight as the child whimpered in his arms. The toddler had a needle in his left arm with three small IV bags hanging from the stand, each bag a different color. His watery eyes were so big and so blue; and his little pale face was pulled tight with discomfort. Sister Lucia knocked softly on the door and smiled at the man who barely acknowledged her. With no verbal rejection of her intrusion, she tiptoed up to the chair he was sitting in and asked if it was all right if she prayed over his son. The father nodded, then looked her in the eyes and asked her if she really thought it would help.
Lucia answered with complete conviction and total faith, "Yes, I believe the Lord helps us in ways that we do not ask for or understand, but is always best for us. Let's pray to Him to heal your baby."

The father then turned his son, Colin, so that he was facing the Healer. She saw the dark stitches on the side of his head marring his beautiful features. Sister Lucia raised her hands so they were positioned over the surgical site since she assumed that was where healing was needed most. With closed eyes she again began to pray as she had done the other two times. Lucia felt the flow begin to circulate at her fingertips and she opened her eyes to see a cloud of white healing light illuminating the boy's head. His father looked dumbstruck. After a few minutes, the boy stopped whimpering and seemed to fall into a quiet sleep. Lucia thanked the father for letting her pray over his son and turned to leave the room.

The father seemed to come out of his daze and reached out to grab her arm, "Ma'am, what just happened?"

Lucia smiled and told him that she thought God was listening tonight. Then she left, heading to the room across the hall that had several beeping machines.

The next child was an older boy who looked to be about eleven years of age. The name posted outside of the room was Bryan Withers. He was alert and alone in the room. Sister Lucia noticed that his bed was much different than the one's the other children were in. Lucia also noticed that he had several tubes coming into and draining fluid from his body. When she asked if she could come in and pray over him; he nodded but confessed to her that his family didn't go to church and that they really didn't believe in God so much. He proceeded to tell Lucia how he had fallen out of a tree and was paralyzed from the chest down. That explained his labored breathing. He looked down at the sheets covering his body and told Lucia that he was the pitcher on his baseball team, but that was impossible now. He was supposed to play on the All Star Team in town, but the coach had to replace him. Bryan continued telling her that what was worse was that his worst rival replaced him. His replacement was always bullying him. His friends told him how the cruel boy laughed when he found out Bryan was paralyzed. He was trying not to be angry but his tone of voice belied the words he was saying. He had lost everything because he wanted to climb a stupid tree.

"Is this really what God wanted for me?" he asked. Lucia stood by the bed and told him that was exactly what she was going to ask God when she prayed over him and advised him to do the same but it would be best if he left out the angry tone.

The Healer closed her eyes and began her prayers. She quickly felt the energy coming down her arms and out her fingers. Lucia had to shush Bryan when he began shouting, "What the heck?" when his body was covered in a white mist. The energy seemed to be coming out faster and stronger with each healing. So it was not long before Lucia felt the tingling subside. Bryan told her he was feeling kind of tingly all over so Lucia said it was probably best to go to sleep and see what happens in the morning. He agreed and his last words to her were if God healed him tonight he would promise to go to church every Sunday, even if there was a baseball game. Lucia told him she would hold him to that promise.

And so Lucia attended all who allowed her entrance, room by room, praying over terminally ill children, even though her heart broke to see each child exhibiting the signs of a disease that ravaged their little bodies and drained the life from them. She also tried to minister to the majority of parents who expressed heavy doubt as their faith was being tested. With each healing, Lucia could feel the warmth of God's grace and her own energy leaving her body, but she did not give in to the progressive fatigue that assailed her. Her confidence grew stronger with each family, but she could feel her body tiring as she entered the last two rooms. Twenty rooms were on the floor and a child who was very, very sick in each of them.

Almost every family let her in, albeit, a few hesitantly. Unfortunately, there was one young woman, the last room on the floor, who would not allow her in to pray over her son. She practically hissed at Lucia that there was no God and if there was one, how could He let her son suffer so. Her heart was cold and hardened after sitting night and day watching her son deteriorate slowly, and Lucia could not break through. Lucia, drained of energy, became frightened and no longer so self-assured. Up until this point, the nurses had not paid attention to her, but once the mother became loud and started yelling at Lucia to leave immediately, they hurried over asking the Healer to leave the floor. And she did.

Lulu walked out of the hospital visibly shaken by the confrontation of the last mother. Nothing she said made a difference to the poor woman. Lulu could feel her tremendous pain and anguish flowing from her as she sat there watching her dying son. All the confidence Lulu had been feeling was gone and she hurried to her car. The drive home seemed longer than usual, and Lulu was exhausted. She played the scene over and over in her head trying to think of other words she could have used to try to sway the mother, but the woman was past the point of hearing her. So instead, Lulu prayed for the mother since she couldn't get to the son.

When Lulu pulled up to her apartment, she quickly exited her car and practically ran into the door of the building's entrance, all the while looking for anyone who might try to hurt or rob her. She had stuffed the shawl under her coat; it was too precious to lose. As she entered the building she glanced back out to the street and thought for a second that she saw two men standing outside but smiling at her through the glass. She smiled back but dropped the smile when she realized each man had a pair of wings protruding from their backs. She hurried into her apartment and locked the door, turned the dead bolt and hooked the little chain at the top. With her back pressed up against the door, Lulu gave a sigh of relief, thinking of the two angels at the door. Thankfully, God's Divine Plan included a protection package for her.

Chapter V

The alarm went off at 5:00 am. Lulu was exhausted, and for the first time ever, hit the snooze button. Dear Lord, she was tired. She had returned home a little before 10:30 pm and went right to bed. She was so proud of herself for going to the hospital to pray over those sick children. She had hoped she had provided some comfort to them and their families. She still felt unnerved by that one stubborn mother who wouldn't even allow her to step into the room. But now it was time to go to work – her earthly work - and make some money. Lord knows she had plenty of bills to pay. After splashing cold water on her face and drinking a hot cup of black coffee while she got dressed, off she went to the hospital.

On her way to work, she thought about telling Bea, but had come to the conclusion that Bea would probably walk her up to the ninth floor to be admitted to the Psych Ward. Who could possibly believe her story? She wasn't even sure if any of the children were even helped, never mind healed.

She still couldn't believe that a white stream had surged out of her fingertips, "I mean, who does that?" Lulu thought to herself. She wasn't even sure what it was but she thought it might be something like energy – healing energy. She was also waiting for someone to come and arrest her for being in the children's ward after hours and going room to room asking parents if she could pray over their child. There might be a law against that. The nurses had passed right by her like she wasn't there. Lulu wondered if the black shawl made her invisible; dear God, now she thought she was the invisible woman. When she heard the voice in her head, it was so clear and firm; the voice in her head felt so real; but when she thought about it now, she thought she might be delusional. She needed to get to work because her mind was going a hundred miles an hour. She was anxious to see if there was a change in any of the children's condition. That would determine her next move and with that thought, she parked her car and entered the hospital.

    Lulu was in the cafeteria preparing food for breakfast, when the news filtered down from the sixth floor. Nineteen children admitted to the St. Francis Children's Hospice ward seemed to have made a miraculous recovery this morning and nineteen food trays with chocolate chip pancakes and waffles were ordered from the cafeteria. It was also made very clear that this was a rush order. These kids were alert and hungry as could be. In fact, some of them had not eaten for days and were demanding food. No one knew what to make of it. The nurses and doctors were mystified; some called it a miracle. The parents were praising God and celebrating the visit by the woman who healed their children.

Lulu stood at the counter mixing the pancake batter, thankful that she was doing something that did not require her brain to work. The children were completely healed as a result of her visit. She tried to think of alternative reasons for the children to be healed, but then she realized the unknown white mist-like substance coming out of her fingertips must actually have been God's healing energy. Unfortunately, one little boy did not make it through the night. His mother was the only parent on the floor not celebrating his recovery. With this thought, a deep sadness filled the Healer.

    Lulu thought over and over if she could have done something different to get that mother to change her mind, but no, the mother was adamant in refusing her access. Lulu closed her eyes and said a quick prayer for the grieving mother.

    Then, Bea came to her side, "Did you hear? It was a miracle! Blessed be to God! They think some woman in a black scarf healed all the kids on the sixth floor last night. No one seems to know who she was. She just came into the kids' rooms and prayed over them and left. No one saw her come and no one saw her leave. Some of the parents said they saw a white mist come out of her hands while she was praying. Can you imagine that? White. Light. From. Her. Fingertips. Hallelujah! Everyone thinks she was an angel." A sneer from their supervisor in their direction stopped Bea's ravings.

    "Let's get these kids some food," Bea said loud enough for the supervisor to hear.

    Once all the food was cooked, plated and topped with the metal cover, Lulu's supervisor asked her if she could bring the food up to the sixth floor, but Lulu was afraid that she might be recognized and she was just not ready for that. She made some excuse and ran to the bathroom to hide until he found someone else. She stood alone in the bathroom contemplating the results of her visit last night. Could the rumors really be true? Did God really choose her to heal all those children? She could not believe what she was hearing and was trying to process it, but Bea knocked on the bathroom door telling her to hurry because there was a huge line of hungry people waiting to be served. Lulu rushed to assume her position in the cafeteria line, putting her thoughts behind her.

    All day, the hospital staff was buzzing about the miracle in Pediatrics. Some of the rumors claimed that the woman was seen ascending back to heaven on a cloud. The authorities could not find her on any video surveillance. Each child that Lulu prayed over was in the end stages of their illness, some with just hours to live. However, each one she had touched was completely healed, even the boy who was paralyzed from the chest down. He had already called his coach to tell him he was ready to pitch again. Lulu could not believe all the chatter. Hair and eyebrows were growing again, pale chalky skin turning a healthy pink tone, dark black stitches disappearing and there were no surgical scars to be found anywhere on these children. The results were not only amazing but also truly miraculous. Everybody in line added a different version of the events that led to the total healing of nineteen terminally ill children, some moments from death. Lulu listened to all of it, as did Bea, who of course added her own opinion on what had happened. She even mentioned Lulu's dream and maybe that was a foretelling of what happened last night. Lulu nodded and stood quietly not saying anything.

    Later in her shift, several of the hospital's Pediatricians came down for a late breakfast. Lulu could not help but overhear the conversation taking place in front of her. It was her favorite doctor, David Woods, who was talking about the one child who had passed early in the morning. Apparently, the mother had forbid the woman in the black scarf from entering the boy's room. The mother became loud and the nurses had to get involved, but for the life of them, not one nurse could describe the woman in the black scarf and no one seemed to see her leave. She just disappeared.

As the distraught mother was leaving the hospital without her son, she heard how every other child was healed by that woman; realizing that she had ultimately caused the death of her own child. Thankfully, her husband was with her because she became inconsolable after running room to room to see every child sitting up in their beds completely healed. They were conversing happily and animatedly with their parents. The doctor continued saying that several of the kids even spoke with the woman who healed them; one promising to attend church every Sunday if he was healed.

"The kid was a paraplegic, from the chest down and now he's sitting up feeding himself. How the hell do you explain that?" he asked his colleague.

Lulu heard a nurse behind the doctor say that all the kids were being examined and made ready for discharge. No one knew what to make of it. The head of Pediatrics had called an emergency meeting with all hospital leadership and Pediatricians to discuss the possibilities that could have caused nineteen terminally ill children to recover overnight.

Most of the doctors were too afraid to say it was a miracle or that God was even involved, but Dr. Woods proclaimed to all his colleagues, "There is no doubt in my mind that this is the work of the Lord. Not one single doubt."

Lulu was so happy to hear how all the children had recovered so quickly and gave thanks to God, but her heart grew heavy thinking of the woman who forbade her to enter the hospital room where her son lay dying. Even with all the good news surrounding Lulu, she felt helpless and powerless to do anything for that poor mother.

As lunchtime approached, her supervisor again asked her to deliver food trays up to a floor. It was not the sixth floor, so Lulu readily agreed. She delivered the trays and was on her way back to the cafeteria. She knew she was supposed to use the staff elevators when working, but they were further out of the way, so when she heard the chime of the visitor elevator near her, she hopped on without thinking. She stood staring at the doors hoping no one would report her when she felt a set of eyes boring into her. Slowly she turned and recognized the very familiar boy staring at her. It was Bryan standing on his own two feet with a huge smile on his face as he was looking right at Lulu. She did the only thing she could think of and raised a finger to her lips to prevent him from revealing her secret. Lulu was afraid to move and chided herself for using the visitor elevator. Bryan's parents were standing on the other side talking to each other. Lulu was so nervous; she couldn't even process what they were saying. Bryan kept moving closer and closer to her as Lulu stood ramrod straight not knowing what he was about to do.

Suddenly, he quietly whispered, so that only she could hear, "See you at Church Sunday, Sister." Lulu couldn't suppress a smile and then the elevator doors opened and she quickly strode out towards the cafeteria. Right before the elevator closed, Lulu turned back and gave Bryan a wink and he ran his fingers over his closed mouth as if zipping it shut. Thankfully, her secret was still safe, but for how long?

Lulu got home from work a little late that day. She looked all around the street to see if she could see those two men with wings on their backs again, but Lulu noticed that the whole street seemed deserted, which was highly unusual. She wondered if Gabriel had sent the two angels to watch over her.

"I'm sure God wouldn't want anything to happen to me, especially since I live in this dangerous neighborhood," Lucia considered as she entered the building. As soon as she walked through the door of her apartment, she checked the side table to make sure the black shawl was still there and it sat as she had left it. She raised it to her nose to smell the beautiful scent of roses. She knew that St. Mary loved roses and was convinced that the shawl had been touched by her hands. She started thinking of Gabriel's visit, the black shawl and the healing of all those sick children. She could not believe that God had chosen her, and still had some doubt as to whether she was really the right person to carry out this mission. She prayed the Lord would continue to give her direction on where to go next; but not tonight, because, in truth, she was completely exhausted. She couldn't wait to jump in the shower and go to bed. Thankfully it was Friday and she had the weekend to recover. Just before she drifted off to sleep, she again prayed that God would help that poor mother.

Chapter VI

Lucia rested the entire weekend. So on Monday morning she reported to work totally invigorated with energy. Earlier that day, Bea had shared with her that someone at her church had said their nephew was recovering from losing his legs in a roadside bomb attack in the Middle East. He was a soldier in the United States Marine Corp and was supposed to get married on his next leave home. The poor soldier was only twenty-nine years old and had refused to see anyone but his mother. He would not even let his fiancé visit and had told her to find a real man for a husband. The girl was heartbroken and refused to leave the hospital, sitting day and night in the waiting room hoping he would change his mind. Bea had said the fiancé's name was Deanne or Diana, something like that. Lulu took this as a sign as to what her next mission would be.

She waited an additional evening until she was able to overcome her fear, and on Tuesday evening, she donned her black shawl and decided that she would drive over to the VA Hospital. Lucia did not know the area well, so she left a little early and got there slightly before visiting hours were ending. She parked her car and walked through the parking lot. When she got to the elevator, she really did not know where to go. Someone got in and pressed the button for the 7th floor. Lucia followed the person off the elevator not really knowing what direction to take. She looked to the left, then to the right and before her eyes sitting in the waiting room, all alone, was a beautiful young woman looking distraught.

Lucia walked into the room and sat near the woman. She asked her if she was waiting to see someone. The young woman's eyes watered as she looked at Lucia, unsure of whether she should respond or not. Lucia just knew this was the girl Bea had told her about.

When Lucia held out her hand, the woman took it and cried out softly, "No, my boyfriend won't see me. He thinks he is not good enough for me since he lost his legs in that damn war. I can't make him listen to reason that I love him any way he is. I don't care about his legs."
Lucia squeezed her hand in response. She could feel the pain in this woman's heart and remembered when her heart ached in that same way when her husband discarded her.

Lucia stood up and took a deep breath and asked her, "What is his room number?"

It was the first room on the right. The nameplate outside the door read Sergeant Major Robert G. Walsh. He was a bilateral amputee. She knew that because even at a distance she could see his stumps were uncovered, probably so he could be constantly reminded of his loss. The second thing Lucia noticed was how his chocolate colored eyes glared at her with a coldness that reflected his ice covered heart and contrasted with his warm brown skin. She was surprised that he even let his mother in. The Healer could feel the tension and power radiating from the strong hard muscles along his shoulders and arms. If he had his legs, his demeanor would have truly scared Lucia. The thickness of his anger and hostility permeated the room. This was nothing like the children's ward, except for that mother who wouldn't let her near her son. Lucia decided she would proceed carefully.

His mother sat quietly by his side. She was a large woman with black curly hair. Lulu could see the protruding black bags under her eyes, even though her skin was very dark. Crying had caused her cheeks and nose to appear red and irritated. Lucia knew she was praying, her lips silently moving. Robert turned from Lucia and began staring out the window aimlessly. She knocked softly and entered the room slowly so as not to be confrontational. Without smiling, Lucia solemnly asked if she could pray with his mother for him.

    He swore and ordered Lucia to "Get the hell out of my room."

    Immediately, his mother stepped in and reminded him that no son of hers was allowed to speak to anyone like that, especially a woman of God.

    She then took Lucia's hand and guided her to outside his room, pleading, "My son is a good man, Sister. A mother couldn't be prouder, but this has certainly caused him dark times. He refused to see a counselor or anyone with a similar condition to show him he still can live a full life. He has lost his will to live and has even refused to see his fiancée, Diana, and she won't leave the hospital. I just don't know what to do to help him… or her." Lucia told her that she could not enter the room unless he allowed it. The mother then begged Lucia to try just one more time. Lucia could see the desperation in her sunken brown eyes as she too was suffering from the loss of who her son used to be.

    Lucia walked cautiously to the side of the bed and explained to Robert, or Bobby, as his mother called him, that she was there to pray with him or for him.

    His mother added that Bobby was an altar server for their local church when he was younger, and Bobby responded with a shrug, "Yeah, and look how God repaid me."

Lucia said, "Sometimes God gives us trials that we don't feel we deserve, but only God knows why he has brought such pain and suffering to us."

Lucia then suggested bringing his fiancé into the room, explaining that the more who prayed together, the louder the message God would hear. He shrugged his shoulders that Lucia took as reluctant agreement.

His mother ran out of the room to get Diana and when they returned the young woman was wiping her hopeful eyes. She glanced at Lucia as if to say how did you do this? A shocked Diana stood stiffly in the room, afraid to say a word in fear that he would demand she leave. She couldn't believe that she was standing so close to him. She had not seen him in days, but besides the beard now growing on his face, she noticed that his eyes had grown harder and colder towards her. He had thrown her out of his room the first day she had come to see him. Bobby was so angry at her. He told her to sell her engagement ring because no way would he allow her to marry half a man. What did this tiny wisp of a woman with small brown curls escaping from the black shawl on her head say that would change Bobby's mind?

Bobby seemed undecided if he had made too hasty a decision allowing Diana back in his room. He had told her to leave; what was she still doing here? He would wait until the woman left, and then he would tell Diana she needed to move on. There was no future with him. What did this crazy woman do to him? She was just giving him false hope that he could get his legs back. As he was about to shut this little get together down, Lucia felt his apprehension growing out of control, so she quickly grabbed Diana and his mother to gather around the bedside, ignoring the fire emanating from his eyes and the smoke from his nose. Sister Lucia adjusted her shawl and took a quick smell, which always gave her the strength and conviction of St. Mary. She asked his mother and Diana to hold their hands over the space where his legs had been. She then informed them to close their eyes and concentrate on the prayer, which Lucia led. The familiar tingling began to run down her arms as she prayed and then witnessed again thick white energy emanating out of her fingers over the area where Bobby's legs used to be. She also felt tremendous warmth and energy leaving her body. Please dear Lord, she mumbled, let this man's legs be restored, or at the very least not be so filled with hate and anger. When Lucia chanced a quick peek at Bobby, he was turned away from the healing with his eyes closed tight. Lucia continued the prayer until she could feel the energy and tingling slowly fade.

Once Sister Lucia stopped praying, both his mother and Diana opened their eyes and they all made the sign of the cross. His mother than turned to Diana and asked her to stay with Bobby while she went to the bathroom. She then looked at Lucia and nudged her head to the doorway. Bobby offered no resistance so both Lucia and his mother left the room. Lucia turned as she reached the door and saw that Diana had taken Bobby's hand in her own and he did not recoil.

Standing outside the room, his mother grabbed Lucia's hand and squeezed it, saying, "You are the angel that healed those children at St. Frances' Hospital, aren't you? I have been praying for so long, I can't believe God sent you to us. I saw God's healing light coming from your fingers. I just know God is giving us our miracle."

Lucia explained to the woman that she was not an angel, just someone who believes in the power of prayer. "I think the miracle here is that he is letting Diana in. We could hope for more, but we will ultimately need to put our faith in God's plan for Bobby."

When both women returned to the bedside, Lucia admitted that she was unsure if Bobby would ever get his legs back. Bobby was hesitant; he still was not sure of what was going on. He tried to quell the feeling of hopefulness he felt, he was also afraid to ask if she was the same woman who healed the children with cancer at the hospital in the neighboring town. Instead, he just nodded. Diana was still sitting beside him and was holding his hands tightly. Bobby could not deny how good it was to finally feel her next to him again.

Just as Lucia was preparing to go to the next room, a message popped into her head. Making the sign of the cross, she looked at Bobby and told him to try and get some rest; he would need it in preparation of what was to come. Sister Lucia extended her arm to shake the mother's hand, but his mother grabbed her and gave her a big hug. Before she left for the next room, Lucia instructed the mother not to tell anyone yet of her visit. If she did, then Lucia would be unable to heal anyone else tonight. The mother obliged, understanding the importance of Lucia's mission to heal as many people as possible.

In her mind's eye, Lucia could see Bobby and Diana holding a small baby. The soldier was standing tall with two good legs by Diana's side. The anger and coldness Lucia had seen in his eyes was long gone and replaced by a warm loving glow. He was still certainly a force to be reckoned with, but Lucia could see the baby having him wrapped around his tiny finger. Yes, it would be a strapping boy, just like his father. Lucia smiled at the bright and promising future awaiting the couple. Now, if she heard the Lord's message correctly, that man was in for a long and painful night; he would need Diana by his side.

Chapter VII

Lucia stood outside the next room along the hallway hoping that the hostility she received from Bobby would not be repeated here. The nameplate outside the doorway read Private Vincent Landry. From the outskirts of the door, Lucia could see a young man in a wheelchair, his body angled to one side and his head bobbing up and down. There was an ugly jagged scar across the left side of his shaved head. His eyes turned to Lucia and she could see that his right eye was half closed and the right side of his mouth was drooping down. His right arm hung loosely on the side of the wheelchair and his hand was clenched in a tight fist.

He was alone in the room and Lucia glancing around did not see any cards or flowers or any other evidence that family or friends had come to visit. Lucia did not feel any emotion or hostility coming from the man, which gave her confidence. However, this lack of an energy field, good or bad, from the man confused Lucia who was an emotional empath by nature; it was unsettling to confront someone so devoid of feeling.

Lucia knocked softly on the door as had become her way and asked if she could come in. He raised his left hand and motioned her in. Wearing only scrub pants, she could see the hard muscles across his chest that rippled when he turned toward her. His eyes were a dull, lifeless green that regarded Lucia as she stood there. The left corner of his mouth lifted but seemed to be a forced gesture.

She introduced herself and instantly knew she had to do things a little different with him; so instead of asking to pray with him, she asked if he would like a visit. With a shrug of his shoulders, she entered and pulled one of the chairs so that she sat across from him. She asked some simple questions: where are you from? How long have you been here? Do you have any family? He had some trouble verbalizing his answers but Lucia was patient and allowed him the time as he struggled to make his mouth form the words. Lucia could see how much energy it took for him to answer her. However, when she asked if he had someone special waiting back home for him, his affect changed from flat and emotionless to one of a brooding, deep despair. He shook his head and she could see his eyes water as his distorted face became defeated and his shoulders slumped. Lucia reached out and grasped his left hand, which in turn held hers tightly. She closed her eyes and could immediately see in her mind a younger healthier Vincent with a pretty young girl with long blond hair. They were both laughing at a party, then walking along the river holding hands, and finally the both of them sharing a goodbye kiss as he boarded a train. Lucia could make out the tears on the girl's face and a diamond on the fourth finger of her left hand. In an abrupt change, these beautiful images of love were replaced with scenes of gunfire and explosions. Lucia saw the bodies of many soldiers lying across a field covered in blood and there in the middle of the scene was Vincent. His head was covered in blood and his body looked lifeless. Medics ran around the field checking the men for any sign of life. When one of them got to Vincent, he yelled to his fellow medics that he had a pulse but it was very weak. The medics brought over a stretcher and quickly put Vincent on a waiting helicopter.

It seemed Vincent was sending Lucia visions of his life prior to the brain injury and the explosion that caused it. Slowly and with great difficulty, Vincent told Lucia that he had a girlfriend, Sadie was her name, and he loved her very much. He told Lucia that it was just hard enough trying to get through each day since the explosion. He seemed to accept that his life had taken an unexpected tragic turn and he wanted no pity or sympathy from anyone. He had chosen to go it alone and not only did he break off their engagement just the other day, he also had her promise not to call him or come see him. He told her it was time for her to move on because there would be no life with him.

Lucia immediately thought of Bobby doing the same thing, pushing Diana away, when in reality, Bobby and Vincent both needed the love and strength these women could give them. Vincent wanted Sadie to remember him whole, not the broken man sitting in a wheelchair the rest of his life. Lucia was filled with sorrow for this poor young soldier. His injuries guaranteed a severely challenging existence and because he so loved Sadie, he did not want her to suffer with him.

     Lucia sat for a while receiving one vision after another of Vincent and Sadie and their short but loving time together. Suddenly, two nurses, one, a middle aged woman with short brown hair and the other a tall, lanky young man, entered the room stating it was time for Vinnie to get back into bed. Lucia rose from the chair and walked to the corner of the room. The nurses prepared the bed and wheeled Vincent next to it. The male nurse lifted the top half of Vincent's body while the other nurse lifted his legs. At each action, they informed Vincent what they were doing, but never allowed him time to comment. The female picked up the meds she had brought into the room and watched as Vincent swallowed them down. They took his vital signs, then, covered him with the blankets. As an afterthought, the male nurse connected the call button to the bed rail and told Vincent to call if he needed anything.

The same nurse looked over his shoulder and with a smile called out, "Good night, soldier. Get a good night's rest because you have a lot of physical therapy scheduled tomorrow." Then, he turned the light off, leaving only the small light over the sink on.

At no time did either nurse acknowledge Lucia standing in the corner of the room. Lucia did not know what to think. Was she invisible to everyone but the patients?

She looked up to see Vincent just staring at her with his one good eye, until he found his voice and asked in an excited and barely audible thick speech, "Are you an angel? Are you the one who healed all those kids on the Pediatric floor?"

Lucia stepped forward and shrugged her shoulders. She was still new at this and wasn't sure if complete healing was guaranteed. Vincent raised his good arm and reached for Lucia. When Lucia reached his side again, he grabbed her hand and tried to tell her in his mangled speech that he did not deserve God's forgiveness.

With tears flowing down his face, he spoke clearly, "I am not a good man. I have killed people."

Lucia could see the toll her visit had taken on Vincent. His face was ashen and his limbs were trembling more with each effort to speak. Stress lines marred his forehead and his breathing was labored. His tear-streaked face broke Lucia's heart. An overwhelming profound pain that had engulfed his soul replaced the lack of emotion that she had felt when she entered the room. He turned his face from her in an attempt to hide his suffering and guilt.

Undeterred by his words and actions, Lucia closed her eyes and made the sign of the Cross over her chest and began to pray. She soon felt the energy building in her core and spreading down her arms to her fingers. In the silence, Vincent turned to look at the small woman by his side and saw that she was deep in prayer. He watched as she raised her hands over his head, not knowing what to expect. Suddenly, a white swirl of static energy flowed from her fingertips and encircled his head causing a heated tingling sensation that seemed to attach to every nerve ending in his head. Vincent tried to move his head side to side but he could not; neither could he find the words to speak to this strange woman praying over him. The white mist surrounding his face and head blinded his eyesight. Even though all those things should terrify him as he had suffered so much loss of function after his accident, he was pulled to just accept what was happening to him. With a deep sigh, he closed his eyes and settled into the pillow behind his head and succumbed to the gentle peace that seemed to fill his body.

    It seemed like forever that Lucia stood over the soldier. She could still feel the energy flowing from her hands. Lucia smiled, thinking that Vincent needed a heck of a lot of healing and she had a good feeling that God would grant this man a miracle. She finally felt the force abate and she opened her eyes to find Vincent in a state of tranquil sleep. She could actually visualize the regeneration of cells taking place and the limp and flabby muscles of his right arm becoming firm and strong. She imagined the same was happening to his right leg. Lucia was amazed to see the red jagged scar over the left side of his skull shrinking and turning a light pink color. She could see the muscles of his right eye and side of his mouth that were drooping and flaccid, tightening and puckering to match the left side of his face. Lucia, again, made the sign of the Cross and gave thanks and praise to the Lord.

"This is incredible. Maybe I am the right person for the task," Lucia thought.

The Healer readjusted her beautiful black shawl around her head and shoulders. She took a deep breath and could still smell the rich and floral fragrant of roses. The breath seemed to replenish her energy level and with unwavering resolve strode towards the next room. She had a new confidence and was determined not to let anyone refuse her entrance. There would be no one else dying because they were stubborn and angry at God for their condition.

"I may be small, but I am mighty," Lucia thought the words in her head; now she just had to believe them.

While walking to the door, Sister Lucia saw his cell phone light up. She saw the name Sadie across the top and without a second thought, answered the call.

Before Lucia could say anything she heard a woman speak. "Hello, Vincent, please don't hang up," the woman on the phone said with a thick southern drawl.
Lucia answered and asked if she was looking for Vincent Landry. She then informed the woman that he could not come to the phone but asked if this was his fiancée. When Sadie responded that it was, Lucia strongly encouraged her to come visit him the next day. The woman responded tearfully that Vincent made her promise not to come.

Lucia laughed, "Oh that. He was out of his mind with drugs. He really, really wants to see you. I mean you still want to marry him, right?" "Of course," she responded, "I love him." Lucia smiled, "Well, see you soon, drive careful," and hung up the phone. She quickly left the room as she had more work to do.

Chapter VIII

Lucia waited patiently outside the next room when she saw two nurses tending to the soldier inside. After a few minutes, they walked right by her as if she was not even there. Neither made eye contact or reprimanded her for being there after hours. The Healer walked into the room and found Matthew sitting in bed with bandages wrapped around his eyes.

He seemed to sense someone in the room and called out, "Did you forget something?" thinking it was the nurses again.

Lucia stepped up to the bed and softly spoke to this young handsome man with the cutest dimples, "Good evening, Matthew, I just came to visit the floor tonight." He turned his head in the direction of her voice and she saw him sniff the air in front of her and grimace. "Wow, that's some strong smelling perfume. Is that roses?"

Private First Class Matthew Johnson granted Lucia permission to come into the room after she introduced herself. Upon entering, Lucia noticed the white cane in the corner of the room, confirming her assessment that Matthew was blind. When she asked to pray over him, he firmly insisted that she should help the other soldiers on the floor. He told her the only praying he would do was for a quick death so that he could join his fallen brothers. He did not see or want any future for himself and Lucia grew afraid that he would fulfill his own prophecy if given the opportunity. Poor Matthew was in a deep and dark depression after surviving a terrible explosion. He had lost his sight but felt he should have lost his life along with his squad. Again, Lucia's heart broke for him, as it did for all the rest of these soldiers that were maimed from the war.

Lucia encouraged him to tell her what happened and they talked for quite some time, as he told her about the friends he had lost. He revealed that his four marine brothers had died in the explosion, while he had lost his sight. Matthew could not come to terms with the fact that he had survived. He often said that he would gladly have traded places with any one of his friends. They were far better men than he. Her eyes watered as he poured out the events of that horrible day.

As he spoke, Lucia prayed, "Dear Lord, how can I help him? He has lost the will to live. Please I need guidance."

Matthew told her how a bomb had exploded and the shrapnel had hit his face, especially his eyes. At this distance, Lucia could now see the deep scaring marring his handsome face. As the only one of his squad to survive, this tough marine expressed no anger or hostility, only a dark hopeless resolve to join his brothers. He was trying so hard to be a strong and brave soldier but expressed that this life was over for him. Lucia could not think of any words that would bring him comfort; she didn't even know where to begin in helping him deal with the loss of his friends and the loss of his sight. Instead of speaking words of comfort, Lucia reached for his hands and started praying. She could feel him squeeze her fingers encouraging her to continue.

In response to her prayers, the room slowly began to fill with a thick white fog that rose up from the floor. Lucia became frightened not knowing what was happening; she was used to this white mist coming from her hands, but this was something new and it wasn't coming from her. Suddenly, four figures were forming around the bed, getting darker and clearer with each second. The man to Matthew's right was really tall and big. He had to be over six feet and his broad shoulders would have made anybody get out of his way. His face was covered with dark course hair, but she could see the snarl on his lips.

He came closer to Matthew and started yelling, "What the hell are you talking about, Matty?"
The same soldier pulled harshly on the bandages covering Matthew's eyes and threw them to the floor.

He then gave a sarcastic smile and in a high pitch sing song voice chided Matthew, "Ooooh, look at them baby blue eyes shining bright. You always did attract the best girls; that's why we went drinking with you. It certainly wasn't for your winning personality."
Then the four men broke into a chorus of laughter.

Eyes that were just a few minutes ago white and void of any ability to see were now very wide, very blue and very alive; even the scars on his face had disappeared.

Stunned, Matthew choked out a cry, "Oh my God, you're all here. I can't believe it!" Matthew formed the biggest smile on his face. He could see them – all four of his closest friends that he served with were standing around him and they were no longer laughing.

The four soldiers were dressed in army camouflage green and still had helmets on the head. They took turns yelling at Matthew telling him he was a poor excuse for a marine.

"What happened to Semper Fi? It means always faithful to the Corp in life and death. You don't just give up," another soldier reprimanded him. This one had a cigar hanging from his mouth, but Lucia could see no smoke. He wasn't as tall as the first man, but still he was a big guy with big hands.

Lucia noticed that he had a plain silver band on the third finger of his left hand. "By the way, tell Alice I'm sorry. I promised her I would come back, but shit happens, ya know. Just tell her I'm okay and give her this for when my son gets older."

Lucia could see that he handed Matthew a gold watch. Then the man stepped back. Lucia could see him wiping his eyes trying to be inconspicuous.

The third man was small with an easy smile. He reached over and slapped Matthew across his face. Then, he grabbed Matthew for a warm and loving brotherly hug.

Matthew laughed, "Come on, Benny, people are going to start talking." They all snickered. The fourth man had remained quiet until it was his turn. Then in a thick New York accent, he told Matthew in a gruff tone how they had died so he could live and he was wasting their sacrifice.

Lucia stood stunned and speechless. She watched the miraculous exchange play out before her. Matthew tried to say he should have been with them, but they were having none of it. The man named Benny spoke up telling Matthew that they had seen that blonde nurse popping into his room frequently throughout the day, "I know you couldn't see her, but let me tell you, she is beautiful."

Then they all started yelling at Matty again for not acting on the chick's flirty banter and constantly rubbing against him. "Hell, you were not even her patient and she comes in here every hour! Hey, if you're not interested, maybe we should trade places."

Matthew was crying as he told them how guilty he felt. They argued back, there was no guilt to be had. Their number was up and they were quite happy. The first soldier who had spoken seemed to be the leader and placed his hand on Matthew's shoulder. He informed Matthew that this was a very special visit, they probably couldn't come back to see him, but they wanted him to know that they were watching and he better shape up and ask that girl for her number or when he did die, they'd be waiting to kick his butt clear across heaven; and yes, there was a heaven.

Carmen, the soldier with the thick New York accent, explained that they were sent to tell him that he owed the "Big Man upstairs big time. He had to get his ass to church and volunteer his sorry self to help others in the community."

Matthew could do nothing but shake his head in agreement and promise he would do as they said. They all put their hands in the center of the bed and yelled loudly, "Oorah." The men proceeded to shake hands and say their good byes. The white fog slowly dissipated and Matthew's colleagues faded away reminding him of his promise.

Matthew sat quietly in the hospital bed looking at the watch in his hands. It took a few minutes for both Lucia and Matthew to absorb what had just happened.

Lucia spoke first, "Well, that was completely unexpected. I guess you better get that nurse's phone number before you are discharged tomorrow, huh? And don't forget to get that watch to Alice."

Matthew looked at her and whispered, "Holy crap! Did God just bring back my buddies to say goodbye?"

Lucia was still shaken by what had occurred, and answered with a nod of her head. This was incredible, unbelievable and so much more than healing with her hands. Matthew smiled at her; well maybe smile was the wrong word because it was more of an ear-to-ear grin; and those big blue eyes were so bright and beautiful. It was getting late, so she reminded him of what the "boys" had threatened and how important it was for him to return to the church, be a good soldier for Christ.

Lucia instructed Matthew not to bring attention to his visual recovery until the morning so that she could have time to help others. He then became excited and questions poured out of his mouth. He never even gave her a chance to answer before he asked the next question. Lucia finally told him that she had to go, never giving him one answer to his questions. His reluctance to let the Healer leave led her to promise that she would meet with him soon and they could go into more detail. Lucia had to laugh to herself because even though she was initiating the healing, she was certainly not responsible for it.

Lucia walked to the door and turned to wave good-bye to Matthew who was still shaking his head in disbelief and repeatedly thanking her for what just happened.

"Don't thank me," Lucia replied, "I'm just the messenger."

In her head, Lucia was thanking God for this gift that was helping those who had no hope. She was witness to miracles she could never imagine.

Chapter IX

Jack, or Corporal John P. Jackson as he was known in the army, had invited her in; "Sure, come in," he said. He was older than the others and you could see the trials of his life reflected in the deep lines of his face, a face that was covered in gray grizzly end-of-day shadow. His upturned mouth gave the appearance of a smile, but there was a hard edge to his eyes he could not disguise.

"What can I do for you, Sister?" he asked as Lucia wandered further into the room.

Jack wore only hospital scrub pants with one leg cut off at the stump; so one could see immediately that he was missing his left arm and left leg below the knee. There was only about five inches of his arm that hung from his shoulder with the dark ugly jagged scarring at the base that she had seen on Bobby's amputation; she could not see his stump but imagined the scarring was similar. Her heart ached at the ugly cost of war paid by the blood and body parts of good honorable young men who believed in a nation and its leaders.

While she stood and watched, Jack lifted his body from the wheelchair using his remaining arm and leg. Lucia could see the muscles ripple across his chest and back straining to support his huge frame. If she had to guess, she would say he had weighed about 250 pounds before the loss of his limbs. He could have been a linebacker. He must have been a formidable foe in battle, and even with the missing limbs; he wore his pride and strength like armor around him. His welcoming smile did not hide the rage and resentment simmering underneath his façade.

He hopped from the chair and used a bar hanging over the mattress to pull himself into the bed. He raised the head to a sitting position and leisurely drew the covers over the bottom half of his body. His face was red and his skin had a sheen from sweat, demonstrating the immense effort it took for him just to get into bed. His refusal to ask the Healer standing right in front of him for help demonstrated his stubbornness not to seek support from anyone. He was determined to prove that the loss of two limbs changed nothing for him. He would take care of himself. Lucia stood quietly to the side watching. There was no way Lucia was going to offer to help. The proud soldier would have thrown her out of the room.

After he caught his breath, Jack turned his head to Lucia and nodded. He was ready for her. He knew she would talk to him about religion, but he had abandoned those things long ago. And so before Lucia could even speak, Jack pounced and let her know what he thought about her God and faith. He told her how he grew up well connected to the religious community in his home town. He volunteered as a boy and attended church with his family every Sunday. He never questioned his beliefs or had them tested until he stepped on the IED. He survived the explosion and still felt the anger of how he and his platoon had walked into a trap. Some would say he was lucky, he lived. Most of the men died when the Taliban surrounded them in an open field until reinforcements rushed in. Jack saw that his leg was missing and his arm was shredded. He begged and pleaded for God to take him, too. He prayed and prayed that he would wake up from this nightmare. It seemed like hours that he lay in what he thought was mud or was it just all the platoon's blood that had seeped into the earth. Even now, he remembered hearing the loud gunfire, men shouting and moaning, and the smell of copper that overwhelmed him. The medics who finally came in thought he was dead, but no such luck.

Jack continued, explaining his lack of faith to Lucia. Even though he had lived his faith, believed in God, and tried to be a good Catholic; God had done nothing for him when he needed Him most. He grew up believing that if you did the right thing, God would always have your back. So strong was his faith that he added his crucifixion cross to the chain of his dog tags when he signed up. (Sister Lucia noticed that only the dog tags hung from his neck now.)

"So, Sister, do I believe in God?" he asked as if she had spoken the question, knowing he never gave Lucia a chance to speak. "I don't know; does God believe in me?" he laughingly answered. "Look, I'm just trying to get through this life the best I can with one arm and one leg. What is this about? What are you REALLY doing here?" he brusquely asked her.

The smile was gone. His cold response made Lucia shiver. She could see that his connection with God was something he had lost long ago on a bloody battlefield. Lucia stood with her back straight and her chin up ready for a fight. She refused to fail again. She stared at Jack, taking in the firm set of his jaw and tightly closed lips; the creases around his eyes and the deeper ones on his forehead were well earned. His eyes were as hard as granite. Such a different appearance from when she had first entered the room. He was very good at pretending indifference but in the dark of night, she saw the pain and anguish of a broken man.

As if on cue, one of the nurses walked in with a hot coffee in one hand and brought Jack his medicine in the other. She walked right past Lucia not giving her any recognition. Handing him first the medicine, then the coffee, she asked him how he was doing as he swallowed the pills. He gave her that fake smile and made a funny comment. The nurse was older and Lucia could tell she had worked with soldiers for a long time. She understood the emotional trauma each soldier came with and respected the choices they made in their care. Some of the men went all in with physical and occupational therapy; and consenting to counseling that rarely alleviated the pain. Others, like Jack, refused all help except for the medicine that never quite masked the physical and emotional pain he was dealing with.

The nurse asked if he needed anything else and when he shook his head, she said good night. When she turned to leave, she looked directly in Lucia's direction but made no sign of awareness of her presence at all; it appeared that Lucia was invisible to her. Jack definitely noticed. Lucia could see his eyes narrowed and his forehead wrinkled.

He waited until the nurse was well down the hallway before he commented, "I don't think she even saw you, what are you an invisible angel sent to save me?"

Lucia laughed and asked him, "What if I am, would you let me pray over you then?"

She did not let him see her shock that the nurse could not see her. She attributed her invisibility to her shawl. Jack stared at her and contemplated his next move. After a few moments, Jack confessed that he didn't think God would send an angel to him. Unfortunately, he felt that God had abandoned him long ago. Lucia then told him that she did not believe that. She confided that she too had something really bad happen to her, not as bad as Jack; but she could see how Jack would feel that God didn't care.

Negotiations were prolonged and intense until he finally agreed to let Lucia pray over him. Her persistence wore him down and Lucia could see the pain medication clouding his decisions.

He smirked when she mentioned regrowing his arm and leg, "Do you think God would waste a miracle on me, Sister?"
Smiling, Lucia offered her small hand out to him and he grabbed it with his big strong grip and they shook. If the limbs grew back, he said he'd return to church and attach the crucifixion back on his chain (a small but important concession); if not Lucia would visit him every Sunday to play poker. Lucia informed him that she would see him at church on Sunday because she had enough faith for both of them. In the back of her mind, she questioned the deal because she had never played poker in her life. Reprimanding herself, she pushed those thoughts away because tonight Robert and Jack were going to have a very rough and painful night growing arms and legs.

Once he agreed, Sister Lucia stood over Jack and began her whispered praying. She could feel the heat flaming out of the center of her body. More specifically, she thought it was coming from her heart and felt it travel up to her shoulders and down her arms and out her fingertips. She was so centered on the swirling heat producing in her body that she almost missed the deep rumble of his voice reciting the Our Father along with Lucia. She opened her eyes ever so slightly to see Jack with his eyes closed and his hand held up in front of him. She repeated the prayer over and over and he followed her lead.

The white healing energy flowed heavily out of her hands and over his missing arm and leg. The white mist floated in a circular pattern over the area looking almost like the funnel of a tornado. Around and around it flowed until it seemed to have churned itself out. Already, she could feel a strong turbulent heat transferred from her hands and hovering over missing limbs.

She looked up at Jack and his eyes were wide with fear and amazement. Apparently he had opened his eyes when he started feeling the intense heat at the tip of the remaining arm and leg. He threw the covers off his lower body and he could see the skin around the stump was changing from the existing angry purple and reddish scarred skin color to a healthy whitish pink and it was slowly spreading.

He looked up to Lucia and his voice was weak and frail, "Sister???" She just raised her eyebrow and returned his question with a knowing look.

She readjusted her scarf and turned to leave. Looking over her shoulder, she reminded him not to disclose their conversation until morning to which he only nodded. Again, she reinforced that the process would be painful and that he needed to be strong. He just looked at Sister Lucia with complete incredulity as the realization that he really might be getting his limbs back; that this might be really happening, left him unable to speak. He felt the growing burn and tingle in both his arm and leg stump. He alternated looking at Sister Lucia, his missing arm and his missing leg until finally he accepted that maybe God hadn't abandoned him after all. He had tears in his eyes, but he was determined not to show any weakness and informed Sister Lucia that he had crawled through hell with one arm and one leg blown off. Nothing could scare him anymore, but then his eyes bulged as the pain worsened and he saw the skin on his arm growing. Lucia smiled and was truly surprised at the hope emanating from his eyes. Sister Lucia squeezed his only hand and told him she would see him soon as she fully expected him to uphold his end of the bargain by attending Sunday mass.

"Try to get some sleep, Jack. It's going to be a rough night," Lucia told him as she walked out the door.

Once she was out in the hallway again, Lucia paused to reflect on her last four visits and was so glad that none of them had turned her away. She thought of the young woman who refused to let her come in the room to pray over her sick son; the poor child then passed on the next morning. She prayed for her again as she walked towards the next room because she could not fathom how the mother was dealing with the outcome of her actions.

Chapter X

It was after 11:00 pm when Lucia had visited all the men on the floor. None of the soldiers were wounded as seriously as Bobby, Vincent and Jack, so the visits were shorter and the healings requiring much less energy. Several had wound infections that had already responded to medication and were being discharged in the morning. Others were in for non-life threatening maladies. None of them refused her offer to pray over them and she hoped it helped.

Lucia was exhausted but satisfied that she was able to meet with every patient and pray over him or her. As she quietly walked down the hall to the elevator, she began hearing the loud moans from the men as they healed. She couldn't believe that the limbs were regrowing; but then thought, God could do anything. Everyday her faith grew stronger as she witnessed the miracles that occurred. As the nurses ran by from room to room, she realized that again none of them had acknowledged her.

"It's got to be the scarf" she thought and laughed. "Dear Lord, this was a great, great night. God is truly merciful."

As she was exiting the front door to the hospital, she saw that a car was parked in front of the emergency department to her right. The woman exiting the car looked like it could be Becky, so she ran over to see her. The man and woman seemed frantic and were trying to get the small child out of the car seat, which seemed to be stuck from what Lucia could hear. Once Lucia got close enough, she could see that the woman was not Becky but noticed her tear stained face. Lucia could not help herself and asked if she could help them in any way.

The man quickly said no and tried to nudge his wife who was now holding the child in her arms toward the ED entrance. The woman looked at Lucia and noticed the black shawl over her head.

"It's you isn't it?" she asked Lucia.

The man stepped forward between his wife and Lucia and thanked Lucia for her concern but they had to go.

"No," screamed the woman, "It's the Healer." Turning toward Lucia, she pleaded, "I beg you, please help my son. He's only four years old."

Lucia was very tired from the evening's work and did not know if she had any healing energy left in her.

Lucia pleaded with the wife not to scream. Taking a deep breath, the Healer raised her hands and asked the mother to pray with her. The father moved out of the way so Lucia could get closer to the boy.

"Please help him," he asked of her.

Unbeknownst to Lucia, one of the children she had healed had been their neighbor and he knew exactly what she had done. Had he not known the little girl Lucia had healed, he may not have believed the miracle. However, he had visited the child two days before Lucia had seen her and thought then that she was not long for this world. The father saw her today playing in the yard like she was never sick.

The small boy had cystic fibrosis and was always getting respiratory infections that required hospitalization. The father couldn't believe their good fortune that God had sent His angel to help their son. His wife handed the boy over to the Healer and Lucia took him to the nearby bench and was concerned at how thin and light he felt in her arms. She began to pray over him and soon the healing energy flowed out her fingertips to be absorbed into the boy's chest. The parents could already see his respirations were not so deep and raspy and his ashen color was brightening to a light pink. The little boy smiled at Lucia and leaned forward to give her a weak hug. Lucia told the parents to still bring him to the ED to be examined, but she implored them to leave out any mention of her to the hospital staff until the following morning. They agreed.

The husband thanked her as he took the child from Lucia while the mother gave her a quick hug and whispered, "God bless you, Sister."

By the time Lucia got to bed, it was after midnight and before she knew it the alarm was going off. She hit the snooze button for the second time in forever because she was still quite tired from the previous night's outing to the Veteran's Administration Hospital, or VA as it was known throughout the community. Lucia struggled to get out of bed when the snooze rang again. Oh, dear, she was so tired. She even thought about calling out, which is something she rarely did. No, she had to go in, staffing was short today. She would have to take in extra black coffee to get through the next eight hours. Her bones ached and she could barely find the energy to get dressed. The scarf was thrown on the chair next to her bed so she folded it and put in her dresser. Her thoughts wondered to last night's outing and hoped that God had provided some relief for the soldiers from their suffering. One glance at the alarm clock gave her the motivation she needed. It was almost 5:30 and she had to be in by 6 am. She hurriedly got ready and ran out the door.

At the hospital, Lucia began preparation for breakfast. She immediately started the coffee, which she needed badly. She started thirty minutes earlier than her best friend Bea, and no one else really bothered with her since Lucia was always so quiet and never seemed interested in their gossip. Only with Bea did Lucia discuss the latest bits of news and usually she was the listener and nodding her head as her friend spoke. Bea had a flare with words and Lucia so enjoyed listening to her go on and on.

As the cafeteria filled, Lucia felt the excitement in the air as all the staff was buzzing about another nightly visit by the Heavenly Angel, this time at the VA Hospital. All the doctors and nurses were saying, "Ten wounded soldiers healed at the Veteran's Hospital. Two of those soldiers regrew their limbs. REGREW THEIR LIMBS! Can you believe it? One of the soldiers regained his sight and he said he saw his dead friends – in his room. Another had a traumatic brain injury and was paralyzed on his right side. This morning, he's alert and awake and moving his arms and legs perfectly. The scar on his head is completely gone! They all said that woman came to them -the one with the black scarf. They think it was the same angel who came here to the children's wing. They can't find her on any of the surveillance tapes and no one knows who she is. Everyone is saying that she must be an angel. I mean how else could she escape the surveillance cameras? I don't know about you, but I am going back to church."

Lucia couldn't believe it. She was so happy for all of them. She hoped Sadie got there okay. Lucia was sure Vincent would be so surprised and happy to see her. All those wonderful men healed by God. She already knew Matthew had regained his sight. Lucia could feel her chest swell with the announcement and knew God had truly been with her at each bedside both last night and the week before.

She started to think of other floors she might visit when she tripped and almost fell on her face. Thank God, Bea was there to catch her. "Hey, Lulu, wake up, these people are hungry this morning. What do you think about that woman healing all those soldiers? Do you think she's an angel from Heaven?"

Without waiting for a reply, Bea proclaimed, "Arms and legs grew back and one blind guy got his vision restored? Can you believe it? God is certainly good! Do you think she would give us the lottery numbers?"

With that last line, Bea burst out laughing and when Bea laughed you could not help yourself from joining in. Lucia loved this woman so much. She had been her lifeline when her life was falling apart. She struggled with whether or not to tell her, but again, Lucia thought she was too drained to make any important decisions today. She just had to make it to the end of her workday, and with that she yawned so loudly, Bea began laughing again.

Bea always looked everyone in the eye when she served, but Lulu kept her head down while serving the people. She always felt intimidated by the doctors and nurses who passed through the cafeteria line. They rarely paid any attention to her or thanked her for her service, but that did not bother Lulu. These people were very smart and had very important jobs. Lulu was glad she could do her part in this big hospital and never really liked being in the spot light. She could only hope that her anonymity continued for as long as possible.

Later that day, she heard one of the nurses in the food line mentioning Dr. David Woods. He was one of the young residents who was always so polite to Lucia when she served him. He was one of the few doctors that always said thank you. Apparently, he was asking all the nurses on the Pediatric cancer floor if they could describe the woman who visited the children and healed them all. He also had been sleeping in the Pediatric Cancer floor's waiting room every night in anticipation that the woman with the black scarf would return. He had informed the nurses to call him immediately if they saw her. Lucia thought maybe she should just tell him it was she when he came by. Of course you are, he would say, as she stood before him in her blue dress, white apron and matching hair cover. No, it was best that she remains anonymous for now. She couldn't believe that none of the security cameras had picked her up. Lucia guessed that someone up above controlled when she was invisible and still believed that the black wool scarf played some part in whether she was seen or not; but one thing for sure, she had to admit she had no power over it.

Lucia wondered if maybe she should ask one of the nurses why Dr. Woods was looking for her. What if he had an important patient that needed her? What if she had made one of the children's conditions worse? Would he call the police on her? No, she heard all of the children were healed, except for the one. She couldn't even remember the poor child's name. Maybe the good doctor was mad because she didn't do enough to save him. Lucia wracked her brain thinking if she could have done more to convince the mother, but no, the mother never gave her a chance to talk and was adamant that Lucia leave immediately or she would call Security. Lulu sighed and hoped this day would go by fast.

Anyways, she was much too tired right now to make any important decisions. She just needed to get through today and go right to bed. Healing seemed to drain all the energy out of her body and she made a commitment that she would start taking vitamins every day to hopefully make her stronger.

Lucia took a deep breath and then set her mind back on her task at hand, "Would you like mashed potatoes or fries with your meal?"

Chapter XI

It was several days after Lucia's visit to the VA Hospital that her beautiful Becky called again, "Mom, how are you? How's work?"

She told Lulu how she was pretty busy with her job. Then her daughter dropped the bombshell that she and Artie were fixing up an apartment to share. Lucia stayed silent on the phone. Becky knew her mother did not like Artie. He had a terrible temper and could not hold a job. Becky talked a little more to fill in the silence and then quickly said goodbye and promised to visit Lucia in the upcoming weekend.

It had been many months since Lulu saw Becky. At least her daughter called every two to three weeks. Both mother and daughter were tired of arguing about her boyfriend. Lulu had decided to make a major effort not to comment on him to Becky anymore, but sometimes she couldn't help it. Artie was just so bad for Becky and when Lucia said something about him, Becky would warn her that she had already alienated her brother; did she want to alienate Becky, too? So, Lulu remained silent. She wanted to say that she did not alienate her son, but that her father had poisoned his mind and bought his loyalty. Sadly, she was too weary from the divorce to argue anymore. So, after their last fight, Becky did not call Lulu for over a month and refused to take her calls. When she finally did call, Lulu said nothing further about Artie. Unfortunately, her daughter had become more distant and curt in their conversations. In order to mend their fragile relationship, Lulu was forced to bite her tongue and was determined to keep their conversations up beat and away from the topic of Becky's boyfriend. She did not want to lose her daughter who she so desperately loved. Becky was well aware of how her mother felt. There was no need for the mother to say anymore.

Thankfully, Lulu was still connected to her son on Facebook as part of his friends group. They were always posting pictures of themselves with her ex and his new wife, at restaurants or at his father's beautifully decorated house, all of them smiling. This broke her heart. She never commented or liked the page in fear he would delete her from their friend's list. At least this way she had some connection with him even if from afar. It was a rare occasion that Lulu would see Becky in any photo posted. After the divorce, her husband tried to buy both their son and daughter with all kinds of gifts, laptops, iPhone, and money. Her son took it all, but Becky would not take a thing from him. This seemed to anger her ex who frequently yelled that she was just like her mother. In rare moments, Becky would call late at night crying and tell Lucia what her father had said. Lucia would listen and say the words a mother says to comfort her child. Since she started seeing Artie, those late night calls have ceased.

Lucia's thoughts then turned in another direction. Where should she go tonight? Her exhaustion was gone after four nights of deep sleep and a static energy was unsettled in the pit of her stomach, almost like telling her it was time to heal again. She thought it would be good to go back to the Children's Cancer Center, but was unsure what would happen if Dr. Woods was still there. Maybe she would remain invisible and she could just go unhindered room to room. She doubted she would meet any resistance after her last visit. So, in her mind, it was settled.

She waited until 8 pm and then donning her long black wool scarf, she took a long whiff of the rose scent that brought her such strength and comfort. On her way to the hospital, she thought about what she would say if Dr. David stopped her. He was such a nice man. She hoped he was not mad about the little boy who had died. It was her first night and she was not so confident on what she was doing. Had she known the power of the gift she was given to share with the sick, she probably would have pushed a little harder.

She entered the hospital door and took the elevator up to the sixth floor. She walked by the waiting room, and sure enough, there was Dr. David Woods on his computer. He looked so tired. She hoped it wasn't because of her, why was he so determined to find her. None of the other doctors seemed as intent on locating her. Lucia had heard all the doctors talking about her, some saying she was a gift from heaven, some were skeptical that she even existed, but her second night out at the VA hospital was surely causing the cynics to rethink their position.

Room to room she glided with no opposition, in fact; the families welcomed her with open arms, praising her. She stopped them immediately, instructing them to give their praise to the Lord. She was but an instrument of His mercy. After each healing, she strongly advised the families to return to the church in gratitude, giving thanks for God's grace. She asked them to strengthen their faith and those of their family and friends with dedication and support to their local communities. She also warned them not to discuss her visit with anyone until the morning. All of them agreed, never thinking of putting their children in jeopardy; instead they watched as their child's illness just faded away.

Time passed quickly and Lucia was again pleased with how receptive the children and their families had been. Many of the parents participated in the praying, some stood by watching in wonder as the energy floated from Sister Lucia's hands. The children were too sick to have any input except to weakly smile when she left. The nurses went about their business and though a few nodded and smiled, not one stopped her.

As she was leaving the floor, she again saw Dr. David sprawled out on the couch. He appeared to be in a deep sleep and Lucia was hesitant to disturb him, but felt sorry for him waiting every night for her. She softly shook his arm and his eyes shot open. He realized immediately who she was and seemed to have lost his ability to speak. Lucia smiled and apologized for waking him. He must be so tired and she had heard how he had camped out here each night waiting for her. She could not leave the floor without speaking to him. Dr. Woods was raised Catholic and had a deep faith in God, but he was so busy he rarely was able to attend Mass. However, with Sister Lucia standing right in front of him, he was awe struck knowing he was witnessing someone involved in events of a divine nature.

Dr. Woods finally asked her who she was, where did she come from, who gave her healing powers. He spoke quickly, asking one question after another. He was afraid she would disappear and he would lose his opportunity. He became a doctor to help the sick and this woman was healing them. How could he be the only one here? How could no one else want to find her? Being awakened abruptly while he was in such a deep sleep, David knew he was making little or no sense. He asked her to get coffee but she refused. She told him her name was Sister Lucia and then said she had to go, but that she would contact him in two or three days for that coffee. "How?" He asked.

She replied with a laugh, "The Lord just channeled me to heal twelve children; I believe He will help me to find you."

She started walking away, then turned and spoke, "Do not follow me, Dr. David. And there is no need for you to camp out here anymore. I will find you in three days. Okay?"

David agreed, and he knew deep down that he had no choice. As she got on the elevator, David packed up his things and went home.

He welcomed the soft, comfortable bed in his small two-bedroom condominium not too far from the hospital. He would see her in two days. He would wait patiently but anxiously as she asked, because he was going to ask her for a big favor. He was the doctor of the one child who had died the night of her first visit to the children's cancer floor. He needed her to see the mother that had unknowingly condemned her child to death by refusing the Healer's entrance to his room. The mother and father were inconsolable and he had prayed to God for His intercession to help these parents. While attending the funeral of the boy, Dr. Woods had heard voices coming from the altar.

"Find her," they said. "Find Sister Lucia."

He looked around but no one seemed out of sorts. That evening, after work, those words played over and over in his head. He packed up a few things and drove over to the hospital. So began his mission of finding the Healer. He just knew she would come back and she did.

When Dr. Woods returned to the Pediatric floor in the morning it was with no surprise the kids were jumping on the beds and running around the halls. Several nurses were chasing them, trying unsuccessfully to get them back in their rooms. Dr. Woods saw his patient among the runners. He quickly scarfed him off his feet and carried him back to his room over his shoulder. The boy was laughing as the young doctor tickled his side.

Dr. David couldn't believe that this boy was practically on life support yesterday afternoon and here he was today running around causing mischief. His parents ran to the doctor after he had dropped the boy on the bed. Hugging the doctor, they told him how the Healer had come to their son last night. They had followed the woman's direction not to tell anyone until the morning. Looking at their son, Dr. David could see their love and immense relief that he was no longer sick.

"Do you think she cured him?" the parents asked.

Dr. David told them that so far none of the healed children had any reoccurrence of their disease and all of them had resumed their previous activities with no ill effects.

The boy was already dressed and pressuring his parents to take him home. Dr. David said he wanted to examine the patient first and get some blood work before he left. The boy was not happy about that, telling Dr. David that the woman said his outside body would be fine but she told him to attend Mass every week in order to heal his spiritual body.

Then he added, "I didn't know I had two bodies, Dr. David."

Once the chocolate chip pancakes were brought to the room, he settled down and exclaimed, "Well, maybe we can go after I eat my pancakes, right, Mom?"

Dr. David gathered his supplies and drew the boy's blood while he was happily eating his breakfast. The doctor listened to his lungs, which previously were filled with fluid but were now clear to auscultation. His heart rate and respiration were normal as was a quick physical exam. David could not think of a reason to keep him any longer and gave him the thumbs up to leave. He gave instructions to the parents to make a visit with him in a few days and walked to the elevator. As he turned the corner, he saw one of the cafeteria women getting into the back elevator. She was small with brown curly hair. God, if he didn't know better, he could swear it was the Healer.

Chapter XII

Dr. Woods waited impatiently. On the third day, he was beginning to doubt whether she would keep her word. Of course she would, she was sent by God. How could she lie! He was no good to anyone that day. He hadn't slept well and he could not get his mind off of his impending meeting with the Healer. He kept himself visible throughout the day; performing as much work as possible by the Pediatric waiting room he had met her at.

David's thoughts went back to when he had first heard about the Healer. He had been on the floor the morning after Sister Lucia's first visit to the Pediatric ward. He had arrived early because he knew his young patient was in the last hours of his life and he thought it only right that he be there with the parents. When he arrived on the floor in the early morning, the floor was buzzing with excitement. He could feel it and it made the hair on the back of his neck stand up. The nurses were all conversing; the families were gathered in the hallways talking amongst each other, but no one was quiet. He was shocked because the floor was always so quiet and depressing, hell, it was the children's cancer ward. These kids were really sick and yet everyone was exuberantly celebrating. And then he heard laughing and giggling. He turned toward the first room and saw a young girl jumping on the bed. He turned to the room across from it and saw another boy doing the same thing. Two other young kids in Johnny coats were running down the hall. He had been here yesterday and these kids had tubes coming out of every orifice of their body. They were on death's door. What the hell was going on?

One of the nurses saw Dr. David and ran over. "David, it's a miracle, almost all the kids have made a full recovery. I mean I can't believe it but their hair has grown back and their vital signs are perfect. We are checking their lab work right now, but they are all packing to go home. They said an angel came last night and cured them all, well, almost all."

David stood frozen. He couldn't believe what she was saying. Almost all the kids were healed; what did she mean by almost? Was my patient one of them?

The nurse called out after him, but Dr. David was running down the hall to his patient's room. He saw immediately that the door was closed and bile rose up to his throat. No, dear Lord, please don't let it be him. He walked in the room and there he lay alone, a deep dark death tinge had already settled on his lips. Joey's parents were already gone, for which Dr. David was filled with gratitude.

David stood just inside the door, unable to get any closer to the body. One of the nurses came in and reached for his hand. She relayed to the grief stricken physician that the mother was the only parent to refuse the Healer access to enter the room and pray over her son. She told him how they had tried to keep the children's joyful cries quiet in the morning but it was impossible. When the mother saw all the healed children running around and all the parents laughing and hugging, she fell to the ground.

Her husband had to carry her out as she was tearfully screaming, "What have I done?"

The nurse squeezed David's hand and told him that it wasn't his fault; he did all he could do, as did the nurses. David stood frozen staring at the boy's body, still in death.

The nurse continued talking to David. "Who could have predicted God would send an angel to heal their kids?" she softly whispered.

David had lost a few patients, but this one was by far the hardest. Over the course of the boy's illness, David had gotten to know him quite well and he really liked him. Dr. David knew his mother had shut down emotionally and the father was left to deal with his son's terminal illness alone. The parents had refused hospice services or any counseling support.

David continued standing, barely breathing, thinking how he had spent time shopping and watching television over the past few days when he should have been sitting by the parent's side helping them prepare for the boy's death. David thanked the nurse and backed out of the room and walked brusquely to the end of the hall where the public bathrooms were. He threw the door open and slammed it shut, locking the door. He barely made it to the toilet when he emptied the contents of his stomach. Then, David sat on the floor and wept.

The boy's name was Joseph, or Joey as he preferred, and he was ten years old. He loved baseball and talked about it all the time. He also liked video games so Dr. David had a Nintendo Switch set hooked up in his room. He was such a great kid who had certainly pulled the short straw in life. He suffered through it all, the chemo, seizures, headaches, yet he always smiled when Dr. David walked in the room. When Joey was able, David would stop his day and play a video game with him until Joey said he was tired. For the first time in a long time, David prayed and asked God to give him the strength to face his parents. He was sure that Joey was in a much better place where he would never have to endure the painful and agonizing effects of his disease and chemotherapy again.

At 2:00 pm, the Healer still had not made contact with him. He was getting very nervous or maybe he was just hungry. He had not eaten all day, as he was filled with apprehension of meeting with Sister Lucia, but now he was starved. The good doctor told all the staff on the floor to contact him immediately if anyone came looking for him. He double checked that the ringer on his phone was on high, then set out for the cafeteria.

The cafeteria had only a few visitors, most of the lunch crowd had cleared out and Dr. Woods could hear banging and clattering behind in the kitchen. As he was walking toward the food line, several of the residents came up behind him. They greeted him and began to harass him with questions as to whether he had found the woman in the black scarf yet. They had heard how he had been camping out in the Pediatric waiting room every night; however, their cynical tone and laughter led him to deny any contact with the Healer. They continued to tease him as they piled food onto their cafeteria tray.

One of the more serious young doctors asked him how the family of the young boy who died was. Dr. David just shrugged and his eyes watered. David was so lost in that thought, he barely heard the small cafeteria woman in her blue dress and white apron and hair cover; ask him if he was all right.

"Yes, I'm fine," he answered.

As he went to move on to the desserts, he realized he had heard that voice before. He quickly looked back and saw the woman smiling at him.

She pointed at her watch and said, "Hi, Dr. David, could you wait for me at a table in back? I could meet you in half an hour. That's when I get out of work."

David couldn't move. She was here all the time; he remembered her always serving him with a smile. He couldn't believe he did not recognize her sooner; he had been to the cafeteria at least six times in the past three days.

Before he could say anything, the residents behind him started yelling, "Come on, David. Get out of the way." Lulu had already turned to serve the next person in line. The young doctor realized that no one knew who this woman was, so he kept walking the line. It was important that he kept her anonymity for he desperately needed her and he didn't want other staff getting in the way of their meeting. Dr. David grabbed his tray and two cups of coffee and went to sit at the furthest table in the back of the cafeteria to wait.

It was a little after 3:00 pm when Lucia sat down next to David. He didn't mind that she was late; he would have waited all day if he had to. Lucia took a sip from the coffee she brought with her, closed her eyes and then took a deep, deep breath.

"What do you want from me, Dr. David?" she asked.

No need to beat around the bush, David guessed, "I want you to visit the mother who would not let you into her son's room. He died the next morning, you know. I was his doctor."

Lucia replied without hesitation. "Fine, let's go."

David had spent the last two days formulating an extensive and lengthy argument as to why Sister Lucia should go. He needn't have wasted his time. Lucia took a final sip of her coffee and grabbed her coat and bag. He could see part of the black scarf escaping from the pocket of her coat. He jumped up and followed Sister Lucia to the parking lot.

As they walked to Dr. David's car, Lucia confessed to him how she carried a heavy guilt with the death of the boy. "I tried everything, but the mother would not let me in. She even threatened to have me arrested," Lucia told him. "I have relived the interaction over and over, but I can't think of anything I could have done to change her mind. I'm so glad you are taking me to her, Dr. David. I know she must feel devastated. I need to help her and her husband."

David didn't think there was anything the petite woman could have done but if she could cure cancer, maybe she could lessen the mother's pain and guilt. He had called Joey's father the night before and the father shared that the loss was devastating to them both. He confided that his wife had mentioned suicide. The father had also expressed that if he was there, he would have definitely let the woman in. Although, the mother had turned her back on God and religion upon the diagnosis of her son, the father still believed and prayed for a miracle every night. He just couldn't believe that his prayers were answered and his wife slammed the door closed in the angel's face.

Dr. David assured him that he had found the woman and was bringing her to the house the next day. The doctor also asked that he keep that information to himself as the woman had agreed to come as long as she maintained her anonymity. Both men agreed it was for the best as they could not predict the mother's reaction. In the middle of the conversation, David could hear the mother wailing and praying for death. The father thanked the doctor and disconnected the call to provide comfort to his wife.

Dr. Woods drove the short ride to Victoria and James' home. Sister Lucia did not ask any questions or make any comments the entire ride. He could see out of the corner of his eyes that she was praying the Rosary. Her lips were moving but no sound came out. Her eyes were closed and her face looked so serene, so at peace. David asked Lucia what she thought she could do for the couple.

"Honestly," she answered, "I don't know but the Lord had directed you to me and knows my heart was broken over the boy's death. I will see what the Lord has planned when I get there."

David nodded and thought, "Not only does she heal, but she gets messages from God. I wonder if she also received a visit from the angel."

Chapter XIII

It was well after three when they arrived at the house. Sister Lucia donned her black wool scarf over her head. She looked almost ethereal. A neighbor was in the kitchen cooking and acknowledged Dr. David and Lucia with a nod of her head then returned to stirring the pot. James told them that Victoria had refused all food since her son's death more than a week ago. Victoria had no family, as her parents had died several years before in a car accident. James was also an orphan. It appeared that this couple had no real support system to deal with this tragedy.

David asked where Victoria was and James led him and Sister Lucia to the bedroom. Sister Lucia could see James's face was red and swollen from crying but nothing prepared her for the vacant and empty vessel of his wife staring at the wall beside the bed. Her face was gaunt and drawn and she seemed oblivious to our interruption. When James spoke to her, she just smiled and turned away to face another focal point on the wall. Lucia asked Dr. David to make sure they were not disturbed under any circumstance and to stand guard outside the bedroom door.

Lucia sat next to Victoria and spoke softly and melodically into her ear. Whatever she said seemed to bring Victoria to the present. She whipped her head around and sobbed uncontrollably into Lucia's lap. She just kept repeating how sorry she was for not letting Sister Lucia into the room; she had been so angry with God for making her little boy suffer. She was riddled with guilt believing his death was her fault. Lucia just stroked her head and repeated comforting words. Once her crying seemed to be waning, Lucia softly raised her head up so that she could see her face. She then asked James to sit on the other side of her.

Lucia held both Victoria's hand and that of James.

In a quiet voice, she spoke, "What I am about to do cannot be spoken of. What I am about to do cannot be repeated. If you speak of it, it will never happen again. Do you both agree?"

They looked at each other with only a moment of hesitancy on their faces, and then both nodded, trusting Sister Lucia to end this nightmare they were in.

Sister Lucia closed her eyes and began to pray, then asked Victoria and James to do the same. From the corners of the room, white smoke billowed around the three of them. Victoria seemed not to notice as her eyes were closed in prayer, adhering to Sister Lucia's instruction, but James clung tighter and tighter to Sister Lucia as with each passing minute the room filled more and more with a dense smoke until nothing was visible.

James called out in panic, "Sister?"

Lucia replied reassuringly, "It's okay James, keep praying."

Then, slowly the dense white fog began to clear. They were no longer in Victoria and James' bedroom. Actually, they were in a living room and sitting on a couch. James' eyes had been open throughout in fear of what was happening, when suddenly he could barely make out two figures across the room. Slowly, they came into focus. He was speechless as he stared at the couple before him. It was Ellen and Zach; Victoria's parents smiling and holding their arms out to them.

James shook Victoria and said, "Oh my God, Vicky, look who is here."

Victoria opened her eyes in disbelief, "Mom? Dad, is it really you?"

She was up on her feet and into her mother's arms. James ran to her father for a warm embrace.

They were all crying, with Victoria telling her mother about Joey.

Her mother just nodded and smiled, "We know dear, he is with us."

Victoria sat with a confused look on her face, and suddenly she heard someone running toward the house pushing a door open and letting it slam shut. Then there was running feet headed toward the room they were in. And there he was, standing before them with his bright blue eyes and pink cheeks. James and Victoria could not even move as they took in the dramatic change in their son's appearance. No longer thin and emaciated, no longer was his color ashen and pale. He had at least another 15 to 20 pounds on him and he was so beautiful and healthy.

The moment was broken when he ran into Victoria to hug her and almost knocked her over. She was so overwhelmed with emotion that she could not speak and instead just crushed him to her.

Joey finally complained, "Hey mom, I can hardly breathe."

She released him reluctantly only when he pushed at her so he could hug his dad, who also held him tightly to his chest. James broke the hug to give Sister Lucia a questioning look, then, thinking better of it, returned to hugging his son. He didn't want to know how this was happening. He kept his eyes closed, smelling the warm sweaty smell of his son and thanking God for every moment he had with Joey.

Victoria was blissful; there was her son looking so good and her parents. My God, she missed them so much. Her mother guided them into the dining room to eat, commenting that Victoria looked more like death then they did. Before long there was so much chatter and so much to catch up on, with Ellen constantly telling Victoria to eat or she would spoon-feed her. Sister Lucia stayed on the couch, dismissing their invitations to join them.

After eating, it was Ellen who broke the news to Victoria. As much as they all missed them and wanted both Victoria and James to stay, their time on the earthly dimension was not up yet. Victoria tried to interrupt, but Ellen stopped her with a hand raised to Victoria's lips. Ellen explained that her daughter and her husband had much more to do. There was a plan and they had to abide by the rules.

When Victoria's eyes welled up in tears, Joey gave her a hug, "Mom, I know you're sad that I left you, but Gram and Gramps are great.

Ellen, chimed in, "This is non-negotiable, however, this is not your last visit here. God knows of your loss and with His good grace is granting special visits for both you and James. Now let's enjoy this visit."

Victoria was so happy to be with her son and parents. She wondered if it was real when Joey grabbed her arm to get her attention and excitedly told them, "Hey, Mom, Dad, there is someone I want you to meet."

A small child with long blonde hair entered the room. She shyly walked up to Victoria and bowed her head.

Smiling, Victoria took her hand and asked, "Hello, what's your name?"

The little girl said nothing but climbed on her lap and held Victoria tightly. Victoria sensed something special about her; she looked like a mirror image of herself at that age. Victoria looked at her mother silently questioning her. Ellen nodded and smiled. "She is waiting for you and James," her mother informed her. James was watching the exchange transpire and was in complete wonder.

"How can this be," he thought.

The little girl climbed off Victoria's lap and walked over to James. She held her arms out and James swooped her off her feet and into his arms. She held him tightly and whispered in his ear, "I can hardly wait" and gave him a big, beautiful smile.

Reluctantly, James put her down; even though he wanted to continue holding her, protecting her. He couldn't believe he was holding the little girl that they would have in the near future. James was speechless, as was Victoria. The little girl waved and walked out the door throwing kisses at both of them. Right before the little girl walked out the door, she called out, "I would really love to have a pink teddy bear. Joey said you would get it for me." Then, she ran off.

Victoria and James looked at each other and broke out in a contagious laughter. Oh my God, had they just seen their future daughter. Victoria had not laughed in a long time; it changed her whole face. James noticed and kissed her. Then, he thanked God over and over in his head.

Victoria's mother, Ellen, smiled and said they needed to get busy because that little girl had been coming over every day waiting for Victoria and James to arrive.

"She won't replace Joey, but she will fill your hearts with lots of joy and happiness," Victoria's mother told them.

Not to be forgotten, Joey interrupted, saying, "I really like the name Rachel and I told her all about you. She can't wait to be born. So you see, Mom, Dad, you gotta go back. But don't worry; you will be back to visit before you know it. Maybe you can watch my game next time."

Victoria held Joey tight to her but he squirmed away.

"I don't want to rush you but my friends are waiting for me," the healthy boy told them.

With that, Lucia stopped praying and said it was time to go back.

Victoria gave a worried look, but her father stepped in with a hug and spoke, "Honey, don't ruin that beautiful face with ugly tears. You need to take care of yourself and James. I promise, we will see you soon. Now, where's that million-dollar smile?"

James put his arm around Victoria holding her close to him. It had been so long since he had held her like this; he truly missed her closeness. The way she snuggled against him seemed to confirm that she had missed him too.

Victoria and James joined Sister Lucia on the couch and the three joined hands in prayer. Again, the room filled with that white fog. James was unable to see his hand in front of his face. Sister Lucia reminded both of them to pray and give thanks to the Lord. Seconds later, the fog cleared and they were back in the bedroom. Victoria's face was no longer gaunt and wasted, but rather possessed a budding radiance, as was James's.

Victoria stared at Sister Lucia, "Did that really happen? James, tell me you experienced the same thing, too? Oh my God! I can't believe it. Sister, when can I see them again? This is incredible!"

James pretty much repeated what Victoria had proclaimed. Both were in disbelief. They believed they were "gone" for at least 4 to 6 hours. Victoria gave Lucia the biggest hug and smiled. "Thank you. Thank you. Thank you."

Lucia responded, "I am only a messenger, thank the Lord, Victoria. He wanted you to know how important you are to Him and how much He loves you. Now, remember, not a word to anyone. Okay?"

Victoria and James wondered how they could keep this wonderful magnificent secret, but agreed and hugged each other.

Lucia opened the bedroom door and their stood Dr. David as instructed.

"How's it going?" he whispered.

Sister Lucia smiled and turned back to look at Victoria and James who stood holding each other and grinning ear to ear. David peeked into the room to see the couple in each other's arms and laughing.

"You were only in there for fifteen minutes. What the hell did you do?" exclaimed Dr. David.

"Nothing" laughed Sister Lucia. "Let's go, I am tired and have to work tomorrow morning."

In truth, Lucia was having difficulty explaining what had occurred in the bedroom to herself. It almost seemed like someone else had taken over her body and she just acquiesced to the higher power. She reminded herself that she was just an instrument that the good Lord used and she was okay with that; especially with outcomes like this.

Sister Lucia was holding her Rosary and quietly praying on the way back to the hospital. David was dying to ask what had happened. After a while he could no longer contain his curiosity and finally asked what miracle took place in the room.

Lucia just replied, "God is really, really great, Dr. David."

David thought for a moment and replied, "After seeing the smiles on Victoria and James's faces, I believe He is, too."

Chapter XIV

Dr. Woods brought Sister Lucia back to her car and she left him with strict instructions not to expose her identity to anyone and he reluctantly agreed. He just felt that she could help so many people. She explained that the time was coming but not yet. So he nodded in agreement. When she got out of the car, she informed him that she would see him tomorrow night when he would accompany her on her healing rounds. He readily agreed. He asked for her number and was surprised when she gave it to him without hesitation. He then called her phone so that now they could get in touch with each other.

Sister Lucia wished him good night and advised him to get a good night's sleep. She saw the dark circles under his eyes and his rumpled clothes caused by his apprehension and anxiety of having to wait three days to see the Healer again. Concerned, she also told him to stop worrying so much; God had a plan and advised him it would really be for the best if he would just go with it. That's what she was doing she told him. Dr. David watched her as she got into an old beat up Toyota. It made him think of how Jesus was born in a manger and how material things did not matter in this life. It seems God chose this woman because of the wealth of her faith and not because of the amount in her bank account.

On the drive home, David reflected on the evening's events. Something big had happened in that bedroom, of that he was sure. Sister Lucia would not share the details, but David believed that God had allowed Victoria and James to see their son healthy and happy once again. He could not fathom what else could have transpired that would have changed Victoria and James's tragic devastation to the smiles and giggles when Lucia had finally opened the door. Was there no limit to what Sister Lucia could do?

All that was happening made him reminisce on a strange dream he had long ago. At eighteen, he had debated whether he would attend medical school or prepare for the ministry. Both vocations called to him equally. It was a difficult decision for him and David had prayed relentlessly to God for an answer. Then, one night, a deep male voice woke him from a sound sleep. There stood a well-built man with curly black hair, large eyes and a mouth that turned up in a half smile looking almost like a smirk, David thought in his sleep fogged mind. A white linen cloth was draped strategically over one shoulder, covering most of his torso with a gold braided cord around his waist. He had large gray-feathered wings protruding from the sides of his back that made a low flapping sound. If that wasn't strange enough, the light surrounding him was like a white cloud but had balls of lavender, blue, green and pink gliding through the white aura.

Then the angel spoke. "David, the Lord has sent me to give you his answer. He wants you to be a Healer of the sick, but know a time will come when He will need your help to save His people from Satan and all the evil spirits who prowl about the world seeking the ruin of souls."

By this time, David had pushed himself up to a sitting position and shook his head side to side in an effort to shake himself awake. This was no mortal man he thought but was unable to fully comprehend what was happening.

Finally finding his voice, David asked, "Who are you?"

The angel answered, "I am Gabriel sent by God to give you His message. In the future, a Healer will need your help. You must not fail to help her, David."

Gabriel then waved his hand. All of a sudden David became overwhelmed with a sense of peace and calm as he fell into a deep sleep.

When David woke in the morning, he thought that angel visiting was a dream, but nonetheless, did as the messenger commanded and decided to apply to medical school. After taking a shower and dressing for the day, David noticed something sticking out from under the chair in the corner of his room. It was a long gray feather. He was dumbstruck. David never shared that dream with anyone; they would have thought he was crazy. He has kept that feather to this day in the top drawer of his dresser as a reminder of the angel's visit. Always, in the back of his mind, he had hoped he would be ready if and when God called to him.

College and medical school were so demanding that, unfortunately, his faith had been pushed further and further to the back of his priorities. There were times when he was deeply ashamed by this, but then another emergency would come up and his thoughts centered on saving the life in front of him. He chose Pediatrics for three reasons a) his best friend in grade school died of leukemia, b) he liked kids a lot, and c) he thought that he could make a difference and be a caring and compassionate provider to children who were terminally ill.

Over the last ten years, whenever David thought about the message he received, he had convinced himself that it was a dream and inconsequential; even though he found that feather. Now, after all the healings performed by Sister Lucia, he just knew that this was the time the messenger referred to. All these thoughts were running through his mind during the drive. He almost missed the turn for his street and with a final thought he had made his decision that he was attaching himself to Sister Lucia who he was sure was sent by the Lord. He was determined to help her as best he could. The time the angel had spoken of had come and he was ready.

The events of the last few weeks confirmed to him that God did exist, and he was omnipotent. Sister Lucia often had said she was an instrument of God's love and grace. Well, so will David be. He might not be able to heal, but he certainly would contribute where and whenever he could. So he would go see Sister Lucia at the cafeteria in the morning to receive direction. Little did he know that Sister Lucia woke up every day and put her complete faith in the Lord as to what would happen and just kept praying she was good enough to meet God's expectations.

The next morning, David walked into the hospital; he was full of energy from a great night's sleep and open to whatever the day may bring. Unfortunately, he didn't get very far. His friend and colleague hurried toward him and inquired if he had been successful in finding the Healer?

David didn't want to lie so he responded with a question, "Why? What's up?"

The other doctor was Gerald Fitzpatrick and had been a kind and knowledgeable mentor to David while he was an intern. However, this morning he looked terrible. He was unshaven and his lab coat was dirty and wrinkled. The whites of his eyes were cloudy and threaded with red lines. He looked extremely tired and the deep stress lines on his face gave David some warning that this encounter was personal.

Dr. Fitzpatrick told him how his girlfriend was diagnosed with a stage four malignancy a few months ago. She was thirty-four years old and had four kids; her husband had died six years ago in Iraq. Understandably, the children were having a very tough time. The mother had little to no familial support and her local parish had paid for her treatment because she had adamantly refused offers by Dr. Fitzpatrick to pay any of her medical bills. In fact, she wanted to break up with him because she didn't want to make him carry her burden, but he would not abandon her in her time of need. Regrettably, she failed to respond to the chemotherapy and her disease had rapidly progressed. Neighbors had taken in the kids, but it was only temporary.

The woman lay dying as the two men spoke and social services staff was preparing to put the kids into the foster system. He had a meeting with the caseworker to see if the kids could stay with him. They had planned to get married in several months and now it was too late. His girlfriend was barely conscious. David could hear the defeated tone of his voice and how his friend felt so helpless and powerless in this situation.

He pleaded with David, "to keep trying to find that woman. She is Janet's only hope." David grabbed his arm in a show of support and noticed the man's eyes were filled with unshed tears.

"I love her, David. I can't imagine living without her," Dr. Fitzpatrick told him.

Then he quickly excused himself and ran to the elevator, as he was late to his meeting with the case manager.

David didn't know what to do. Well, that's not really true. He did know what to do, but he was not so sure that Sister Lucia would appreciate what he was about to ask her to do. She had flat out told him that she was not ready to "come out"; but he had to help his friend. He practically ran to the cafeteria where she was working. Lucia saw him and immediately knew that there was an urgency and desperation as he ran past the staff in line and quickly approached her. Deep concern was etched on his face with an undercurrent of regret.

Lucia looked up at the good doctor as he apologized profusely again and again,0 and then whispered, "Please, someone needs you badly."

Lucia nodded, acknowledging that she needed to go with Dr. David and accepting it was the Lord's plan that she could not hide who she was any longer.

Bea was working right next to her, "Lulu, what does Dr. Woods want from you?"

Lucia turned to her dear friend and said that she had to go. She gave her a big hug and walked swiftly to the locker room to change.

Bea just stared after her thinking, "What in the Lord's name is going on?" "Lulu, where are you going?" Unfortunately, Bea had attracted the attention of all the people in the cafeteria line. All the doctors and nurses looked from Bea to Lulu to Dr. David and a few of them were able to connect the dots.

One of those intuitive persons standing in line was one of the nurse managers, Mary Ellen Simmons. She was a devout Catholic and ran the hospital Rosary group every morning. She was one of the first to make the incredible assumption that the cafeteria worker had something to do with the healings that had occurred on the Pediatric floor. The entire hospital was aware that Dr. Woods was searching for the Healer. Mary Ellen could see Dr. David's pleading look as he spoke quietly to the cafeteria server and the worker's resignation when she put down the serving spoon. All the staff in line watched as the small woman left the serving line and walked in the back. Dr. Woods followed her while the tall black cafeteria server named Bea continued to call after the smaller woman who had left.

The nurse manager saw Dr. Woods speaking to Dr. Fitzpatrick right before he came into the cafeteria. She knew Dr. Fitzpatrick's girlfriend was very ill and made the assumption that was the urgent request Dr. Woods made to the woman. Mary Ellen called the floor she knew the girlfriend was on to see if she was still alive and when the charge nurse confirmed that she was barely hanging on, the manager told her to clear the floor and hung up. She was sure that was where they were headed.

Mary Ellen quickly put her tray back and walked swiftly out of the cafeteria with her phone to her ear. She was texting all the charge nurses to write up a list of the sickest patients on their floor who had stopped responding to treatment and their room numbers. The nurses were all badgering the manager with questions but she would not hear of it. She stopped them and told them to get their lists and bring them to the ninth floor STAT and to clear their own wards quietly without garnering too much attention.

"We need everyone's prayers that Dr. David found the Healer," she told them. Then, as an afterthought she added, "I think David is bringing her to the ninth floor."

Soon, the elderly nurse manager heard the beeping of messages pouring in. One after another they came. Mary Ellen was on her way up to the floor but quickly turned and ran to the cafeteria staff exit. She would wait for them there and hoped the woman would agree to help the nursing staff. Sister Lucia had changed quickly and donned her long black wool scarf. She used to think that the scarf itself was powerful but now she knew it was given to her to bring her strength and comfort in stressful times, like today. She felt her head pounding and her hands trembling in fear. She walked out of the locker room to where Dr. David stood waiting for her and they headed to the staff exit.

As Mary Ellen sent the final text, she saw Dr. Woods leading a small mousy woman wearing a black shawl out toward the elevator.

She ran over to them and Dr. Woods called out to her, "Mary Ellen, what are you doing here?"

"Come with me," the manager said, "we need to use the back elevators."

Lucia was wringing her hands trying to pray but was just too nervous. She did not know Mary Ellen, but she had walked by her Rosary group sometimes and wished she could attend.

Once they were on the elevator, Mary Ellen introduced herself and confirmed they were heading to Dr. Fitzpatrick's girlfriend. She pushed the button for the 9th floor; all the while Dr. David had his hand on Lucia's arm. No one spoke as they traveled up to the floor.

Chapter XV

Once at the nursing desk, David asked what room Janet Murkowski was in. The elderly white haired nurse looked at Mary Ellen, then Dr. David and Sister Lucia.

When she saw the black scarf around Lucia's head, the charge nurse exclaimed, "Is this the Healer? It's her isn't it? Sweet Jesus! The patient's in room 910 - down the hall on the left hand side. Wait, I will bring you there."

The charge nurse talked as she hurried down the hall, "You know Ms. Murkowski is doing very poorly. I don't think she will make the morning."

Mary Ellen followed along with Lucia and spoke, "All the nurses throughout the hospital are on alert to look for you. We have a list of our worst patients that could really use your help. I know you've only been to Pediatrics but if you could just see a few people this morning. Please, there is nothing else we can do."

Lucia did not answer, but walked into the room of an obviously very, very ill woman. Lucia remembered the nurse telling her she was only thirty-four years old; however, the woman lying in the bed looked like an old woman who was barely responsive. Sister Lucia could see her disease and the effects of the chemotherapy ravaged the poor woman. Her once long wavy red hair was gone, and her face was void of eyebrows and lashes. One could barely make out the freckles that had taken on a grayish hue across the patient's pale and gaunt face. The woman's breathing was raspy and erratic.

All around the room hung pretty colorful pictures drawn by her children. All the drawings had scribbled messages saying you are loved in different words. Lucia's heart was heavy with hurt for these poor children. There were no flowers or balloons to brighten the white sterile room. Wrapped tightly around the woman's hands were the crystal blue beads of a Rosary to which she clung tightly even in her comatose state. Lucia politely asked the nurse manager and charge nurse to leave and shut the door. Thanking them for walking her to the room and taking such good care of this patient.

It wasn't until Lucia walked closer to the bed, that she saw a thin figure sitting in a chair beside the woman's bedside. It was a boy no older than twelve or fourteen with shocking red hair. He wore a white shirt that blended with the white of the sheets on the bed, which is why she did not notice him at first. His arms were wrapped around his mother's arm, which rested limply next to him. When he looked up, Lucia could see that he had been quietly weeping, as his face was wet from his tears. Noticing the intrusion, he quickly wiped his face and tried to sit straight up. He checked his mother to make sure she was still breathing and let out a relieved sigh.

"Can I help you?" he spoke with a control beyond his years.

Lucia stopped and stared at the boy. It was times like this that she did not think she was strong enough. The young son at his dying mother's bedside broke her heart. She pulled the shawl close around her and the fragrant aroma seemed to give her the strength Lucia was lacking. Dr. David walked over and introduced Sister Lucia and himself. The boy looked at Lucia and gasped.

"Are you the Healer?" he asked.
Lucia could see the sadness and worry disappear as hope lit up his whole face. Lucia nodded and smiled.

"You know your mother is very, very sick. I am going to need all our prayers to try and help her, but that may not be enough," she spoke to the boy.

The boy shook his head side to side. "You're wrong Sister, I made a deal with God that if He sent you here, I would bring my brother and sisters to church every Sunday and then, when I turned eighteen, I would join the seminary. He sent you in answer to my prayers. I have faith, Sister."

The boy, now filled with lots of hope and energy, told Lucia about his brother and sisters. He usually took care of them but he didn't want his mother to die alone, so he had a neighbor watch them while he came to the hospital. He had all but given up hope. He told the Sister and Doctor how as the oldest, his father would assign him as the man of the family whenever he was deployed. When his father died, the boy did his best to help his mother and siblings, but he was only thirteen. When she got sick he just felt so helpless. He didn't think Child Services would let him take care of the three younger kids.

He prayed night and day for a miracle, "And here you are, Sister."

Lucia asked the boy what his name was and he told her proudly, "Simon, after one of Christ's apostles."

She smiled, and then instructed David to place his hands next to hers.

"Pray hard David", she told him, "this woman is really, really sick."

Lucia could not feel any of the warmth and tingling she felt prior to any healing she had done. This woman's life force was completely depleted and death was seconds away and Lucia was not sure she would be enough, but continued just the same. Let God's will be done, she silently prayed. With little hope but great faith, she and David raised their hands over the woman's cancer ridden body.

As both of them prayed, Lucia again witnessed the familiar white energy oozing from her fingers. The substance seemed to penetrate every part of the patient's body. Lucia did not waver as her own energy left her and David stood stoic with his eyes closed while he prayed. All of sudden, Lucia could feel herself drawing from David's own energy and passing it on to the woman lying in bed, a new phenomenon that had never happened before. After a few minutes, David took a quick look at what was happening and saw a white stream coming not only from his hands, but saw that Paul had extended his hands next to Lucia's, adding to the white mist flowing freely from Sister Lucia hands and Janet's fading aura sucking up all the white energy they emitted until finally the woman was surrounded by heavenly healing light. Both Dr. David and the boy were astounded by what they were seeing but both of them closed their eyes again, continuing to pray with the good sister.

Unbeknownst to them, Mary Ellen and the charge nurse who had escorted them to the room had set up a barricade outside the door. The stalwart nurses refused to let anyone enter the room. The woman's boyfriend and provider, Dr. Gerald Fitzpatrick, was called in by the social worker who was refused access to the patient when she came to get the son. Once Dr. Fitzpatrick arrived and was told that Dr. Woods had brought the Healer to see Janet and even he would have to wait until they finished; the doctor told the social worker to leave, she was no longer needed and joined guard at the door.

Someone had called security and several of the nurses were gathering outside the door, but Mary Ellen stood firm. No one was going to interrupt whatever was going on in that patient's room. Instead, the deeply religious nurse manager asked the faithful to join her in prayer. So as the crowd grew, everyone was invited to join hands and participate in the circle to silently pray for the total healing of Janet Murkowski. No one who was asked declined.

After what seemed like hours but was only about twenty minutes, Dr. David opened the door.

Dr. Fitzpatrick, who was not a small man, grabbed David in a big bear hug, "Thanks David. Thank you so much"

Dr. Fitzpatrick then burst into the room to see his girlfriend. There she was sitting up in bed holding Sister Lucia's hands, weak but a grateful smile on her rosy-cheeked face. Her son sat proudly right next to her on the bed.

Janet looked up at her doctor's stunned expression and in a weak voice whispered. "Hi, Gerald, I think I am going to be okay now."

Sister Lucia smiled at the woman sitting up in her bed and responded, "You know it was your faith and love of God that has saved you. And your son played no small part."

With that, Lucia ruffled his already messed up curls and told the patient, "You need to rest now. Dr. David will check on you later."

As she walked away, she saw Janet and Gerald engage in a warm embrace, her son in the middle of them.

The nurse manager that stood guard at the door met Lucia as she was exiting the room. "Thank you so much for coming, Sister Lucia. As I said before, I was hoping I could introduce you to a few other patients that really deserve your help. You see, me and a few of the other head nurses got together to compile this list."

She reached into her white coat pocket and pulled out a crumpled piece of paper with names and room numbers. "We, I mean, the entire nursing staff, we're all on alert for you, Sister. Please, Sister."

Sister Lucia graciously took the list and smiled, "Of course, Mary Ellen, and thank you for your help. Can I expect the same from every floor?"

"Definitely" replied Mary Ellen, "I can come with you if that's okay. I can guard the doors. No one will get by me. And if it helps, Sister, I can pray outside the door like I did before. I had everyone who came to see what was going on, join a prayer circle."

David looked over at Sister Lucia for an answer. He was still reeling from watching Sister Lucia work and being a battery for her during the healing. Lucia was a little worried; she really did not want to bring any attention to herself.

When she expressed the same to Dr. David and Mary Ellen, it was Mary Ellen who spoke up, "I am so sorry, Sister Lucia, it is much too late to worry about that. The whole hospital knows you're here."

Chapter XVI

As they walked closer to the nursing station, Lucia could see a number of security officers pushing a large crowd of spectators back and the crowd was growing rapidly. They were all calling to her and most had their phones out filming. Lucia wasn't sure she was going to be able to get to other floors and became a little frightened.

David, wonderful Dr. David, stepped up in front of Sister Lucia, blocking their view and started shouting, "Sister Lucia is trying to help people and you are in her way. Go back to your floors and for heaven's sake put those cameras away."

Mary Ellen was simply stellar with her authoritative commands as she directed security and her floor staff to clear the halls.

The Manager then pulled out her key chain and had Lucia and Dr. David follow her down the locked back stairwell to one of the floors on the list. Swinging the heavy door open, the trio ran down the stairs to the floor below. The other Charge Nurse met them at the bottom of the stairs and escorted them to the patient's room. Security and the floor nurses had already cleared the ward. Sister Lucia entered the room and quietly asked the woman lying in bed if she could pray over her. It seemed like everyone knew about her already and the woman grabbed Sister Lucia's hands and tearfully kissed them.

Then the patient looked up and proclaimed, "The Lord has heard my prayers."

While they were in the room, Mary Ellen guarded the door faithfully. She made a few excited phone calls to her fellow nurses throughout the hospital to keep their hallways clear at all costs – The Healer was coming, then she folded her hands and started praying. Unbeknownst to anyone, Mary Ellen had been a nun before leaving the Order and changing her career to nursing. At the convent, Mary Ellen had felt like she was not doing enough of the Lord's work so every day after dinner, she spent her evenings praying to God for direction. After weeks of this routine, the nun woke one morning with perfect clarity of what her future should be. She met with her Mother Superior to discuss her wish to leave the order, and with her supervisor's blessing, went to nursing school. She relayed this information to Lucia as they walked through the hospital. She told Lucia that she couldn't help but think that the Lord had directed her to this moment in time. With conviction, Mary Ellen told Lucia that she would not fail her or Him.

Dr. David had to navigate himself through the menagerie of machines and tubes surrounding the woman as Sister Lucia had accessed the only opening to the woman's bedside. Once he maneuvered his way to a small space, David again joined Lucia in prayer at the bedside extending his hands over the patient's small frame. This time David kept his eyes open to watch as the flow of energy engulfed the woman until finally it looked like her body and soul was completely filled with healing light. It was absolutely beautiful to watch the process and he, too, felt himself filled with the Lord's love.

It was pretty incredible, that the trio went from floor to floor with minimal encounters or obstructions. Visitors were directed to stay in the patient's room and the waiting rooms were closed while Sister Lucia was on the floor. The nursing staff was amazing, Lucia thought, they are truly God's Angels. Patient to patient she went, all of them very ill, most terminally, but none had compared to Janet. No, she had taken a lot of energy to heal, which is why she needed Dr. David. She used him like a battery. One day she will let him know.

All in all, there were fifteen patients on Mary Ellen's list. All the patients and their families welcomed Sister Lucia and her healing prayer, some held tightly to her hands and seemed so afraid to let her go. Lucia reassured them that she had done all she could do but the extent of the healing was up to God. She had encouraged them all to continue practicing their faith through prayer and Communion and for those who had grown distant from God, she asked them to return to the church and actively practice their faith. God is the way – the only way to salvation she told them.

When she had finally left the last patient's room, Lucia was hungry. She hadn't eaten since breakfast and now it was way past lunch. She didn't think she could return to her job after today and didn't even want to think about tomorrow.

She asked Mary Ellen if they could get something to eat when a security officer came running over to them practically shouting, "People are pouring into the entrance of the hospital and the Emergency Department is looking all over for you."

David responded first, "What's going on? Sister Lucia is leaving now."

The security officer spoke to Dr. Woods but never took his eyes off of Lucia, "I think you all should take a look at the front entrance first. I have my whole team down there trying to organize a line of people waiting to see the Healer."

The security guard escorted them to the front entrance and what he had reported to them was confirmed. Large crowds of people were being corralled into a single line along the wall and that line stretched around the building to the outside and was growing. Security and the administrative staff were in the front entranceway trying to manage the crowd. Mary Ellen walked over to one of the nurses trying to organize the line of people and whatever Mary Ellen said; the younger nurse nodded her head in agreement. Mary Ellen was on the phone immediately and directed maintenance workers to set up tables and chairs by the door and along the line, too. She would begin screening those in the line and take children first. Dr. David and Lucia, both overwhelmed, agreed. Dr. David looked down at Lucia and asked her if she had a little more energy.

"Did you say a little more energy, David? There are hundreds of people here! You need to get me some food, lots of food. And don't forget some dessert!" Lucia countered and walked over to the first person in line.

David looked over the large crowd of people standing in line and then back to Sister Lucia.

He could already see the white light of healing shoot strong from Sister Lucia's fingertips and shaking his head, he thought, "It's going to be a very long day."

He ran to the cafeteria to get Sister Lucia some food. Bea was there and provided several sandwiches and added a dozen of chocolate chip cookies to the tray,

"They are her favorites," she exclaimed. "Tell her I forgive her for not telling me."

When David returned, Lucia took ten minutes to eat a sandwich and two of the chocolate chip cookies. She washed it down with coffee and then returned to the line.

She dragged David with her and instructed him to do as he did before and provide an additional boost of energy while she performed the healing. He was honored – honored to be here with her, honored to be part of this miracle, honored to be a part of God's plan. And so he silently stood next to Lucia and closed his eyes in prayer.

Mary Ellen was superb in directing the patient traffic and when doctors and nurses were crowding the area to watch Lucia work; she reprimanded them all and directed them back to their workstations. As the manager was ensuring a smooth and efficient patient flow through the hospital entrance, she noticed security placing room dividers to make a single line and to provide some privacy as Sister Lucia healed. Mary Ellen asked the security staff rather loudly who ordered the room dividers. She thought it was a good idea but she wanted coordination and as she had assumed charge, she wanted to know who else was giving directions.

A sixtyish well-built man in jeans and a Henley shirt came strutting over to where Mary Ellen was asking security staff questions. He had an easy smile, but Mary Ellen was not fooled. He was a lean mean fighting machine. The muscles rippled under his shirt and the manager also saw the gun holstered under his leather jacket.

"Hello, I'm Jacob Bronson. I'm Head of Security for the Archdiocese and was asked to help out here. I don't mean to step on your toes, but I think we both want everyone, especially Sister Lucia, to be safe."

Mary Ellen nodded and conceded that she would abide by his assessment. She told him she was happy he was here since she was overwhelmed with all the sick patients coming in. She had already established perimeters for people to be seen. They were not seeing any routine illnesses, so those people were redirected to a triage area. Mary Ellen already knew that Sister Lucia had cured cancer, liver, kidney and heart disease, and though unconfirmed, she heard that limbs were even regrown. Mary Ellen made a note to confirm this.

Thankfully, visiting hours were over at 8pm. The hospital security had stopped the line at 7 pm and closed the entrance except to the Emergency Department, and even then there were five security guards posted at the entrance to screen patients arriving. Most were coming to see Sister Lucia, but the guards informed them that she had left for the evening. They assured the people that she would be back again and advised them to look out for notices announcing when.

Lucia, Dr. David, Mary Ellen and staff that were recruited to help sat in the deserted waiting room. All of them were overwhelmed and exhausted from the day's event. Most of the support staff had left after the last patient and the maintenance crew was cleaning up the area. Lucia could feel people staring at her, but she was too exhausted by the number of sick who came to her for healing. I'm sure Dr. David is too, she thought.

Acknowledging her uncertain future now that she was outed, it was not so surprising that her eyes watered when she spoke, "I am so sorry to have caused such disruption at the hospital; believe me it was never my intention."

David placed his arm over her shoulder. She was such a tiny thing, he thought.

"This is no one's fault," he told everyone. "This was bound to happen sooner or later. Sister Lucia, you have been given a tremendous gift from God." He then looked at the few administrative staff still there. "If you don't want her here, say it now. I will take her over to the Veteran's Administration Hospital and see if they will give her space."

The Hospital CEO stepped forward and spoke, "This is St. Francis Hospital. Our mission is to serve the faithful who are sick. What would God think if we turned away the precious gift Our Lord has sent to us? Sister Lucia, please give us a couple of days to prepare. I will let Dr. Woods know when we are ready for you again"

He then turned to Jacob Bronson and a small group of men to begin planning for Lucia's return.

Lucia could think of nothing but going to her small apartment and jumping into her bed. David was off talking to a few of the hospital administrators.

She heard him say, "I know, this is absolutely incredible. It's a miracle."

She again wondered why God had chosen her and not Dr. David. He was young and full of energy, and from what she could gather, he was pretty spiritual. With a sigh, she hoped that the Lord was satisfied with her work today.

Chapter XVII

Dr. Woods had insisted that Sister Lucia stay at his home because no one really knew or could predict the repercussions of Sister Lucia going public. He had spoken to the head of security that told David he would arrange for discreet security around David's apartment. Lucia didn't want to impose, but in truth, she was a little scared of what could happen if anyone found out where she lived. Also, she had nowhere else to go. Lucia wasn't sure if she should share that she had seen two guardian angels outside her building on one occasion. She never saw them again, so could not vouch for their continued protection of her. Her neighborhood was filled with nefarious criminals and she had become a prime target. Bea was her only friend and she had her husband, four kids, her in-laws and two dogs. Lucia knew her friend would make room for her, but it would be a big inconvenience for Bea and her family. Her Toyota was left in the employee's parking lot at David's insistence.

Lucia did not have to report to work the next day as Mr. Kingston, the Hospital CEO, had said it would be too disruptive, but she did want to call Bea as soon as she returned home that night to explain what had occurred. As tired as Lucia was, she became extremely anxious thinking if she did not work, she would not have any money. If she did not have any money, where would she live, how would she eat or pay for gas. God forbid if her old car broke down.

She did not want to be any more of a burden, but she could not help the sobs that escaped as she sat in David's car staring out into the night sky. David was on the phone talking to someone but Lucia was lost in her own thoughts and did not pay attention. One look at the Sister and he quickly pulled the car over and reached over to squeeze her hand. She unloaded her fears to him as the tears flowed down her face. David could understand how she was filled with uncertainty; he could not believe how his own life was impacted, but hers was a mega shift. She reached in her pocket for some tissues and dried her eyes. Her black shawl was on her lap. She lifted it to her face and inhaled deeply; appreciating the calm and comfort it always brought her. David assured her that no matter what happened, he would provide for her; however, in his mind, he could not imagine the Catholic Church stepping in to assume responsibility for and control of Sister Lucia who had been consecrated by God Himself.

They arrived at David's place and he showed her around the condominium. Lucia took in the spacious open floor plan and the huge window that gave her a beautiful view of the harbor. She could see the lights from the ships passing by in the dark of night. There were no curtains here and she agreed that the view was so breathtaking that nothing should impede it. The kitchen had stainless steel appliances and a granite counter top. Wistfully, she recognized that it was the same pattern she had in her home in the suburbs. The dining room set was a dark brown with chair seats covered in rich cream upholstery. Lucia noted that the walls were bare as was the counter and tabletop. His home was filled with tasteful furniture, but Lucia could tell it was definitely not lived in. As if David could read Lucia's thoughts, he shrugged his shoulders and told her he spent most of his time at the hospital, so he was rarely at home.

The bedroom he escorted her to was almost as big as her tiny apartment. She even had her own bathroom and shower. Dr. David must be rich, she thought. Again, the bedroom furniture was a masculine dark brown with cream and turquoise linen and a comforter to match. Lucia ran her hand over the bed and could feel the soft velveteen material. She couldn't wait to get in the bed. David had brought her some shampoo, soap and towels for her to use. He was always so thoughtful and considerate towards her. Lucia thanked him and told him how lovely his condo was. She knew she would enjoy her time here; there were no gangs, gunshots or cars racing at night.

Lucia placed the black shawl on the chair in the corner of the room and followed David back to the kitchen. Just as David was showing Lucia how to use the Keurig, the doorbell rang. Who could that be, Lucia thought, maybe he has a girlfriend. She certainly did not want to be an intrusion into his life. She hurried to the door to tell him that she wanted to go home, when to her surprise she heard the most beautiful voice she knew.

Bea stood in the doorway with a bag filled with her clothes and personal items she thought Lucia might need. Lulu ran to her friend who had at least ten inches on her, and gave her the biggest hug.

"How did you know to get my clothes? Lucia asked.

She then found out that Dr. David had been talking to Bea in the car and asked her to bring some things to his house. Bea had told him earlier that she had a key to Lucia's apartment. Human Resources had given David Bea's number while everyone was sitting in the hospital waiting room.

Bea looked down at Lucia and asked, "That wasn't a dream you had, was it?" So, she and Bea sat at the table while she filled Bea in on all that had happened. Bea sat quietly, nodding her head as Lucia talked. David brought over some coffee for the two women who barely acknowledged him as he busied himself around them. Listening to Lucia tell Bea what happened, filled in a lot of the missing pieces for him.

He heard Lucia describe the angel that woke her as she slept in her apartment. The description matched the same angel David saw in his dream that night long ago. Then he thought about the large gray feather he had found long ago that he kept in his top drawer, and finally admitted that it was not a dream. God sent a messenger to him to ensure he was in the right place when the Lord initiated his Divine Plan. God certainly played the long game because he was now twenty-eight years old and here he was, right in the thick of it – exactly where he was supposed to be.

David couldn't help interjecting himself into the conversation to tell both Lucia and Bea his experiences as a young man. Both David and Lucia compared descriptions of the angel, and determined that, yes, it was the same one. David even brought out the feather he found under the chair the next day after the angel's visit. Bea asked to touch it and David handed it over to her. Bea closed her eyes as she ran the feather along the side of her cheek.

"This feather came from one of God's Archangels. Do you realize that this feather has been in the Lord's presence?" Bea informed them.

She was spellbound. It was too much for the spiritual woman and she began to tear up.

Lucia tried to comfort the woman by holding her hand.

Unexpectedly, Bea grabbed both her hands and told her she was blessed to know a woman chosen by God, "I watched you work in the front lobby and I saw the white energy come from these hands, Lucia. I always knew you were special."

And then Bea couldn't help herself and added, "I hope that damn husband of yours rots in hell for what he did to you."

Lucia laughed and told Bea that she was so far past that. Her husband no longer had any power to hurt her.

Lucia then divulged what Mary Ellen had told her earlier about her experiences as a young nun and her decision to leave the convent to be a nurse. All this disclosure left the three of them flabbergasted and took quite some time to digest the enormity of how the pieces were coming together. Bea was the first to break the silence by slapping the table and declaring that she had no such experience and she felt left out. Then, Bea gave the most heartfelt laughter saying she was going to insert herself into God's Divine Plan anyway. Lucia supported this full heartedly and for the first time tonight; she had a smile on her face and the tension lines disappeared.

David swore he saw a white aura shadowing Lucia's body as the two women laughed and discussed different scenarios that might occur in the future. Bea made her promise to be readily available if she burned her hand on that darn stove she had to cook on or if she cut herself with a sharp knife. Both of these accidents had apparently taken place in the past. Lucia raised her right hand and solemnly promised to heal both accidents should they occur again.

At that promise, Lucia gave a huge yawn and Bea took that as time for her to go. Lucia held Bea's hand as they walked to the door. Both of them were whispering softly to each other but from what I overheard, Bea was reassuring Lucia that she would be there for her no matter what. The good friend then instructed the good Healer to rest and not to worry.

"Remember what I always say," Bea told her. "If God brings you to it, he will bring you through it."

With hugs and long good nights, the door finally closed.

Sister Lucia grabbed the bag Bea had brought to her and headed for the bedroom. As if she had forgotten about him, she turned half way down the hall and said goodnight. David heard her door close and went to sit on the couch in the living room. He could see how Sister Lucia was overwhelmed. After attending medical school, David committed himself to Pediatric medicine and though he thought about his faith, it had assumed a back seat to his career. Now he realized that his destiny was preordained the night of the angel's visit. He went to the kitchen to retrieve the gray feather and returned to the couch.

David wondered what would have happened if he had chosen to join the seminary, in spite of the angel's message. Even though he had followed God's given direction, he felt he had done so at the expense of his beliefs. Faith is just so abstract and life had a way of taking your attention from what was truly meaningful.

"Well," he thought, "Thank God I did listen to the angel's message."

Just a small shift, the slightest change, would have taken him away from his destiny and he would not be here with Sister Lucia sleeping in his guest room. As he thought about the evening's events that had occurred, he lay his head down on the couch, making himself comfortable and then continued thinking of all he had learned tonight. He stared at the feather and remembered what Bea had said; the feather had been in the presence of God. David continued to stare at the feather and reflected over its origin, and before long, he gave in to his exhaustion and fell asleep.

Chapter XVIII

In the early morning hours, Gabriel materialized into the living room and saw David sleeping soundly. He saw the long gray feather resting on his stomach and was pleased that the man had kept it all these years. Standing over David, Gabriel took the small vial of oil from his side pocket and poured some on his fingers.

He made the sign of the Cross over David's forehead, lips and heart; speaking God's Grace, "May your thoughts be free of impurity; may your words be filled with kindness; may your heart be overflowed with love."

David murmured and shifted on the couch but did not wake. Gabriel lifted a blanket that was thrown over a chair next to the couch and covered David; then he drifted down the hall and opened the door to see Sister Lucia sleeping in the bed.

"Ah", he thought, "Everything is going smoothly according to God's Plan. He will be very pleased."

The next morning, Lucia woke to the sound of the tugboat horn blasting. She was glad that her bedroom window faced the harbor; watching the ships induced a calming effect on her. The sun was just rising over the horizon. Lucia had slept like a rock. She felt so safe in David's home. She went thru the bag that Bea had brought her and found her slippers and robe. Thankfully, Bea did not bring her raggedy old robe and slippers, but found the newer robe she kept in case she was brought to the hospital. She went out to the kitchen hoping she beat David in preparing the coffee. She was going to make him the best breakfast. Unfortunately, when she opened the refrigerator, all she found was a small container of milk and a couple of beers. Well, this wouldn't due, Lucia thought.

She got her phone and saw that she had many messages from unknown numbers so she ignored them. She found her old grocery app and began placing an order for home delivery. She bought enough for at least two days, until the next anticipated healing event, if Mr. Kingston was correct. She found some frozen breakfast sandwiches, so after preheating the oven, she opened the door and to her surprise, found the inside of the oven to be in pristine condition.

Lucia smiled, "I guess he really doesn't cook."

Waiting for the breakfast sandwiches, Lucia looked around to find David sleeping on the couch, still in his clothes from the night before. A blanket was haphazardly thrown over him and the angel's feather was lying on the coffee table. Feeling her stare, David opened his eyes and jumped off the couch. He apologized for sleeping in the living room but Lucia assured him, it was his home, he could sleep wherever he wanted. David felt an oily substance on his lips and wiped it off.

"What the hell is on my mouth?" he thought.

Lucia prepared the coffee; she had watched Dr. David make his coffee many times when he came to the cafeteria so she knew exactly how he liked it.

Lucia had set the table with dishes, which she had washed before setting them on the table, along with his coffee. She had found placemats and put them down so as not to burn the previously untouched table. She gave him two breakfast sandwiches and watched him devour them. She offered him a third and he took it. Lucia laughed when he commented that they tasted so much better when Lucia made them. She then told him how she had ordered food for delivery and would be making supper tonight. He was thrilled and told her it was a very long time since he had eaten a home cooked meal. He insisted on paying for the food and left his charge card on the table.

When it was time for Dr. David to leave, he called Jacob Bronson to ensure security was in place. Lucia assured him she would be home all day cooking supper and watching television, but in reality, she knew that she would spend most of her time sitting on the back porch watching the boats go by. She had already fallen in love with the sounds of the tugboat horns that seemed to go off time to time. She also watched the water skiers and the parasailers floating above the ocean. She couldn't wait to be outside and smell the salty air and hear the seagulls squawking.

The time seemed to fly as Lucia spent most of the day sitting outside until one of the security men brought up her delivery order and brought the bags to the kitchen counter. Then she went into action to make Dr. David the best meal he ever had. Lucia made everything from scratch and realized that it had been so long since she had done that. Like David, she relied on frozen prepared meals for herself, but not tonight and she was so excited to be cooking for someone. She even invited the security men, but they declined. Lucia would bring them something later. They were so kind helping her with her delivery.

She had tried going through her voicemail but it was mostly reporters or crank calls calling her a fraud. There were more than a few callers making accusations that she was possessed by the devil or that she paid the families to say that she healed them. Lucia did not understand how or why they would think that way. Unfortunately, she had to go through each one in case Becky had called. Lucia's daughter would not know how to find her if she needed her, so Lucia had left a message at the number Becky had given her several months ago stating she would not be home for a while and was staying at a friend's house. Later, she had called Dr. David and asked him to invite Mary Ellen to dinner. The displaced homemaker had made plenty of food.

Dr. David and Mary Ellen showed up together and Lucia had everything ready. She was worried that they would not like her cooking, but there was very little of the meal left in the serving dishes after everyone had eaten. Dr. David had really attacked the prepared food and Lucia told herself that she would make more food tomorrow and put some in separate containers to freeze. Then, he could heat them up in case Lucia returned home. She really was unsure how long she would be staying here, but David assured her that she was welcome for as long as needed.

In two days, David and Lucia had made a good team and David seemed to appreciate Lucia's efforts to make his condo homier. It seemed David had not entirely unpacked when he moved in and Lucia had found boxes stored in the closet. In the boxes, Lucia discovered some really nice pieces that David had collected and she placed them around the living and dining room. Most of them were colorful and added just the right amount accent to complement the dark brown furniture.

Lucia would retire to her room once the kitchen was cleaned after dinner and David would take over the couch and watch one of the ball games. Lucia didn't mind, she could continue watching the ships pass and listen to the waves crashing to shore. It also gave her time to say her daily Rosary. This was so much better than sitting in her old green chair all alone. If she got lonely she just went out to the kitchen and David always had something nice to say to her.

The morning of the third day, David told Lucia that Mary Ellen had contacted him last night and informed him the Hospital CEO had designated a space for Lucia and it would be ready for tomorrow at three o'clock. The posters had been sent out; the parishes were notified, as were the doctor's offices to contact their patients that met the criteria. Anyone with a curable or short-term illness would not be allowed in. Mary Ellen was handling admission criteria and Jacob was handling security.

Lucia was conflicted. The past few days were idyllic. She was truly at peace and loved watching the harbor activity day and night. Then, she reminded herself, she had a job to do. Many people were counting on her, and, in truth, she was well rested and never more prepared. She had noticed that the more people she healed, the faster the current of energy seemed to flow; in addition, her strength seemed to be improving. She was tired after healing all the people that showed up at the hospital entrance but she wasn't as tired as she had been when she had left the Pediatric ward on that first night. She said a quick prayer to the Lord that she could handle all the people they anticipated.

David, reading her apprehension reassured her, "Don't worry, I'm sure everything will be fine. I won't leave you."

Chapter XIX

As promised, Mr. Kingston, and the security team had developed a plan for Sister Lucia to return and administer her healing to the community. In the back of the hospital, there was the old Emergency Department that was vacant since it was relocated to the front of the hospital several years ago with an updated floor plan. He ordered it cleaned by housekeeping and then assigned Mary Ellen to arrange staffing with volunteers. Many of the hospital nurses were anxious to participate in this truly extraordinary event.

Advertising was kept to a minimum and the executives decided to rely mostly on the posters they faxed out and word of mouth. The hospital had set up a special hot line to inform callers when the next event would be. Mary Ellen had made contact with front line staff of the surrounding parishes; unfortunately, the religious community was reluctant to endorse Sister Lucia's work, even though they admitted the healings themselves were miraculous. Mary Ellen had made several phone calls to the Bishop and the Archbishop who resided in town, however, none of her calls were returned.

Dr. David, who had attended to his patients earlier that day, picked up Sister Lucia and brought her to the hospital. She draped the scarf over her head and prayed while David drove in silence. Dr. David was lost in his thoughts about the strange over whelming feeling of peace he experienced upon wakening in the morning the first night Lucia stayed over. He also couldn't explain how he had some kind of oil on his lips and forehead and then there was the blanket covering him on the couch which when he asked Lucia, she denied putting the blanket on him. No other strange things had happened since that morning, but David was still mystified.

Once they arrived at the hospital, David was hoping that today was less chaotic than the first day when both Lucia and he were taken by surprise by so many people coming to the hospital to be healed. Mary Ellen had reassured him that she had a lot of volunteers who would keep the flow organized and moving. Dr. David had gotten some of the more religious residents, like himself, to help the Healer if needed.

Lucia and Dr. David came through a side door as directed and received a warm welcome by the staff and volunteers. Then, they were guided to a small room, which held an old table and a couple of metal chairs. Lucia could see there was a more comfortable cloth armchair in the corner of the room. Volunteers were tasked to keep the crowd organized and as quiet as possible in the old ED waiting room. Lucia observed the people praying softly. She felt the praying would help her immensely and she told Mary Ellen that. She also advised her to inform the people that she was only a messenger and God would give each of them what He felt they needed. Mary Ellen went off to inform the volunteers to deliver that message to everyone.

Prior to opening up the doors to where the healing would take place, Sister Lucia was escorted by Mary Ellen and Security with David trailing behind her to "visit" some of the very sick patients in the hospital. As before, the floors were empty of visitors and patient doors were closed, although she could feel some cracked open enough to feel the watchful gaze of family in with the patients.

She could also hear their whispering, "Oh my God, it's her. She's here and she's wearing the black shawl," coming from behind the doors.

First stop was Pediatrics and Dr. David accompanied her inside every room, while again, Mary Ellen stood guard. There were only a few children who needed her and their parents welcomed her into their rooms. The lack of confidence and insecurity she had felt on that first night were gone. Sister Lucia strode into the rooms with a smile on her face and the black shawl draped over her head and resting on her shoulder.

She engaged warmly with the children and tried to put them at ease before she lifted her hands over their small bodies and began to pray. David stayed to the side as Lucia had instructed him to do saying she would call him over if she needed him. The stream of white energy that flowed from her fingertips seemed much faster and stronger than ever before. It also seemed to stop much faster. The children were mesmerized. David thought that Lucia must be getting stronger because before they had even left each room, the children seemed to improve before their very eyes. Some of the parents dropped to their knees before her, but Sister Lucia gently helped them up explaining she was only the messenger. She repeated her usual encouragement that they needed to go to church and give thanks to God there.

Mary Ellen directed them to a few more rooms and Lucia laid her healing hands on each of them. Dr. David noticed that she still seemed quite energetic after expending a lot of energy to the sick. As they entered the last patient room, Lucia took in the elderly woman with the younger one holding her hand. The older woman looked pale and frail with many bruises on her arms and chest. She was introduced as Mary O' Rourke and her daughter Erica.

Sister Lucia sensed this was a much different scenario than she usually was dealing with. She didn't know how but she just knew. That just knowing sense was happening a lot now. Lucia smiled at the older woman and complimented her on being named after St. Mary. She then told her that she thought her shawl was a gift from St. Mary as it held the strong aroma of roses and brought Lucia peace and comfort.

Mary asked if she could smell it and Lucia stepped closer and the elderly woman inhaled and agreed it definitely carried a beautiful scent of the flower. The daughter opened her mouth to speak but Mary held up her hand to silence her. It was then that Lucia saw the younger woman was quite distressed with eyes that were red from crying.

Mary then spoke with a strength her frail body betrayed, "It seems my daughter asked for your presence here today, but I want you to use your gift for her. I am ready to meet my maker and my husband who died and left me ten years ago. I have lived a long and full life and I have no regrets. I do not want you wasting your time and energy on me, but I would greatly appreciate it if you could ease my daughter's pain and suffering after I pass."

Her daughter moaned and the tears started again, "Please, Mom, please don't do this." The mother held her daughter as she cried and shooed Sister Lucia from the room. Lucia turned to Mary Ellen and asked her to arrange for a priest to bring Communion to the woman and make sure she received Last Rites, although with a name like

Mary O'Rourke, Lucia couldn't see anyone keeping her out of Heaven.

Lucia felt the daughter's pain and her thoughts went to her own daughter. "Would Becky cry if I was dying?" That was an answer Lucia did not want to consider. She had not heard from her daughter in several weeks and she was so worried about her. Lucia made a note in the back of her mind to call Becky again tomorrow. She just hoped she would answer.

The three of them used the back stairs to get to the old ED as Mary Ellen had informed them that there were many people waiting. Lucia asked if there was food, thinking maybe Bea would be the one to deliver it. Lucia was feeling a little melancholy after that last patient and thinking about Becky. Bea always lifted her spirits when she was sad. Dr. David seemed to sense this and told her he would ask that Bea bring some sandwiches and chocolate chip cookies to the area. Lucia smiled. David seemed to be getting pretty good at anticipating Lucia's needs. Then she remembered how the angel had visited him too when he was eighteen. God probably knew she would need someone young and strong to help her on this journey.

David already had his phone out making the request. Sister Lucia looked down the hallway and even from this distance she could see the crowd of people waiting in line for her. As they got closer, she could see many of the adults and some of the children were holding the Rosary beads in their hands and they were reciting the Rosary with a nurse who was standing on an elevated platform. Those that didn't know the prayer stood with their heads bowed in reverence. God Bless them all.

Lucia could see some of the nurses she recognized from the floors she had visited and they all waved to her. She also saw that security had installed metal detectors at the front and four large security men were standing guard to make sure that everyone passed through. Lucia was shocked. Metal detectors, really! In addition, patients in wheelchairs were being inspected by nursing staff before entering the waiting area. Security was really stepping up their game. Maybe she shouldn't have told Dr. David about those prank phone calls.

Lucia was just getting ready to go to the front when she heard Bea make her entrance. Apparently, security tried to stop her and that was their mistake. She told them in a loud and firm voice that Lucia was her best friend and they better not mess with the Healer's best friend. When David nodded, they let her pass through. She brought Lucia a plate filled with her favorite cookies.

Bea was so thoughtful and gave Lucia such support, "You're gonna need lots of sugar to make sure you heal all those people showing up. I brought you extra for later." Lucia quickly ate a few cookies and then announced to whoever was listening, that she was ready.

Chapter XX

Sister Lucia waited until the Rosary was finished before taking her place in front of the makeshift stage. She directed one of the volunteers to bring the children first. As she was waiting, she looked over to make sure Dr. David was nearby. There were a lot of people and she hoped she would last as long as the line. She knew she was getting stronger after each healing and thanked the Lord for giving her His strength. She would need it today.

The children came forward - some in wheelchairs, some carried by their parents with so many different ailments but all possessed the same look of hope and faith in their eyes that Sister Lucia would cure them. The energy flowing from her hands came fast and furious, so different from the initial days when she first started.

When Sister Lucia felt a little tired, she would raise the black shawl to her nose and inhale deeply. She also felt David's hand on her back and she knew he was contributing to renewing her energy reserve. After an hour of standing, Mary Ellen brought a chair over for her to sit. That woman was literally a Godsend. Lucia sat and found it so much easier to continue.

On occasion, Sister Lucia would scan the room to see if it was clearing, but no, there were still many, many people sitting in the chairs provided and others standing around patiently, waiting their turn. She did notice an increase in the number of security and bouncer looking men standing along the sides to ensure her safety; but Sister Lucia had to chuckle to herself, she had the Lord and all His angels on her side. She never doubted her safety.

Two hours into the event, Mary Ellen announced that Sister Lucia would be taking a short break for sustenance and escorted the good Sister and Dr. David into one of the small rooms around the main waiting area. Lucia walked in and found a huge spread on the table and standing off to the side was her very best friend, Bea.

She floated into her arms and hugged her tight and Bea responded in kind. Bea had already made her a plate with her favorite sandwich and cookies, and then demanded that she eat all of it because there were still a lot of people who were depending on her.

Then, she looked at Lucia or Lulu as she always had called her and said something that filled the Good Sister with resolve and confidence, "God has chosen the meekest of us to be the strongest. He chose wisely."

Lucia hoped she was right.

The fifteen minutes flew by and again Sister Lucia made her way to the front of the room. She had taken care of most of the children that were brought to her and now was working on the adults. Again, some were in wheel chairs, some had white canes and others came forward and she could see the disturbances in their auras and provided the soothing white energy necessary for their healing. That was another new phenomenon; she could see the auras of the people who came to her. Not only did she see the different colors surrounding them, but she also saw when the energy was missing from the diseased or affected part of the body. That was where she focused her healing.

Few of the people spoke to her except to thank her and squeeze her hand in gratitude. She thought that was odd that no one really spoke to her but it certainly moved the line along and significantly limited small talk. One by one they came forward with their heads bowed in prayer, just like they were instructed to do by the volunteers up front. Apparently, Mary Ellen had written guidelines for both the volunteers and the people coming in; including that recipients were expected to give thanks to God by attending church and receiving Communion. This incredible woman had already started several Bible study classes and was encouraging large businesses to arrange space for employees to pray the Rosary every day.

    One of the men who approached her knelt before her unexpectedly. She reached for his arm to pull him back up, but he stayed on his knees and responded, "Sister Lucia, my good friend Matthew sent me. He was one of the men you cured at the Veterans Administration Hospital. He was blind and after you prayed over him, he was able to see again. He advised me to come here today thinking maybe you could help me. I don't really have a disease or missing limbs, but, you see Sister, every time I close my eyes to sleep, I see the faces of all my army buddies who died around me. Then, I get a panic attack and it becomes impossible to sleep. Is that something you can heal? I don't think there is anything that will help me; I turned my back on God so I'm sure he will turn his back on me."

    Lucia looked into his eyes and saw that not only were there dark red veins throughout the whites of his eyes, there were also large puffy dark circles under them. His cheeks were sunken in and his clothes looked several sizes too big. His face was gaunt and she could see his aura surrounding him was dark and murky. He reminded her of Victoria, whose child had passed.

Instead of pulling him up to her, Sister Lucia knelt down before him. She took his hands and while she confirmed that she knew he had believed in God but had lost his way; streams of white light were going from Lucia's hands into the soldier's. She explained that God had asked her to help him find his lost flock of which Kevin was one. He opened his tired and wasted eyes in surprise.

"How did you know my name?" he asked.

Sister Lucia just winked at him, "God told me," she answered.

Once the energy had stopped, Dr. David came forward and helped both of them up. The soldier stood staring at Lucia in disbelief of what had just occurred. The burden he carried felt so much lighter and his mind had a clarity that had long been absent. He tried to close his eyes and conjure up his dead buddies, but the only thing that came through were visions of the happy times of his life -- his wedding day, the birth of his daughter, the birth of his son. What kind of magic did this woman possess?

Lucia shook his hands and whispered in his ear, "The Lord will someday give you the memories of your friends again, but he wants you to concentrate on all your good memories, for now. He also said to tell you that he has a plan for you and he needs you mentally and physically strong. Go with God, Kevin, and for crying out loud, get some sleep! Oh, and tell Matthew I send my best."

Lucia turned back to the line and Security escorted the soldier to the exit.

Some cases were easier than others and some Lucia knew she could not heal what was destined to be. So, when family members brought an elderly mother or father to her, she concentrated more on those that would mourn the passing of their loved one. In an instant, an idea formed in her head and she called out to Mary Ellen asking her to spend time with those she was unable to help. Each time, she would direct this group to Mary Ellen for counseling who after being called for this twice, had maintenance workers set up a counseling room off to the side where she would call in the hospice nurses to provide comfort to those that were not candidates for the type of healing Sister Lucia provided.

    David still stood behind her with his hand on her back or shoulder all throughout the evening. Security closed the entrance at 7 pm and set two guards outside the door informing any latecomers that the event was over and to call the hotline for future dates and times; a sign with such information was also posted on the window next to the entrance. When the last person had left, Lucia and Dr. David were saying good night and thanking everyone for their help. Lucia noticed some of the volunteers and staff was staring at her in awe, so she walked over to thank them. She found it funny that their eyes immediately went to her hands, but were disappointed when nothing came out of her fingers.

    One of the nurses came over and reached out to hold Lucia's hand. Her grasp was firm and the young woman seemed hesitant to let go. When Lucia looked in her eyes, she saw and felt the pain and anguish reflected in them. The nurse was struggling to keep the tears at bay but was quickly losing that battle. Mary Ellen saw the questioning expression on Lucia's face and quickly realized what was happening. She guided the three of them to the "counseling room." The nurse, Carrie, admitted she was in an abusive relationship and was scared to tell anyone. Mary

Ellen took the initiative and said that although Sister Lucia was very good at what she did, the Hospital had great resources available for employees exactly in this type of circumstance and Mary Ellen would help her access them.

The elderly nurse then waved Sister Lucia out the door, telling her, "I got this." Sister Lucia was tired and completely depleted of energy. She looked at David with a look that said, "Can we go home now?"

David's apartment had become her home for the last few days since it was impossible to get to her little apartment with all the reporters and spectators hoping to catch a glimpse of her. Very few people knew that she was staying with Dr. David and he was happy to have her. She not only cleaned his apartment when he was at work, but also cooked for him when he got home, and he certainly enjoyed the food she put on the table. He was so used to takeout and microwave prepared dishes, but Sister Lucia made sure there was a hot meal of meat, potatoes and a vegetable every night.

As they proceeded to the side exit where his car was parked, a security officer came rushing over. He had a concerned look on his face and informed them that he was directed to escort both of them to the third floor Executive Conference room immediately. When David asked him what this was about, the officer told them that he was not given a reason, but just to bring them there. Lucia nodded and thought; maybe she lost her job for not reporting to work the last few days. As tired as she was, she grabbed David's arm and together they followed the man to the conference room.

Chapter XXI

Several other security officers joined them to surround Dr. Woods and Lucia as they were escorted to the conference room using the back stairwell again to avoid any curious staff that had been on the lookout for the good Sister. All of them eerily silent, almost as if they had gotten caught doing something wrong. The executive officers couldn't object to Sister Lucia healing patients, could they? She wondered if she had done anything illegal.

Sister Lucia did not know what to expect when they arrived, but surely not the horde of formidable men and women surrounding a tall, portly man dressed in a black cassock with a large silver crucifix dangling from his neck. Around his shoulders hung a wool vestment and on his head was a black cap from which she could see short well-groomed gray hair. Lucia could see that his eyes and face lit up when he laughed, but he stopped suddenly when he saw that Lucia had entered the room. The way the cleric held court to those in attendance and the vestments he wore led Lucia to assume he was in a position of authority. She had never seen him before and never at the church she attended every Sunday. There were at least a dozen other clerics dressed only in a black cassock and smaller silver crucifixes hanging from their necks, mingling with the people around the room, everyone chattering loudly about the events of the day. As she scanned the room, she could not identify any of the people who had suddenly become very quiet and openly stared at her as she stood holding tightly to the doctor's arm.

Lucia practically hid behind Dr. David. She was not prepared for this onslaught of silence when the crowd saw her. Everyone's eyes focused on her and no one speaking made her incredibly self-conscious and frightened.

Finally, after what seemed like an eternity, the portly cleric came forward, "Dear Sister Lucia, how nice to meet you."

Lucia wasn't sure what to do so she shook the hand he held forth and she felt the warm inviting energy in the connection. She could see his eyes were the color of the sea, green with flecks of brown and his manner put her at ease immediately. Lucia looked up at Dr. David who just smiled at her, like he was expecting this to happen.

Then, the older cleric spoke to the crowd, "I would ask that everyone please leave the room so that I and the good Sister Lucia and her friend Dr. Woods can speak."

Immediately, everyone filed out of the room, except for two of the priests. Lucia continued to hold tightly onto Dr. David.

The cleric asked if either of them would like any coffee or tea, but both shook their head no. Then he sat on one of the chairs and invited Lucia and Dr. Woods to do the same. He knew both of their names without introduction, and then he introduced himself. He was Archbishop Lucas Corvino and he had been following Sister Lucia's miraculous healings over the past several weeks. With a wide grin that reached his eyes, he said, "Well, let's get down to business, eh?"

Lucia and Dr. David said nothing. David had surmised early on that the church at some point would get involved, just not today; however, Sister Lucia seemed clueless as to the repercussions of her healings.

Archbishop Corvino addressed Sister Lucia directly, "I must tell you when I first heard of you, I thought it was a hoax, but I have spoken to many people, some who witnessed your miracles, and have come to believe that the Lord has sent you. And if the Lord has sent you then it falls upon me to help you. Could you tell me how this ability to heal people came about? Did you have a vision or rather did Our Lord come to you in a dream? The Lord often visits people and gives messages. Is that what happened to you?"

His questions were delivered with kindness and compassion, which made it much easier for Lucia to engage.

"Your Grace, I am only a messenger of Our Lord. He has asked that I bring His flock back to the Shepherd," Lucia responded quietly and humbly.

"Well, you have certainly started that," the Archbishop interjected, "Mass attendance is up 40% since the first night you healed the children. I am so sorry, I have interrupted you, please go on."

Lucia explained about the angel's visit waking her up from a deep sleep and how she found the beautiful black shawl in the morning. She also told him how she heard the Lord's voice in her head the next day, or at least she thought it was the Lord's voice, to go pray over the children in the hospital. She was unaware of the full impact of her prayers over the sick or that the Lord was healing through her until the next morning. She also told him that after each visit to the hospital floor, she became overwhelmed with exhaustion. It took about two days to recover her energy after each night out, however that recovery time was becoming less and less each time she healed. She also told him she was feeling stronger and less exhausted after each healing. It seems the more she did, the stronger and faster the energy flowed.

The Archbishop did not say a word for several seconds. Lucia watched as he closed his eyes and began praying. It was not long before his eyes opened and he spoke, "God is very, very good, would you not agree Sister Lucia?"

Lucia nodded.

The Archbishop continued, "You are not going to like what I am about to propose, my dear Sister, but as God has sent you to us, I feel God has tasked me with the responsibility to protect you. As we speak, there are hundreds of people gathering around the hospital and countless media agencies trying all different ways to get to you. I imagine that your apartment will soon be surrounded and even your car will be under surveillance. I am also aware that there are people out there that wish to harm you." Lucia gasped.
Archbishop Corvino took a deep breath, "I have been sent to verify your authenticity, however, I believe the healing of the terminally ill children and the growth of the soldier's limbs has done that. Correct me if I am wrong, Sister, but I believe one soldier even had his sight restored. You have been very busy with the Lord's work." The Archbishop lost his smile and his expression became serious and grave, "Given all that I have learned, I strongly implore you to come under the protection of the Church."

Sister Lucia was speechless, what exactly was the "protection of the Church" that the Archbishop spoke of? What did that mean? The Archbishop turned to speak to the two priests who had stood silently behind him and whispered something Lucia could not hear.

When they left, he turned back to Lucia and Dr. David with a smile, "I think it best that you be moved to a secure location. I have arranged to have all your things brought there, as well as your car. Please, Dr. Woods, help me convince the good Sister that this is for the best. I will do everything in my power to keep her safe."

Like Sister Lucia, David was stunned; he had expected this but now that it had happened, he was at a loss for words. What the Archbishop said made a lot of sense. Now that Lucia's identity has been unmasked, because of David, she would be sought after by the good intentioned as well as the bad.

Dr. David looked at Sister Lucia and reached for her hands, "I agree with His Grace, Sister, he is the only one that can provide the protection you will need. This is the public's response after being known for a few hours, what will it be tomorrow or next week?"

Lucia slowly nodded in agreement but deep inside she was very worried about what would happen to her.

The Archbishop slapped his knee and said, "Well, I am so glad this is settled. Sister Lucia, I will escort you to the convent to meet Sister Louisa. You will love her. And, Dr. Woods, I will have you escorted back to your home. If there is a problem, I will give you my assistant's direct number to call. We will do our best to help you. I don't keep a phone, you know, the only communication I seek is a direct line to God, don't you agree, Sister Lucia?" and he laughed.

The Archbishop looked at his watch and turned toward Lucia, "My car should be ready by now, Sister Lucia; may I help you with your shawl? May I touch it?"

Lucia handed the scarf to the Archbishop.

"Oh my," he exclaimed, "It smells of roses!"

Lucia agreed, "It was left on my table, the night after the angel's visit.

The Archbishop commented, "Such a beautiful gift from heaven,"

As the trio of them exited the conference room, Lucia noticed that the crowd had not dispersed.

One woman came forward and kissed her hand, "God bless you, Sister."

Another few men bowed as she walked by. Repeatedly, she heard people shout, "Bless you, Sister, God bless you." She smiled at everyone as security and priests quickly surrounded her. Through the corner of her eye, she saw Mary Ellen pushed to the back of the crowd. She broke through the line and walked over to her.

Opening her arms to the elderly nurse, she said, "Thank you for all your help, you are truly one of God's Angels sent to earth."
She looked back to find Dr. David but he was already gone. Oh my, she thought, I didn't even get to say good-bye. She was then ushered into the elevator.

The Archbishop kept his hand gently on her back to guide her through the hospital to his waiting limousine. The sentry of security and priests towered over her as they walked, keeping a tight circle around her. She began to feel overwhelmed and short of air because of the limited space left to her by the tight security field around her.

Thankfully, they made it to the car and the Archbishop assisted her in.

Sister Lucia took a deep breath and then inhaled the aroma of the shawl draped around her. She needed its strength as it became quite apparent that her life was changing and would probably never return to normal. Again, she questioned if she was really the best candidate for the mission. Lucia couldn't help the tears forming in her eyes and the tremble of her lip.

Archbishop Corvino noticed her obvious discomfort and fear and took her hand in his. "Please, good Sister, do not fret. God has given the world such a great gift and I cannot imagine that he would pick a woman who did not possess enough love and faith to carry out His mission. In His power and wisdom, He will give both of us direction and strength," he then laughed and continued. "Strength you will need once you meet Sister Louisa."

Lucia was taken back by his words, forgetting her tears and fears. Immediately, she was filled with a nervous curiosity, "Who was Sister Louisa?"

Chapter XXII

It was a long ride to Our Lady of the Blessed Heart Convent. The Archbishop kept the conversation light, telling Lucia stories of Sister Louisa. They had served the same community when he was a newly ordained priest and she had just taken her vows. Now, he was the Archbishop and she, Mother Superior of the Convent, but still they collaborated whenever they could to support the people in their community. He advised Sister Lucia not to be intimidated by Sister Louisa's rough exterior for this only covered up her soft soul underneath.

"Although, sometimes I think the softness is buried too deep," the Archbishop joked.

Upon arrival, a stout nun in full black and white garb walked briskly to the car and opened the back door, leaning into the back seat she voiced her irritation, "Lucas, what is the meaning of this emergency you have? And are you so busy, you could not pick up the phone and call yourself? I am a busy woman trying to run this Convent on the small pittance you allocate to me. What lost kitten are you bringing to me this time?"

The Archbishop smiled at Sister Lucia and then directed his attention to the nun. "Sister Louisa, I would like you to meet Sister Lucia. Sister Lucia is going to be staying with you for a while, dear kind hearted Sister."

"Don't sweeten the pill, Lucas," she responded with a stern grimace.

Then she turned to Lucia and smiled, well, it was really more of a smirk, "Welcome, Sister Lucia, it is so nice to have you come and stay with us. I am sure you will find the accommodations to your satisfaction."

Lucia looked over the nun standing before her. The nun stood erect, shoulders back and chin tipped up. Her dark eyes looked fearless and seemed to penetrate right through Lucia, looking for any signs of weakness or fraud. Lucia looked down trying to escape her perusal but after a few minutes of silence, Lucia peeked up to see the nun's assessment was still taking place. Lucia was too frightened to even extend her hand in friendship.

The Archbishop, noticing Lucia's discomfort, smiled and asked if they could continue their conversation in Mother Superior's office. Sister Louisa gave him a puzzled look but immediately spun around and started for the massive wooden door at the front of the Convent. The Healer remained surrounded by security until they entered the building. As Lucia went through the door, she noticed that there were several black vans that had followed them. Men were jumping out and running to the perimeter where a 12 ft. black iron fence surrounded the entire residence. A jolt of electricity ran down her spine as she realized that the Archbishop had arranged an army of guards and a high iron fence to keep her safe? Was all this really necessary? Taking another deep breath, Lucia followed Mother Superior and the Archbishop down the long dimly lit hallway.

Once they were comfortably seated in Sister Louisa's office, the Archbishop explained that she was the Healer they had heard about and was in need of protection. Sister Louisa listened intently to her friend and showed no sign of emotion or surprise when he explained Sister Lucia's healing ability. In fact, she barely acknowledged Lucia while the Archbishop spoke. He then explained there were already death threats being waged against her and the news media had no regard as to the impact of their reporting that she was a fraud. One of the magazine articles even implied that she was a devil worshipper and her powers came from Satan. Lucia was aghast, she was completely oblivious to the news as she only watched television on occasion and rarely listened to the radio. Working in the cafeteria had been her source of news and she enjoyed listening to the differing opinions from coworkers, staff, and visitors.

      The Archbishop informed both of them that the Diocese was planning a large healing event at the local arena. He asked Lucia if she was ready for such an event and she nodded. She was anxious to do what the Lord had asked of her. She told him she would like to do it tomorrow, but the Archbishop informed her that for such a big event, they would need several days to prepare. He instructed her to rest and told her he would include her in his prayers. The priest rose from his chair and stated that he was leaving her in the very capable hands of his dear friend, Sister Louisa.

      Once he was gone, Sister Louisa continued to show no interest in Lucia and escorted her quietly to her room, which included a bedroom, private bathroom and study. The Archbishop told her that her private things were in the process of being packed and would arrive within the next few hours. Lucia really wanted her phone. She wanted to call Bea and David to let them know she was all right; and what about Becky? Her daughter had still not returned Lucia's calls. This thought made her very sad. Unfortunately, Sister Louisa informed her, phones are traceable and not allowed per the Archbishop, but there was a phone in Sister Louisa's office that she could make calls on tomorrow.

Sister Louisa bowed when she left Lucia to get settled in and informed her she would send someone shortly to bring something for her to eat. Lucia's stomach rumbled reminding her she had not eaten in a while and healing took so much of her energy. The first thing Lucia did was carefully hang her black shawl in the huge walk in closet. In fact, looking around, her designated quarters were spacious and well decorated. The paintings around the room depicted Jesus' life on earth and a replica of the Pieta, on a much smaller scale, of course, sat on a mahogany table in a corner of the room. A large Crucifix was hung over the bed. The room was warm and welcoming in rich hues of green and gold drapes and a fluffy comforter on the bed. It was certainly so much better than what she had in her small apartment.

She wondered who was packing her things and if they were judging her right now. Why her, this small mousy nobody who worked in a cafeteria serving others?

Almost on queue, the voice in her head whispered, "Do you devalue Christ because he was a poor carpenter?" Properly reprimanded, Lucia pulled her Rosary that she always carried with her from her pocket, made the sign of the Cross and began to pray. "Dear Lord, I am yours to command. May I carry out your wishes to the best of my ability and be your vessel for healing in order to guide the lost sheep back to you, their Shepherd?"

Fearing she would fall asleep while she prayed, Lucia sat up straight with both feet on the ground, waiting for her food and for her things to be delivered. She should have called David to bring her things that were at his apartment while she was in Mother Superior's office. She would have to call him first thing in the morning and tell him where she was.

Lucia heard a soft knock on the door and before she could respond, the door opened and a nun entered with a tray of cheese and bread accompanied by a carafe of coffee. Lucia moaned; it smelled so good. The nun introduced herself as Sister Theresa and placed the tray on the small table in front of the window which she presumed would overlook the back of the house. It was difficult to see anything in the darkness of night but Lucia thought she could make out a garden in the light of the moon.

Sister Theresa was tall and thin and looked to be in her late 40's. Lucia invited her to stay and the Sister sat gracefully across from her. As Lucia ate, Sister Theresa informed her that Morning Prayer was held at 6 am and Sister Louisa expected her to attend. Sister Theresa would come get her five minutes before and escort her to the Chapel. The local priest came every day to provide Mass and Communion. After prayer, they would have breakfast and then each of the nuns had chores to perform throughout the day. Lucia would have to check in with Mother Superior to receive direction as to what her daily schedule would entail.

The Sister explained all this in a soft and kind voice. Conversation flowed easily between them and Lucia thought she would like getting to know her better. After she ate her fill, Sister Theresa noticed the Rosary beads left by the chair and asked if Lucia would like company in saying the Rosary to which she gladly accepted.

After reciting the Rosary, Sister Theresa bade her goodnight and quietly slipped out the door. Moments later, there was a harder knock at her door. She opened it to find three uniformed security guards holding several boxes in their hands. Without speaking, they deposited the boxes in the center of the room, bowed their heads and quickly left the room, closing the door behind them.

Well, thought Lucia, "That was a strange and silent visit. I didn't even thank them. Maybe, people aren't supposed to talk here at the Convent."
Surprisingly, the boxes included her things from David's as well as her clothing and sundries from her apartment, but after searching all the boxes, she could not find phone and she had not memorized anyone's phone number. She really wanted to call David and Becky. What if her daughter needed her? How would she know where to find her? She would ask Mother Superior to help her find the numbers in the morning.

Even after all this time, Lucia had hoped and prayed that her daughter would come to her. Maybe she could invite Becky here to the Convent. Of course, she would have to ask Sister Louisa for permission to invite guests, but she hoped that it would not be against the rules. After all, Becky was her daughter and Lucia hoped she was not a prisoner here. Although, after thinking more about the situation, it was quite a long ride to get here from the city. She was not sure if Becky would have transportation. She would talk to Dr. David tomorrow and hopefully he would agree to bring Becky to the Convent. Since her phone was taken away, Lucia would keep calling Becky from the Mother Superior's phone until her daughter answered, as she did not think it wise to leave the Convent's phone number.

Suddenly, Lucia gave a huge yawn and realized how tired she was. Today was certainly filled with an unexpected change in living arrangements. Again, she looked around; she thought that the room was not only tastefully decorated, but filled Lucia with a comfortable inner peace. After changing into her nightgown, she crawled into bed and fell into a deep dreamless sleep.

Chapter XXIII

Sometime, in the middle of the night, a bright shining cloud appeared in the corner of Lucia's room. Two Angels appeared out of the light. Gabriel, the larger of the two, looked over at the sleeping woman on the bed.

He turned to the smaller, more feminine angel and spoke, "It seems she has arrived at her final destination. It is apparent that those chosen long ago have accepted their destiny to facilitate success of the Lord's Divine Plan. Everything continues to proceed smoothly as expected. The Lord will be pleased when I report to Him."

The other smaller figure stood gazing at the woman resting in bed. This angel had long yellow hair in a French braid that hung far down her spine. She also wore a white gown that covered only one shoulder, with a cord wrapped around her waist. Unlike Gabriel's gold cord, her's was a light blue that matched the feathers that protruded softly from her back. Her alabaster skin was flawless with only a slight pinkish hue on her cheeks and large violet eyes that radiated compassion and love.

She walked over to the nightstand and placed a Medallion on a silver chain with the beautiful image of the Madonna emblazoned on one side and Louisa's name on the other. It was made of the finest silver in Heaven and was a gift for the Mother Superior as an incentive to assume her role. It was determined that Sister Lucia must be the one to give it to Sister Louisa in order for a strong bond to be made between them. It would also offer the Mother Superior some protection against the evil to come. Demons were already out and about plotting for Lucia's demise. The Healer's survival was of the utmost importance. Mother Superior was unwavering in her faith and now the

Abbey was well guarded and ready. Lucia must be protected.

Gabriel then whispered, "Nanael, let us pray over Sister Lucia, for in the coming days, much more will be expected from her."

Nanael, who had been watching Lucia for quite some time, was confident that Sister Lucia would not fail. The angels raised their hands and in their own dialect recited a litany of angelic prayers for the success of the Healer.

Sister Louisa was up frequently during the night to relieve her old and weak bladder. So, as she rose from bed for the second time that night, she heard strange low grumbling coming from outside her room. Lucia's room was not too far from her own room, and she thought maybe the woman needed something. As she walked down the dimly lit hallway, she noticed a bright, blinding light coming from the bottom of the Healer's bedroom door. She began to walk over to investigate when just as suddenly the guttural sounds stopped and the light was gone.

She carefully opened the bedroom door not knowing what to expect, but only discovered the Healer nestled in her bed. Sister Louisa looked around the room; however, she did not see anything to explain the blinding light escaping from under the door. As she turned to leave the room, she noticed a wisp of white mist floating through the ceiling. She had seen that same mist once before long ago and quickly left the room, quietly closing the door behind her. Overwhelmed, Sister Louisa sat in a chair rather than return to bed. Sleep was impossible as her thoughts turned to events from long, long ago.

Louisa was a recent high school graduate when she entered the Convent against her family's wishes, but she was filled with faith and love for Our Savior. Louisa just knew that it was her destiny to serve the Lord. She took her vows as a bride to Christ and never looked back. Reluctantly, her family attended the celebration and seemed resolved that this was what she had truly wanted.

She rejoiced in prayer and could frequently be found deep in meditation at the altar. Sister Louisa was known to project an aura of purpose and determination to do God's work to all that met her. It was during one of her prayer sessions that she met Father Lucas who had recently been transferred to her congregation. He, too, had a lot of energy, with plans to increase Mass attendance and strengthen the faith of those in the community. Sister Louisa became his willing accomplice. Their bond endured throughout the years and each never letting the other down.

One day, while at the altar deep in prayer, she was overcome with the scent of roses. She noticed that her surroundings were fading as a bright white mist had enveloped her and the altar. The space around her had taken on a soft surreal haze and she felt a soft breeze on the side of her hair.

Suddenly, she heard a woman's voice whisper in her ear. "Sister Louisa, you have chosen wisely to be a maiden for my son. A day will come when you will be asked to assume your role in the Lord's Divine Plan. You must do everything you can to ensure that the Healer is protected. Do not doubt the importance of your task as it may take many years to come to fruition. Messengers will be dispatched to alert you. My Son is with you, always."

Sister Louisa blinked her eyes several times and saw that the room had assumed its usual appearance and the other nuns around her were still kneeling in prayer, undisturbed.

She wondered to herself, "Did that just happen?"

Louisa immediately wiped any evidence of confusion off her face and bowed her head in prayer; however, prayer was the last thing on her mind. She replayed the conversation over and over in her head. Then, the nun began questioning the validity of the encounter she just had. Had she fallen asleep and dreamt the conversation? Did she have a seizure?

Unbeknownst to her, Father Lucas was watching her intently and although, he had never seen anyone in divine ecstasy, he thought that was what he had seen. Sister Louisa's head was tilted up to the ceiling and her eyes seemed to roll back into her head. Her lips were moving but he could not hear any words coming out of her mouth. In addition, a glow surrounded her and made her look ethereal. The incident lasted only a few seconds, until he observed her shaking her head and looking around. Then, she bowed her head and resumed praying.

After Mass, he sought her out and asked what she was up to. Sister Louisa would not meet his eyes and with a guilty tone told him she was needed back at the Convent and had to go. She quickly escaped before he could question her further. Father Lucas never pressed her, but it had taken some time before she was able to meet his eyes in conversation again.

So many years have passed.

Sister Louisa could not stop her thoughts, "Could this be her, the Healer, the one St. Mary told me about that day?"

When Lucas brought Sister Lucia to the Convent and called her the Healer, Sister Louisa was in shock. She always thought it was a dream or something she had conjured in her thoughts. She was completely stunned when Lucas explained Lucia's need for safety here at the Convent; Louisa hardly heard him and did not know what to say so she kept silently nodding her head. She had intently studied the woman when she arrived but could gather no sense of a heavenly aura around her. She looked nondescript and truly scared of her own shadow. Always one to express herself freely, Sister Louisa whispered to herself, "Is this really the woman the Lord has chosen?"

Sister Louisa never told anyone about what had happened, and she certainly could not tell Lucas; although, thinking back to that day, he almost seemed to know that something happened. She had awkwardly avoided him for several weeks until she had convinced herself it was a dream. Lucas would think her daft or senile, but when she saw the same blinding light coming from Lucia's room as what she saw that day at the altar, it confirmed what was already in her heart. The time had come and she, Mother Superior, would rise to the occasion. The Lord had chosen Lucia and Louisa would do everything she could to help her.

Mother Superior then laughed and added a thought to herself, "Don't you worry little mouse, I will protect you."

It was impossible to sleep after this revelation. Sister Louisa wondered what was expected of her. Protection of the Healer, yes, but there had to be more. What did the Lord want her to do? Then, she became overwhelmed thinking that she, Sister Louisa, Mother Superior, had actually been spoken to by the holiest of Saints – St. Mary, Mother of Christ. She had actually smelled the aroma of roses before Mother Mary spoke and then remembered that Lucas stated that Lucia's shawl held a scent of fresh roses. She would ask the Healer in the morning if she could lay a hand on the shawl.

Sister Louisa was old but her faith was strong. She was anxious to speak to Lucia, but it would have to wait until after breakfast. She reached in her nightstand and picked up the pen and pad from the drawer. Louisa would write all her questions down so she wouldn't forget any. Knowledge is power and Sister Louisa thought she needed all the information she could get in order to make an effective and efficient plan of action. Father Lucas used to chide her about her organizational skills but never stopped her because her success rate in their endeavors was outstanding. Lucas had called her late in the evening to notify her that a healing event was scheduled in three days to take place in the local arena. She grabbed her tablet and googled the arena to find it had a capacity of up to 10,000 people. Sister Louisa spent the night identifying all the safety risk factors of having a large event in such a venue and a plan of action for each.

Time seemed to fly by as she worked and before long, Mother Superior could see the sun rising in the east. She put the pad down and rubbed her eyes. She wasn't even tired, so filled with a vitality of excitement. She rose from her chair smiling, stretched her muscles and got ready for the day. First she would speak with Lucia, then, she needed to have a long conversation with Lucas. It was going to be busy day.

Chapter XXIV

Lucia was awakened by a low buzz humming through the walls of her room. She glanced at the bedside clock to see she had ten minutes before Sister Theresa would come for her. She quickly rolled out of bed and headed for the bathroom. She was glad that she had unpacked her frugal belongings the night before. She was ready only moments before Sister Theresa arrived and thought she would have to make her bed later as she did not want to make the Sister wait.

Father Marco was one of the priests who rotated coming to the Convent each morning for Mass. Lucia counted a dozen nuns in the pews with Mother Superior sitting alone in the first row. After Mass, the priest silently left out the side door and Sister Louisa led the others in a variety of prayers. Lucia participated in the prayers she knew and vowed to learn the prayers she had never heard before. How beautiful it sounded to have the nuns recite the prayers in one voice. Lucia was filled with a total sense of peace and belonging. She felt the peace at Dr. David's home but the feeling of belonging here with these women overwhelmed her. She hoped she would be allowed to stay for a while, even though she was not a nun. All those nights she prayed by herself and in desperation. Here she was not alone and prayed with a community with love and exaltation to the Lord. Lucia was finally one of a group and no longer on her own; she had a strong feeling that she was finally in the place she was meant to be.

Breakfast was a quiet affair, and Lucia enjoyed the delicious food. Since she had lived by herself since selling her house, she had resorted to buying store-bought prepared meals. It was not fun cooking for only one person. Preparing evening meals was one of the things she enjoyed while living with Dr. David. Throughout the meal, Lucia would notice the nuns staring at her; however, they would quickly look at their dish when she smiled at them. It seemed that conversation was kept to a minimum at the Convent and completely absent from the breakfast table. Lucia enjoyed the meal and the silence.

After breakfast, Sister Louisa invited Lucia to come to her office and she gratefully accepted, although she informed the Mother Superior that she needed to go to her room for a few minutes first. Somewhat irritated, Sister Louisa agreed to meet with her in half an hour and requested that she bring her shawl with her. Lucia hoped the delay did not jeopardize her request to call David and Bea. She would also try to call Becky, too, but actual contact with her was always sketchy.

Lucia rushed to her room to make the bed and pick up her things so that anyone entering the room did not think poorly of her. As she was making the bed, she noticed something shiny on the nightstand. She picked it up and saw the Madonna emblem that was skillfully carved into the silver. It was beautiful. When she turned the Medallion over she gasped. There carved on the flip side was Mother Superior's name written in a delicate script. Then, she noticed the pulsing emanating from the disc in the palm of her hand. Nothing was on the nightstand when Lucia retired. Of that, she was certain. She also did not think that any of the nuns left it for her. It was obviously for Mother Superior, but why was it left in her room? She grabbed her shawl and promptly made her way to the office; nonetheless, she was unable to deny the shield of protection she felt surrounding her the moment she grasped the Medal. Lucia was quite perplexed as to why the necklace with the stunning Medallion had been left in her room instead of Sister Louisa's. The Lord certainly moved in strange ways, and Lucia acknowledged that she was not meant to question why.

Upon her arrival, Sister Louisa was pacing the room and seemed to breathe a sigh of relief when she entered.

Lucia smirked to herself, "Not so quick with that sigh, Mother Superior," and placed the necklace on her desk.

Sister Louisa was confused as to why Lucia brought her a necklace, and without a second thought, she grabbed the Medallion and looked at the Madonna engraved on the front. The craftsmanship was exquisite; the work was stunning. Then, she turned it over. With wide eyes and an open mouth, Louisa looked up at Lucia, who was shaking her head and explained that she had found it on her nightstand this morning.

Both of them fell into their seats and stared at each other for several minutes. Sister Louisa broke the silence by telling Lucia of her heavenly visit long ago, how she was surrounded with a white cloud and the fragrance of roses. She repeated St. Mary's whispered words and how she had convinced herself that it was merely a dream. She also divulged what she saw last night in Lucia's room.
Now, it was Lucia's turn to have wide eyes and an open mouth. "It seems we both have been enlisted in the Lord's Divine Plan."

Sister Louisa poured them both coffee but admitted she could probably use a stiff drink. Lucia smiled and nodded. She then handed the shawl over to Sister Louisa who brought the woolen cloth to her face and inhaled deeply.

"Yes," she confirmed, "this is the same fragrance I smelled when St. Mary spoke to me. I would never forget that delicate scent."

Lucia then recounted all that had happened to her since the angel first visited her. She also told her how both David and Mary Ellen had received a message similar to what Sister Louisa had been given; however, Dr. David was visited by an angel and not so fortunate to have a visit by St. Mary.

Sister Louisa picked the necklace off the table and placed it over her head. She then grasped the Medallion and was surprised to feel the pulsating warmth emanating off the Medal. What was the meaning of this? The Medallion was approximately three to four inches around. She held it and could feel its power surging through her. She asked Lucia to pray with her and reached out to hold both of her hands. For the next hour they said one prayer after the other in love, in devotion and in gratitude.

Just as they were ending, a knock came to the door.

The Archbishop appeared with an easy smile and greeted them both, "So glad to find the two of you here together and glad that you are smiling, Sister Lucia. I wasn't quite sure if Mother Superior's hospitality would extend to this morning."

He took a seat with them and told them all the news he had to share.

The arena had been scheduled and security had been arranged. Lots of security would be needed he told them. He had been in contact with Rome, but some of the Vatican staff was skeptical and hesitant to publicly acknowledge

Lucia's healing powers being given by God, but privately, he was told, the Pope was praying for Sister Lucia. They also agreed to send a few members of the Pontifical Swiss Guard to offer assistance and guidance, but the Archbishop said they were really sent to validate the healings performed by Sister Lucia.

Sister Louisa then informed them of all her work done last night. She opened her pad and with pencil in hand, she began to read off all the safety risks that she had identified, as well as bullet points addressing those risks. On and on she went until Father Lucas chuckled and asked her if she had slept at all. It wasn't until she looked up to answer him that the priest saw the large shiny Medallion hanging around her neck and resting on her bosom.

"What in the Lord's name is that?" he exclaimed.

Sister Louisa looked down at the Medal hanging noticeably on her chest and said, "Oh, this old thing."

Sister Lucia couldn't help herself and started laughing, "It seems we have to catch you up on all that has happened here over the night."

The Archbishop raised his eyebrow and looked between Lucia and Louisa, "Yes, please do. And start from the beginning because I don't want you to miss anything. It seems I can't leave you two alone for even a minute without some heavenly interference."

Sister Louisa took off the necklace and handed it to the Archbishop. He saw the beautiful image of the Mother Mary and kissed it. He then sniffed the Medal and surely he must be mistaken, for the Medal carried the scent of roses. He then turned the disc over and gasped. There on the flip side of the Medal was Louisa's name clearly engraved in the silver.

"What is the meaning of this?" he demanded.

Sister Louisa dropped her gaze and timidly revealed her heavenly encounter to Lucas and how she was told by St. Mary to help the Healer that the Lord would send. Father Lucas knew immediately of the time she spoke of and her admission validated his assumption she was in ecstasy. He knew something had happened to Sister Louisa and admonished her that it took this long for her to tell him. Mother Superior also told him how she heard guttural sounds coming from Sister Lucia's room last night and the blinding light coming from under her bedroom door.

Lucia quickly interjected and revealed how she had found the necklace on her bedside table this morning. Father Lucas's mind was whirling with all that he had been told by Sister Louisa just now and Sister Lucia yesterday. It seemed the Lord had this planned for a long time. He also felt somewhat disappointed that he had no story to tell. He had never received any visit from an angel and certainly not from St. Mary herself.

Oh well, he thought to himself, he could not be concerned about that. He did not need a heavenly visit to tell him the importance of the time. He was committed to follow the Lord's path and that path was to ensure that Sister Lucia be supported and protected in all ways. He glanced back up to the two women and with a serious face (which was so unlike him) asked to see those notes from Sister Louisa.

Chapter XXV

After an hour reviewing Mother Superior's notes, the Archbishop finally was satisfied and told them they would meet again tonight with Security and the Pontifical Swiss Guard, who should be arriving within the next few hours. Father Lucas instructed Sister Louisa to bring her notes with her. He asked to see the Medallion again and seemed to say a prayer over it. Then, he asked to smell the black shawl that Sister Lucia had been holding. Again, he inhaled deeply and returned the shawl to her. Lucia could see the frown lines around his face slowly disappear; maybe smelling the shawl brought him the same peace and calm it brought to her. He bowed and left for his waiting limousine.

Mother Superior and Lucia went to the dining hall for a light lunch, and afterwards Lucia was handed off to Sister Bridgett for a tour of the Abbey. Lucia was introduced to the other sisters, and each one of them bowed and gave God's blessing to her. Lucia was unsure whether they knew who she was or why she was there, but, regardless, all of them welcomed her warmly and seemed more inclined to converse with her than they had at meals and prayer.

When Lucia inquired Sister Bridgett about this, she responded in a stern and low-pitched voice, "A quiet Abbey is a happy Abbey, don't you know that?"
And then she grinned and so did Lucia.

The tour included an overview of the large gardens in the back of the Convent, both flower and vegetable. In fact, some of the nuns were already there, weeding endlessly and praying for a bountiful yield this summer. She readily volunteered her time for this and the nuns accepted. Thanking Sister Bridgett for the wonderful tour, Lucia ran back to her room to change. Her heart was about to burst; she had missed her garden after selling the house and moving into her small apartment. Her hands were eager to get back into the soil and she loved watching the plants grow to harvest. Practically running back to the garden, the nuns had already set up a stool for Lucia to sit and weed from.

Sister Louisa watched from the window as Lucia hurriedly ran to the garden. Well, Lucia certainly was not what she had expected. The Mother Superior was quite surprised that Lucia had seemed to thoroughly enjoy Morning Prayer, even smiling when she had been abruptly woken from her sleep early this morning according to Sister Theresa. Sister Louisa had expected resistance and some disruption, but instead found that Sister Lucia blended well into the established routine, in fact, she seemed to welcome it. It was only the first day, she contemplated, let's see how it goes over time. She then made a note to have Sister Paul apply the rubber paste on Lucia's shoes. She got a headache this morning from the clatter made by Lucia walking to Chapel.

Sister Louisa's office faced the front of the Convent. She had noticed an increase in the amount of traffic going by today. If the Archbishop had hoped to keep the Healer's identity a secret, she did not think it was a good idea to put twenty-armed guard around the perimeter. However, if the threats were to be believed, Lucas really had little choice but to secure the property. She would remind Lucas that he needed to increase her budgeted allowance as he expected Mother Superior to feed all the men guarding the grounds. Suddenly, she saw a large black SUV speeding up the driveway and swing the car onto the grassy area close to her office. Sister Louisa sat up and held her black habit up out of the way as she ran outside to admonish the thoughtless driver or "selfish twit" as she called out to him to move the car onto the paved area. The Head of Security would hear about this.

After several hours, Sister Louisa walked outside to the garden to check on Lucia. She had been given a big sun hat and gloves and Mother Superior almost laughed at the sight she made. Her face was covered in sweat and dirt but the petite woman had the biggest smile on her face.

Sister Louisa shook her head and addressed her, "Lucia, the Archbishop is on his way back. It might be best if you stopped now to shower and change."
The younger nuns kept their eyes down, and continued working. Lucia nodded and stood up to go. When Sister Louisa turned her back, Lucia removed the hat and gloves and hugged all the sisters. It had been a wonderful day and Lucia had learned a lot about the Convent and its leader. Lucia quickly returned to her room; she did not want to keep the good Sister Louisa waiting too long.

Arriving in her room, Lucia looked out the window to see the sun was starting to set and then quickly noticed the men armed with guns standing guard all around the inside of the fence. This reminded her of the threats the Archbishop said were made against her. Her bedroom was toward the back of the Abbey and beyond the carefully manicured lawn was a forest. Lucia could not see another building anywhere, only flowers and trees. She would appreciate the beauty surrounding her and not dwell on the armed fortress that the Archbishop thought was necessary. She guessed it was the perfect hideout and smiled.

Having fifteen minutes before the meeting, Lucia left her room seeking the telephone in Sister Louisa's office. Luckily she still had the paper in her wallet with Dr. David's number. She had Bea's number memorized so that would be no problem. Lucia hurried to the office thinking that Dr. David was waiting all day for her call. She would tell him how she was gardening all day and hoped he would understand. She wanted to tell him where she was, but she would have to clear it with the Archbishop first. Dr. David was certainly no threat and neither was Bea. They were her family now.

Sister Louisa was doing paperwork in her office when Lucia knocked on the open door.

"May I use the phone?" she asked.

Without speaking, Sister Louisa slid the phone toward Lucia. First, she called Dr. David who anxiously questioned if Lucia was all right. He then informed her that Father Lucas had invited him and Mary Ellen to the planning meeting and that they were on their way and expected to arrive shortly. Lucia told him that she was glad they were invited, as she felt a little nervous since the Archbishop was planning a larger venue for her healing, which meant many more people to heal. They would all get an update at the meeting. Dr. David told her that the hospital patients she had healed yesterday were already showing significant signs of improvement and would hopefully be discharged in the morning. He also shared that all the people she had healed in the old emergency department had responded miraculously. She thanked him for everything and told him she would talk to him more when he arrived.

Her next call was to her best friend. When Bea answered the phone, Lucia informed her that she was somewhere safe and doing well. Bea updated her on all that was happening at the hospital and how Lucia was still the talk of the town. Bea had also gotten some notoriety herself from staff and reporters, but she reassured Lucia that she had turned down all the requests for interviews. After a while, Lucia told Bea she had to go but would keep in touch. Her friend sent her much love and support then ended the call.

Her last call was to Becky, who as usual did not answer the phone. This broke Lucia's heart for she loved Becky so. She left a message telling Becky that she would be away for a while but that she would call her again in a few days. She then told her that she loved and missed her and hoped Becky would answer the next time she called.

Sister Louisa, who had been listening to Lucia's calls, noticed the tears in Lucia's eyes after calling her daughter. The tough old nun came around the desk and gave Lucia a hug. Lucia gave a brief synopsis of her divorce and her son's rejection of her. Then she explained the relationship to her daughter, or lack thereof, to the Mother Superior. The elderly nun then reassured Lucia that her daughter would come around some day, hopefully soon. How could she not when she had the best mom in the world? Lucia smiled and squeezed Mother Superior's hands. It was time for them to meet with the men in the Convent's large conference room. Lucia tried to match Sister Louisa's brisk step, but in truth, working in the garden in the midday sun had taken a lot out of her; so the Mother Superior grabbed her hand and dragged her along.

Lucia was surprised to see a group of tall muscular men standing around the large conference room talking and laughing with Father Lucas. The only man she recognized was Jacob Bronson, Head of Security and two others that were always around him, but she did not know their names. The Archbishop introduced her to the Commander of the Pontifical Swiss Guard, Philip Sorrin, and explained that he and Jacob would be arranging safety and security from now on. He had brought four of his staff with him, and Lucia thought to herself that she would never want to meet any of them in a dark alley. The Commander then held out his hand as he introduced himself and four other men accompanying him. They really were intimidating as they all stared at her.

Mary Ellen and Dr. Woods rushed into the room, apologizing for being late, but Mother Superior assured them they had not started yet. Apparently, Father Lucas invited them at the last minute. The Archbishop asked that they all take a seat and then had everyone introduce themselves. Once introductions were made, Mother Superior was given the floor to review the notes she had made regarding safety and security at the planned event. Jacob and Philip both nodded as she spoke, and listened respectfully. When she finished, Jacob began informing the group that he and Philip had met earlier and toured the venue. Both men took turns giving their opinion and plan to meet all of Sister Louisa's concerns and listed a few others the Sister had not addressed.

Mary Ellen then reviewed her plan for organizing and processing the crowd, then looked shyly at Jacob and asked if he had anything to add. Jacob then shared that he and Mary Ellen had been working on an efficient and effective plan to handle the large crowds expected. They had agreed that more security was being hired and Mary Ellen was recruiting volunteers to triage patients to the appropriate areas. Not everyone required Lucia's healing and counseling rooms would be made available to individuals in need. Philip offered to summon more of his men from Rome, if needed. Lucia just sat and listened as the men and woman spoke. It seemed that they had thought of everything.

After the meeting, Philip came over to Lucia and gave her a warm smile and sat next to her. He then asked her if there was anything else he could help her with. He informed her that the Pope, who although could not give her the support of the Vatican, was concerned for her safety and had asked Philip to do all he could to keep her from harm. The man radiated an aura of professionalism and competency as he sat before her, and his relaxed and easy manner put her at ease. His English was perfect with only a slight accent that she could not identify. Lucia no longer felt intimidated and sincerely thanked him for all his help. She then informed him how she had lived in a very bad section of the city and never went out at night. However, after the angel's visit and she had to go to the hospitals, she noticed that whenever she went out at night, the streets were quiet and empty. She then told him how she had seen two angels standing guard outside her building.

So, she told him, "Not only do I have you and Jacob looking after me, but God has also provided a heavenly layer of protection for me. I have no questions, that between the both of you, I am truly safe and sound."

Chapter XXVI

It was the morning of the event. Mother Superior refused to let Lucia work in the garden. Sister Louisa told her that she needed all her strength for tonight. And Lucia agreed. Hundreds of people were expected and Sister Lucia was very nervous as to how she would help them all. Tonight was going to be a real test of her capabilities, but Sister Lucia closed her eyes and told herself that the Lord would not have brought her to this point to fail. She always told everyone that it was Christ who worked through her and she believed that He could do anything and everything so with that thought she refused to dwell on how many people would come to be healed tonight. Always in the back of her mind was the hope that her daughter would show up at one of the events and they would be reunited.

She was ready long before it was time to go and wandered to Sister Louisa's office. The Mother Superior was reviewing her notes she made regarding tonight, especially those points of concern she identified and steps taken to ensure Sister Lucia's safety. She was so deep in thought, she did not hear Sister Lucia enter the room and was quite startled when Lucia plopped into the chair in front of her desk. Sister Louisa jumped from her seat and grabbed her Medallion, which was never off her body since the morning Lucia gave it to her.

Sister Louisa asked her if she was ready and Lucia gave a nervous laugh; she had eaten a huge lunch at Louisa's insistence, followed by a nap and shower. Lucia rubbed her fingers over the black shawl in her lap drawing comfort from the soft fabric. She was informed that Dr. David would meet her at the arena and she was anxious to see him. She had grown quite fond of the doctor and had come to rely on him for his strength and support.

She thought back to when she was called to pray over Janet, the thirty-four-year-old woman who was in the end stages of her disease. Lucia had used Dr. David as a battery charger and had thought that would probably be the case tonight, too. In fact, she had requested the Archbishop arrange for ten priests who were very devout to be on hand, if needed.

Sister Louisa asked Lucia if she could bring some Rosary beads with her, not for sale but to give to those who had none.

"Of course," Lucia answered. "Just don't accept any money, even if offered for them and direct all donations to the parishes. Don't forget to have one of the priests say a blessing over them before giving them out."

Mother Superior assured her that she had already done that after Mass this morning.

Promptly at two o'clock, the Archbishop pulled up with four large black SUVs. Lucia and Sister Louisa were ready and climbed into the back seat. The driver drove carefully and professionally.

The car was quiet except for the occasional reminders from His Grace, "Let me know if you get tired." "Let me know if you see anything suspicious." "Notify me if you need a break to eat or drink."
Lucia never responded. He was making her more nervous than the first night she ventured out unknowing where she would go or what would happen.

After some time, the car turned off the highway and Lucia could not believe her eyes. There had to be hundreds of people trying to get to the convention center - some in wheel chairs, some in stretchers, and some being carried - all with the hope of being cured. Lucia wondered how many she would be able to help.

A small voice inside her head replied, "The Lord will help all of them."

When the car stopped, Lucia took a long deep cleansing breath. They had arrived at their destination.

The SUV had pulled up in the back of the building to a small inconspicuous door. One of the security guards opened the door to their vehicle and helped them out of the car. Sister Lucia, the Archbishop and Sister Louisa were surrounded by a group of men, none who were familiar to Lucia. The Archbishop and Mother Superior led the procession and Lucia was relegated to the middle. She was beginning to feel quite isolated and alone, when suddenly four tall, muscular men walked toward her. All four were dressed in different military dress uniforms, and they stood straight, tall and strong. Suddenly, Lucia recognized them and her heart filled with joy. Robert, Vincent, Matthew, and Jack – dear Jack, all smiling and Lucia so overwhelmed, opened her arms to all of them. Each in turn hugged her, except Jack; he picked her up and spun her around. Then the four men told her how they all had returned to the Church to give their thanks to God. This was just what she needed. Then, the four of them got into formation, two on each side of her, and proceeded to enter the arena.

They were all escorted down a long corridor lined with security and volunteers from the Knights of Columbus. She knew that because the men had it written on their jackets. They all bowed as she walked past them. Half way down the hall, their entourage stopped and Sister Louisa was directed to go to the right into a makeshift

Chapel labeled the Rosary Station. There were silver and deep purple drapes all around the room with muted lighting projecting a feeling of sanctity. There were rows and rows of pews, which were already filling up. Sister Louisa entered the room and placed a box of Rosary beads on the table, giving Lucia a quick supportive smile, she turned back to lead those in the pews to pray the Rosary.

Already, Lucia could hear Sister Louisa saying, "In the name of the Father and the Son and the Holy Ghost."

As they walked further down the hall, Lucia could see that the path swerved to the right. On both sides of the path, were crowds of people yelling at her, "Lucia, pray for us, Lucia save us." Her mind was swimming. She could barely concentrate. Everyone was calling her name but always in the background she listened for someone special calling her "Mom." Finally, they reached the small stage and in desperation, she covered her ears. The Archbishop saw how the loud chanting was affecting the Healer. Father Lucas grabbed the wireless microphone and in a loud and stern voice demanded the crowd be silent.

It took a few minutes but the noise abated and once it was quiet he instructed the crowd to sit or kneel silently while they said the opening prayer together. After he was finished, Lucia could feel the power surging through the room. She acknowledged Dr. David with a wave although he was in the back corner assisting the nurses where the triage station had been set up. She also saw Mary Ellen with several women standing outside a room that was labeled Counseling Station and waved to her, too.

On the stage, Lucia could see there was a crucifix hanging in the background and a couple of seats along the back wall. She requested the ten priests to join her on the stage, five on each side of her. Sister Lucia donned her long black wool scarf and closed her eyes in silent prayer. When she opened them, she nodded and asked for the first child to be brought forth.

A large man carried a small hairless body to her.

"What is your name?" Sister Lucia smiled and asked gently.

In a weak and whispered voice, the girl answered, "Alexia."

Her mother stood back while Sister Lucia prayed over the girl. She heard the audience gasp as the white healing light flowed from her fingertips. The light enveloped the girl and could be seen being absorbed into her body. Lucia squeezed the girl's hand and gave the mother a reassuring smile.

She turned back to the ushers and said, "Bring the next person please."

And so it went, each patient quietly presented himself or herself to Sister Lucia, who prayed for their recovery and good health. The Healer later found out that the patients were told at triage not to talk to Sister Lucia because it might distract her. Well, it certainly made the healings go much quicker without conversation. A couple of the patient's would try to kiss her hand but she would direct them to Sister Louisa's Rosary Chapel to give thanks to God.

Lucia had lost count and was getting a little tired, so she turned and interrupted one of the young devout priests who had been deep in prayer. He jumped up and ran to her right side. Lucia instructed him to put his hands next to hers and pray.

"Bring the next child, please" she directed the security guard.

The priest seemed taken back when he saw the energy flowing from her hands but said nothing and closed his eyes to meditate as one child after another was brought forward.

Sister Lucia could see Sister Louisa standing off to the side of the stage and as soon as the last child was healed, the Mother Superior sauntered over and announced a short break. Lucia smiled and hugged the elderly nun in gratitude. They escaped to a small room off to the side where Lucia found coffee and other refreshments. There were also pastries and Lucia's favorite, chocolate chip cookies. Lucia grabbed a bunch and put them in her dress pocket for later.

The Planning Group, as Sister Lucia labeled them, had determined that the military would come after the children since Lucia was directed by God and had started her healing in that order. God bless that Mary Ellen was Lucia's next thought. She was leading a long group of men dressed in their military affiliation. It seems she had brought forth members and veterans from the army, navy, air force and marines who had suffered much for our country. Because of the extent of the trauma, Lucia called for another priest to stand to her left side. Six prayerful hands contributed to the steady stream of soft white energy force over the bodies of strong men, who were blind or missing legs and arms. She had tried to explain the pain associated with growing new limbs to the first soldier but he stopped her and told her it was already explained to him.

Lucia found out later that Jack, the soldier she had healed at the VA Hospital, was standing by the entrance to help the nurses and give instructions to the wounded warriors who had traveled near and far for a miracle. Lucia could see him over the crowd showing the soldiers his new arm and leg. He was still in physical therapy but he was getting stronger every day. One of the times she looked over to the area where he was; she could have sworn he winked at her; Lucia winked back.

On and on it went, when she felt weak she just added another priest. The crowds of people praying had remained the same, but the long line of people presented to her had significantly diminished. Sister Lucia was trying her best but the stress and delivery of energy from her body to the sick caused her to stumble and almost fall. Two of the priests quickly caught her and had her administer from a chair where she continued to deliver her healing. Many hours had passed when, finally, Sister Lucia could do no more and without warning fainted in the chair. She was transported back to the Convent via ambulance, with Sister Louisa by her side. Additional large black SUVs filled with security surrounded the ambulance back to the Abbey. David and Mary Ellen had insisted that they accompany her back to the Convent. With Sister Louisa's support, the Archbishop permitted it.

Chapter XXVII

Sister Lucia woke refreshed and relaxed. What an afternoon, she thought. It was incredible. She couldn't even fathom the number of people brought before her. She said a quick prayer to God thanking him for giving her this opportunity to help so many people. Her stomach growled. Lucia was starved and needed food like right now. She was surprised that Sister Louisa had not woken her up for Morning Prayer.

She got out of bed and felt somewhat discombobulated. Her knees were weak and her head was spinning. She went to sit in the corner chair near her bed and that's when she saw him.

"Dr. David, what are you doing here?" she exclaimed.

His eyes opened wide and he jumped from the chair and said, "Oh my God, you're awake!"

Lucia found out that she had been pretty much unconscious for the past two days. All the nuns, including Sister Louisa, David and Mary Ellen had taken turns watching over her. All were very concerned but David and Mary Ellen reassured them that her vital signs were great. She just needed to rest.

Hearing Dr. David yell, Sister Louisa ran quickly into Lucia's bedroom, as did some of the other nuns to check and see if Lucia was okay.

Lucia was smiling, thinking to herself that, "Apparently, Dr. David did not know that a quiet Abbey was a happy Abbey."

Sister Louisa was the first to find her voice, "Do you know you scared us half to death? Lord above."

Lucia could see the strained and concerned face on the elderly nun and solemnly apologized, "But if it is all the same to you, I am so hungry and would appreciate this conversation after breakfast."

Sister Louisa walked away in a huff responding sharply, "Well, if it's all the same to you, we will continue with eating our LUNCH special emphasis on the word lunch. Feel free to join us."

Dr. Woods left to join Sister Louisa at the lunch table while the nuns helped Lucia to wash and change her clothes. They also assisted in walking her to the dining room where Lucia sat down at the table and ate everything they put in front of her. When she finished eating, she again apologized to Sister Louisa who was also in better spirits after watching Lucia at the table eating and looking so well rested.

Sister Louisa left to call the Archbishop and Mary Ellen who Sister Louisa found to be most helpful at the arena and then again, when taking care of Sister Lucia. Mary Ellen had wiggled her way into the event planning meetings, and Mother Superior liked her more and more after each encounter, especially when she found out that she had entered the Convent but left to pursue a career in nursing instead as a way to serve the Lord. Mary Ellen had come to the Convent after work every day to help care for Lucia, who remained comatose and required complete care until the moment she woke up. She was expected shortly to check on Lucia.

When Sister Louisa returned, she shared that the Archbishop was bringing Cardinal Peter Moreno, a guest from Rome with him to check on Sister Lucia. While they waited, the nuns filled her in on all that happened after she fainted.

"Everyone was so scared that you would not wake up," they told her.

She could see Sister Louisa reaching down for the Medallion resting on her chest. Lucia noticed that the Mother Superior did that since receiving the Medal when she was nervous or concerned, so Lucia reassured them all that she was feeling great and wanted to know when the next event would be held. Dr. David informed her that feedback from those who came to the arena reported that their conditions were either fully healed or definitely improving significantly.

When the priests and Mary Ellen arrived, David, Lucia and Sister Louisa met them in the conference room. Cardinal Moreno introduced himself and smiled at Sister Lucia, "I have been told of the gift you have been given by God and judging by all of the people that have been healed, I can see you have wasted no time in doing God's work." The Archbishop then interjected, explaining that Cardinal Moreno had just arrived from Rome to bear witness to Sister Lucia's healings. Cardinal Moreno continued smiling and informed them all that two other women have also come forth with the same ability. One was in France, her name was Sister Juliette and the other came out yesterday in Russia, her name was Sister Sofia. Sister Sofia reported this morning that the angel told her that there would be more Healers coming over the next few months.

Sister Lucia was stunned. There were more like her; she took a deep breath truly feeling like part of a movement. She wondered if she could speak with them, ask if they also received a black shawl from St. Mary. She directed that question to the Cardinal who confirmed that yes, both women had received a black shawl scented with roses. Their stories were similar to Lucia's, including that both of them thought their angelic visitor was a dream, until they saw the black scarf. Two Cardinals have been assigned to meet with each of them to bear witness.

"As am I here to bear witness to you," the Cardinal informed her, "the Vatican is not taking this lightly. The Holy See was hesitant to show alignment, but it seems Jesus is pushing the Pope to acknowledge his Healers and give them all his support."

Dr. David was sitting quietly next to Lucia during the exchange. He squeezed Lucia's hand and then spoke to the Cardinal. "Your Eminence, I would like to bear witness, as you say, to Sister Lucia's ability to heal the faithful. She has accepted no payment or accolades but rather directs those to the Church and Christ. Also, there are a few people who had also been visited by an angel many years ago in order to prepare us for this time to help the Healer fulfill her promise. I am sure once you begin investigating the others, you will find there are some who have been chosen to help those Healers as well. The Lord has been setting up His Divine Plan for quite some time, and those who He contacted sit before you."

The Cardinal lost his smile and stared at David. "Thank you, Dr. Woods; I will make the other Cardinals aware to look for those who may have received a heavenly visit, also." He took another sip of his coffee and contemplated his next words. "I wish I could give you the full confidence of the Vatican, but, many there are hesitant to promote miracles so readily. I will, however, give you my full support for I have visited some of those who have been healed. I have seen the people who have had their limbs regrown and those who were blind now have eyes that can see. I have visited the families and children who were devastated by their disease only to wake up fully recovered."

At this, the Cardinal's eyes watered. He bowed his head in prayer and then came to kneel before Sister Lucia. She tried to grab his arm but he stayed before her stating that in his entire career, he had never felt so close to the Lord than he did now with the people in this room.

To lighten the mood, the Archbishop spoke up and confided to the Cardinal that he did not receive any angelic visit, but he did work with an angelic Mother Superior who kept him on the straight and narrow. Sister Louisa smiled awkwardly and blushed, clutching the Medallion hanging around her neck. The Archbishop rarely gave her praise but when he did she reveled in it. The Archbishop then directed the Cardinal to the Medallion worn by Mother Superior. He told him the story of what had happened only a few nights ago and how Sister Louisa's name was engraved on the back of the medal. After the elderly nun handed over the necklace, the Cardinal studied it closely, admiring the fine craftsmanship and quality of the precious shiny grayish white metal engraved with the Madonna on the front side.

"Well, it seems Sister Lucia does not need the support of the Vatican as you have the weight of Heaven behind you already. I will report back to the Vatican with my findings. The Archbishop tells me that there is another event planned in four days. I will be staying for that and then return to Rome. I would be honored to be one of the priests on the stage with you, Sister Lucia, with your consent, of course."

Sister Lucia smiled and nodded. She was ready.

Sister Louisa practically grabbed the Medallion from the Cardinal. She draped it over her head and then held onto it with both hands. The Cardinal told her he was jealous of her receiving such a priceless gift from the Lord. Mother Superior answered that she was convinced there was a reason it was given but it surely gave her solace whenever she held it. Then, she looked over at Lucia and exclaimed that she would need even more rest over the next four days if the last event was anything to go by.

Chapter XXVIII

After four days of Sister Louisa harassing her about eating and sleeping and taking naps, Lucia was relieved to finally be on her way to the arena. This time there were several more security cars accompanying the Archbishop and Cardinal Moreno when they arrived to pick up Mother Superior and herself from the Convent. Lucia noticed that all the cars seemed bigger and stronger which Father Lucas confirmed that safety dictated that they have bulletproof windows and reinforced steel on the outside. Lucia nodded nervously and Sister Louisa took her hand and squeezed it tight.

Upon arrival, the security staff surrounded Lucia so closely she could hardly breathe. Once inside the door, she told them she needed them to back off so she could get some air and reluctantly, they complied. Again, Robert, Vincent, Matthew and Jack were waiting for her to arrive, so was Dr. David and Mary Jane.

Jack could see how nervous she was, so he whispered in her ear, "" Don't worry, we got you."

Unbeknownst to anyone, Lucia had showed Jack a picture of Becky and asked him to scan the crowds for her at the events held. Lucia prayed every night that God would lead her daughter back to her and she hoped it was His will that they be reunited. She had not heard from her daughter since she came to live at the Convent, but each morning Lucia would reach out to her, however the daughter she loved so much had yet to return any of her mother's calls.

Sister Louisa informed her that she had asked one of the priests to lead the Rosary tonight, as she wanted to be close to Lucia and make sure she did not overexert herself again. Their entourage swiftly walked to the prepared stage. This time there was a dark brown upholstered chair placed in the front of the makeshift stage to accommodate Lucia with several folding chairs provided for the clergy who would help her.

The rows before her were already filled and she could see the line of people standing in the aisles on all sides of the arena. As they started to step onto the platform, Lucia heard someone calling her from one of the rows. She looked up and saw two women waving trying to get her attention. They were at the end of a row and when Lucia saw one of the women was Diana, Robert's fiancée; she broke the line and rushed over to her.

Security went crazy. They were trying to catch up to her but she paid them no mind and embraced Diana warmly. Diana introduced her to Sadie, Vincent's girlfriend, and she gave her a hug, too.

Then Diana leaned over and whispered in her ear; "I'm pregnant, Sister Lucia."

Lucia could not be happier. The Healer placed her hand over Diana's stomach and commented, "Uh oh," to which Diana frowned. Then with a huge smile, Lucia continued, "A stubborn boy, just like his father," and then they both laughed.

She looked over her shoulder to where Robert was standing and he had the biggest smile on his face. Lucia told them that she would arrange a visit soon so they could talk more, but for now, she thought she should follow the stern security staff members who were shooting daggers in her direction. She also had to face a very angry Mother Superior who let her know her little visit was not in the plan.

The line started with children being carried or assisted over to Sister Lucia. They broke her heart seeing such sick boys and girls; their little bodies ravaged by disease. Several of the children were paralyzed by accidents and brought in by wheelchairs or stretchers. For these cases, Lucia enlisted Cardinal Moreno, Sister Louisa and some of the priests at her side. She had told her assistants to close their eyes and pray, with their hands extended over the child. At once, Sister Lucia heard the elderly nun gasp as a strong steady stream of white energy flowed from the nun's fingertips and the others, as well.

She whispered in Lucia's ear, "I can feel the heat coming down my arms and out my fingers."

Lucia smiled and answered, "That means it's working."

The line moved smoothly, each person was instructed as before to limit conversation and not to linger after the healing was given; although, some would continuously thank her for which Lucia responded that this was the Lord's will not hers. Thankfully, several men were assigned to help the parents and guardians to transport the stretchers and wheelchairs out toward the exit. The process was truly a well-oiled machine thanks to Mary Ellen and Sister Louisa's careful planning. She could see that many of the men and women were diverted to the counseling room where Mary Ellen had multiple counselors set up to provide available community resources as needed.

After the line of children was finished, Sister Louisa called a short break and with Dr. David's help, assisted Lucia to the break room. Lucia insisted that she was fine, but the Mother Superior hovered over her like a mother hen, which Lucia appreciated. Lucia sat down with her coffee and cookies – chocolate chip- and was joined by Jack. He had gotten past security by telling them Lucia had called for him. She could see that he still needed a cane to walk but he told her it made him look distinguished. She laughed at him and his smile seemed so smug and content; so unlike when she saw him at the VA hospital.

Jack told her how he was volunteering at the local church and also spent his time at the VA Hospital counseling the veterans coming for care, mostly PTSD, and getting them connected to services. He also informed her that he kept in close contact with Robert, Vincent and Matthew. Not one of them had ever believed in miracles, but since Sister Lucia had healed them, they all had regained their faith, stronger than ever. He then gave her a piece of paper and said that he knew she was very busy but if she could ever come to the VA and just talk to the men, it would help them immensely. She took the address and tucked it in her pocket, assuring him that she would try her best.

As if on cue, Dr. David came and told her it was time to go back. They all assumed their positions on the stage, except Sister Louisa, who had wheedled her way up next to Lucia and assisted in every healing. When a difficult case came forward, she would sometimes pull Dr. David and tried to include Cardinal Moreno as much as possible. She knew it would be draining for them; however, Lucia seemed to be energized as the night went on. In fact, it wasn't very long before Sister Louisa found herself in that big brown upholstered chair. Lucia didn't mind; she was doing fine – until she wasn't.

There was nothing that she could put her finger on. Lucia scanned the room and everything looked in order.

Security was scanning the area. She could hear the Rosary being prayed in the room off to the side. Cardinal Moreno was sitting behind her up on stage and Dr. David was never far from her side. Nothing she could see that would explain the sudden rush of cold tingling snaking up her spine. She could feel the aura around her growing more intense and hostile. She looked around again and didn't seem to notice anything amiss; but something made her stop from extending her hands forward. She looked before her as two security guards brought the young man forward. He was standing with his head bowed but Lucia could not see any break in his aura or identify any area needing energy; however, she could see black angry balls swirling around his head and heart. The confused look on Sister Lucia's face alerted the head of Security who shouted something, but Lucia could not make it out. All motion had slowed down for her and she could not seem to comprehend what was happening. She vaguely heard the screams as if in a tunnel and suddenly she was pushed to the ground, watching as Sister Louisa jumped in front of her just in time to save Lucia from a bullet. Then utter chaos erupted when a mass of security guards grabbed the man, holding him to the ground. People were screaming and fleeing out the exits. Lucia lay on the ground feeling frozen in fear, until she noticed Sister Louisa lying next to her with blood staining her hands and the white bib over her chest.

The Mother Superior's eyes were closed and she did not seem to respond to the events happening around her. Lucia crawled to her side and saw the nun's hands still clenching the Medallion that rested on her chest. There in the middle of the Medal was a small but clearly defined bullet hole. Lucia had difficulty seeing as the tears flowed down her face; she tried to rip the black dress covering Sister Louisa but could not open the fabric to see the wound below.

Dr. Woods rushed over and easily ripped the gown open and began yelling for bandages and a stretcher. Lucia could see a red stain spreading across Sister Louisa's white underclothes. One of the security staff tried to pull her away but Lucia resisted, and tried to place her hands over Sister Louisa's chest to heal her but nothing came out of the Healer's fingertips. Sister Lucia felt frozen and could barely breathe. Her hands were shaking uncontrollably. She tried to pray but could not find the words and could only think, "Please God, no, let Louisa be okay." Before Lucia could try to heal her again, Sister Louisa was lifted onto a stretcher and taken away by ambulance to the hospital. Jack had managed to reach the stage moments before security sealed off the area. He held Lucia as she sat on the stage crying uncontrollably. The Healer was inconsolable; she could not heal the woman who saved her life.

Father Lucas and Mary Ellen accompanied Louisa to the hospital, while Dr. Woods called the ED to let them know Mother Superior was coming in hot with a gunshot wound. Jack and several security guards practically carried Lucia to one of the black SUVs and whisked her away to the Convent. David just managed to jump in the car before it tore out of the arena parking lot. No matter how she protested that she wanted to go to the hospital, the decision was made that her safety was the utmost priority and she could be better protected at the Convent. Dr. David held her as she cried and stayed with her in her room until she fell asleep.

    The doctor received regular updates from the Archbishop and so far Sister Louisa's prognosis was guarded; for although the Medallion stopped the bullet, the impact of the force had broken the skin and cracked several ribs. The woman was still unconscious and Father Lucas was going to stay the night with her. David hung up Lucia's black shawl in the closet where he found a pillow and a blanket. Then, he hunkered down in his favorite recliner that he had slept in when Sister Lucia was incapacitated after the first arena event. He couldn't help but think how that Medallion had saved the Mother Superior's life. He was sure she would be all right. He had faith.

    Outside the Abbey, a battalion of security staff was actively patrolling the perimeter. Unbeknownst to the Sisters, hundreds of threats were made in writing and through the dark web, which accounted for the heightened security. How the perpetrator had gotten a gun past security at the front of the arena was being investigated? Cameras had been set up at every entrance and all through the large arena. The gunman had help and they would find out soon enough who his accomplice was. At this moment, a staff of trained professionals was reviewing the footage of all the cameras. The Commander of the Pontifical Swiss Guard, Philip Sorrin, and the head of Security, Jacob Bronson, worked closely together in order to get to the bottom of this attack. They had already notified the Security teams assigned with the other two Healers to increase their protection. Cardinal Moreno was driven to a small airport where he would take a private jet back to Rome and report his findings.

Chapter XXIX

Lucia woke up before the sun and found David sleeping soundly in the recliner next to her. She thanked God for this man for he never left her side after the shooting. He had been a tremendous support for her. She wasn't sure how the good doctor was able to attend to his practice and all the other demands made of him because of her. He was still in his clothes from the day before and Lucia could see he had taken off his shoes, which were on the side of the chair and his cell phone was resting in his lap.

Lucia shifted over to the edge of the bed filled with doubt and fear, could anyone expect her to continue her mission after the shooting last night? She could not understand how Sister Louisa pushed her out of the way in order to save the Healer from being shot and, ultimately, put her own life in jeopardy. She had taken the bullet meant for Lucia, and again the tears flowed from her eyes. She felt so guilty and then remembered how she couldn't even heal Sister Louisa. What good was her gift if she couldn't use it when she really needed to? She dropped her head into her hands and began sobbing uncontrollably, so loud that David woke up and jumped from the chair.

He tried to comfort Lucia and told her that Sister Louisa would fully recover (hopefully) and that everything would be fine. After she calmed down somewhat, he advised her to go wash up and change and then they could call the hospital and get an update. That seemed to motivate her and she ran to the bathroom to get ready. When she looked in the mirror, Lucia could hardly recognize herself. First, she had a black eye and a small cut on her cheek, which she received when Sister Louisa pushed her down and her face hit the edge of the chair. Both eyes were so swollen from the injury and crying that she couldn't even recognize herself. Lucia dropped to her knees and asked the Lord for the recovery of the Mother Superior, who she had looked upon as a mother figure. Then, renewed with a little energy, she jumped in the shower.

    Sister Lucia would have to inform them that she had lost her gift and could no longer heal, and that alone caused her great sadness since she felt that she still had so many more people to help. Maybe she did something wrong and that's why Jesus took back his gift. She was in the process of working herself up into another round of tears when David knocked at the door to tell her Father Lucas was on the phone in Mother Superior's office and he would meet her there.

    Lucia flew out of the room, wearing a fluffy white robe that was hanging on the bathroom door and ran down the hall after David. When they reached the office, it was David who answered the phone and with Lucia's urging, put it on speaker. Before the Archbishop could even get a word out, a very cantankerous nun was yelling for her clothes and demanding Father Lucas provide transportation back to the Convent or she would call for an Uber. Lucia and David could hear the Archbishop arguing that Louisa had to stay in the hospital until the doctor discharged her. The bickering continued until Father Lucas put his foot down and said that he was in charge and she would listen to him and in response Sister Louisa gave a harrumph loud enough that they heard it through the phone.

After a few moments of silence, Father Lucas came back on the phone and informed them that Sister Louisa had woken up an hour ago and had been giving him and all the nurses a hard time with wanting to go back to the Convent; then he stated loudly and in a very authoritative voice that she would have to wait for the DOCTOR TO ASSESS HER and that SHE WOULD FOLLOW THE DOCTOR'S ADVICE, WHATEVER THAT WAS! Sister Louisa was silent after that. Dr. Woods was sure that Sister Louisa was heavily medicated for the pain caused by the bullet hitting her chest and although the Medallion stopped it, the impact still did damage; but the medication falsely masked pain and made her feel well enough to go home.

As if on cue, Sister Lucia then started yelling at Sister Louisa about how stupid a move the elderly nun had made taking a bullet for her and she told her to never do that again.

After another loud harrumph, the elderly nun answered Lucia, "The shawl was given to you so that you could do your work. I was given the Medallion to protect you. The Lord KNEW this would happen and he protected me while I was protecting you. I will never regret my actions; it was the right thing to do. I just need some Advil."

Dr. David was chuckling at her response and then pointed to Sister Lucia, "Well, Sister, it seems you were crying for nothing, because the Mother Superior seems to be her normal kind, loving self."

Conversation continued about the shooter and the investigation going on but Father Lucas confessed that he had not received any update. He did inform them that he felt it best to stay with Sister Louisa to lessen her arrows when the doctor came in and Dr. David agreed. The Archbishop stated he would call them when he had more news.

Sister Lucia felt like a huge weight was lifted from her shoulders, knowing that Sister Louisa was awake and would be back soon. She told Dr. David she would get dressed now and meet him in the dining room for breakfast. David went to update the other nuns about Sister Louisa's condition, and in truth, he was starving. It had been a long night and the reality of the threats against Sister Lucia had come to fruition. How could someone look at her and what she was doing as demonic or hurtful? He hoped the security would identify the accomplice before the next event. He wasn't sure the Medallion trick would work twice, but then the Lord did work in strange ways.

The Commander of the Pontifical Swiss Guard and the head of Security were still at the Command Center they had set up at the arena, going through frame-by-frame of surveillance video. It was tedious and they were tired but neither would rest until they found who gave the shooter the gun. There were so many people; a handoff of a weapon was pretty easy in the crowded arena. They had focused on six ideal opportunities where the transfer of a weapon could have happened. Now it was just investigating all the people in each of the six frames to identify anyone who looked suspicious.

The shooter was taken to the police station to be processed, but the police reported that he had not spoken a word. In addition, they were unable to identify him. His picture was in no national database and there were no records of his fingerprints. He was kept isolated in a locked cell with no possibility of bail.

Jacob Bronson had made many friends in his career and he made all the right phone calls to make sure that this guy was not let go. Jacob was sure that if he were released, he would disappear and never be heard of again. That's why they were intent on finding his partner before they went underground, if the person hadn't already done so.

The gun gave no clues since the serial number was removed, so Jacob sent it to a local lab that might be able to recover it. He was assured that they would work on it right away, but Jacob knew the process and the system was slow. While he was making his connections, Philip Sorrin was contacting international databases around the world. He, too, had connections and he called them all without luck so far. Philip was also talking to the teams assigned with the other two Healers and arranging maximum protection by recruiting trusted mercenaries that he had served with in his years in the Swiss Special Forces.

They had been living on coffee and cigarettes throughout the night and on one short break, they discussed how the Medallion had stopped the bullet which they were told had been given to Sister Louisa by an angel. Both of them believed in God but had never witnessed such a miracle before. Jacob still had the Medal in his pocket. After close examination, he determined that it had two layers. The outer layer was high quality silver, and the craftsmanship was extraordinary. The outline of the Madonna on the front of the Medal had to be done by someone who was highly skilled with a laser. After they removed the bullet, which had hit the Medallion dead center, they found the inner layer appeared to be a metal they could not identify but was definitely similar to tungsten. He had promised Father Lucas that he would not relinquish the necklace to anyone and Jacob kept his promises.

Back at the hospital, the doctor still had not come and Sister Louisa was becoming more and more agitated and belligerent to the Archbishop and nursing staff, especially when she had discovered they had removed the Medallion from around her neck. She was so angry that someone would touch the heavenly protection she was gifted. She demanded to be brought back to the arena where she was told Jacob was holding it for her. The Medallion was not only a source of protection for her, she felt it had also created an invisible bond that strengthened her connection to Christ and it felt like an important part of her was missing. The Archbishop assured her that they would get the Medallion back before she returned to the Convent and then gave a deep sigh. He hoped the doctor would come soon because he wasn't sure how much longer he would be able to contain Mother Superior. He didn't think she knew how to contact an Uber but she was quite resourceful when she wanted to be.

Chapter XXX

It was hours before the Archbishop and Sister Louisa returned to the Convent. The elderly nun was pale and looked tired, but when Lucia and the other sisters ran to the door to greet her, she shushed them away saying she was fine. They helped her to her room and assisted in getting her into bed. Her face reflected the pain that had returned as the medication wore off. Lucia ran to get her water and her pain medication; and after giving Sister Louisa two of the white pills, the elderly nun sent the others away but asked Lucia to stay with her.

When the door closed, Lucia pulled a chair close to the bed and sat next to the Mother Superior. She could see her Medallion shining bright against her white nightgown, but quickly noticed the small hole that had not fully penetrated the Medal. As usual, the nun had both hands wrapped around the disc and with both eyes closed, she was quietly praying. Lucia waited patiently until she was finished, observing the paleness of her skin and the stress lines across her forehead.

Opening her eyes, Mother Superior grabbed Lucia's hands and thanked her for allowing an old nun to participate in healing the people at the arena. Lucia tried to object, but the nun held up her hand. Sister Louisa continued that she would be forever grateful for the experience that seemed to fill her soul with God's love and the over powering faith she felt as the white energy flowed from her hands as she stood next to Lucia. Sister Louisa was convinced that the Lord had given her the amulet specifically as he knew Louisa would protect Lucia at any cost. She went on to say that it was a miracle and Lucia should rejoice that the Lord so loved Sister Louisa that he protected her from a direct gunshot to her chest.

Lucia could not help herself and broke down in tears. She told Sister Louisa how she had tried to heal her but could not.

"I have lost my gift," she told the Mother Superior, but the Mother Superior would have none of it.

"I am sure you were in deep meditation when you calmly held your hands over my chest, murmuring words of love and adoration to God," she responded. "God did not need you to heal me as he had provided me with a much stronger protection," and glanced down at the Medallion sitting securely on her chest. "Also, I told Lucas to arrange another healing at the arena as there were a lot of sick people who came to see you but didn't get the chance to be healed. We have a lot of work left to do, Sister Lucia" said the nun," And let's start with placing those loving hands over my ribs, they're killing me and I don't like how the pain medicine makes me feel."

Sister Lucia left to go back to her room to get her black shawl. She wasn't even sure it was there; she couldn't remember much of what happened after the shooting. She felt guilty that she had so little regard for such a precious gift. It wasn't like the shawl had any special powers but it surely gave Lucia an immense feeling of comfort and confidence. She found it hung up carefully in her closet and thought Dr. David must have put it away after she fell asleep. She would have to remember to thank him later.

Returning to the Mother Superior's room, Sister Lucia closed her eyes and gave thanks and praise to the Lord, first for His thoughtfulness in giving Sister Louisa the Medallion that saved her life, but also for His forgiveness that she would doubt His plan. Quietly, she prayed with her hands raised over the elderly nun's chest where she suspected the broken ribs to be. The healing mist flowed freely from her fingers as it had many times before seeming to permeate the chest cavity. Lucia continued praying and soon Sister Louisa joined her, although she could see the nun breathing shallow breaths and wincing with pain, which only allowed her to manage a low whisper.

Once the energy stopped, Sister Louisa dismissed her and instructed Lucia to find the Archbishop and get an update on the next scheduled event. Lucia tried to protest but the stubborn nun raised her hand and covered her mouth.

"You are causing me more pain with having to stop your feeble arguments. Now, go find Lucas and let me get some rest," the Mother Superior firmly told her. Lucia bent over and kissed the back of Sister Louisa's hands, which were wrapped around the damaged Medallion, then quietly left the room.

The Archbishop and Dr. Woods were standing outside the door waiting for Sister Lucia. She assured them that Sister Louisa was resting and hopefully would respond to her healing. Lucia silently acknowledged that she would need to recover her confidence quickly as another event was being planned in two days' time. Father Lucas gave a huge sigh of relief, making the sign of the cross over his chest and escorted them to the conference room for an update on the shooting and the planning of the next arena event.

Lucia entered the meeting room and was taken back at the number of people waiting for them. Among the crowd were several priests and the security team of which included Philip Sorrin and several of his staff. Jacob Bronson and several of his team were also seated at the table. There were papers and photographs all over the table, as well as a projector flashing a power point on a screen at one end of the room. There were three seats saved around the table while several men sat in chairs against the wall.

Once Lucia, Dr. Woods and the Archbishop were seated, Jacob started the conversation by giving an update on the shooter, who was still in custody and had been placed in isolation. The accomplice had been identified as one of the security staff named Victor Smith, and whose location was being tracked. The address Victor, if that was his real name, had given was bogus and no one was quite sure how he had gotten through the background check, but Jacob had staff working on finding out. The serial number of the gun was recovered through a special process and it was discovered that the gun was reported stolen three months ago in a home invasion. All available manpower was working on this case to ensure there would be no repeat at the next event.

Once Jacob finished his report, Philip stood up and reported changes in the security plan to ensure the safety of Sister Lucia and the rest of the healing team. He recommended Lucia wear a bulletproof vest and that two security guards stand on both sides of the person presented for healing in order to thwart any further attacks. It was also decided that participants would be strongly discouraged from bringing in any bags and if they did have a bag, it would be checked thoroughly. Participants would be limited to have only one person accompany them; this would also apply to stretchers and security would be assigned to assist these cases. State of the art metal detectors were currently being installed before the check in stations, and mandatory screening for all participants was being implemented before entering the arena, similar to airports. In addition, both nurses and security would now attend the registration desks.

It was agreed that no event would be held until the applications of all staff involved in the event were rescreened, including social media interaction, and background checks resubmitted. An ID badge with special invisible markings would be distributed once employees have passed the above processes. The number of security personnel was being enhanced to include private security professionals. It would take at least four to five days to complete the screenings, so the next event would be held in five days, not two as previously thought.

All of this was flashed on the screen for everyone in the room to review and give feedback. One gentlemen, dressed in a dark suit and tie, who was sitting in the back of the room, frequently gave suggestions and questioned a few of the processes that had been initially put in place, such as the necessity of having four soldiers who were not security staff escort Lucia to the stage. This man had come in late, after Jacob had started giving his report, and had not been introduced. His suggestions generated a lot of discussion and initiated a few major changes regarding how people were lined up. His proposal was to create a line that wrapped around the outside of the inner arena and only have one or two lines in the inner arena to lessen the areas needing close observation by security.

This unknown man seemed quite intelligent, and Lucia could see his reasoning was very objective and unemotional. He certainly impressed Lucia, but when he questioned the need for Robert, Vincent, Matthew and Jack, Lucia stood up and said firmly that the four men must be part of the entrance team; then she sat back down. Her short, uncommon outburst seemed to startle everyone and both Philip and Jacob smiled and explained to the gentlemen in the suit that the four men were patients that were involved in the initial healings and very special to Sister Lucia. The Healer nodded and sat with her back straight and tried to assume as resolute and confident a look as she could muster.

When the meeting was over, the man in the suit made his way over to Sister Lucia and introduced himself as John Anderson, CEO of one of the most established private security firms in the United States. He apologized if he had upset her and had meant no harm. John then held out his hand and Lucia grasped it with both of her own and held it longer than was acceptable. She could feel the man's soul empty of faith and confirmed that John Anderson did not believe in God and told him so. She asked if he would be at the next event and when he nodded, she asked that he stand close to her so that he could see her in action. He agreed, although, he told her he doubted that would change his mind. She told him to bring his son and walked away.

Chapter XXXI

The limo had arrived and Father Lucas opened the door to assist Sister Louisa into the back seat. She seemed to be completely healed and argued with the Archbishop to stop fussing over her. She had also rebuked Lucia when the Healer suggested the elderly nun stay safely behind at the Convent.

Sister Louisa chastised her saying that "she would take her rightful place next to Lucia on stage as directed by the Lord," and then held up the Medallion to validate her point.

Sister Louisa sat next to the window, watching the scenery, thinking how she had never felt so close to God in all her years as a nun as she did when she was praying with Lucia on stage during each healing. She thanked God each night during her prayers that He had chosen her to be part of His Divine Plan and she would not abdicate her duty. Lucia's healing the other night had been quite effective and when she woke in the morning, she returned to her daily routine without hesitation.

Lucia sat next to Sister Louisa and held her hand throughout the ride. She wore the black shawl in hopes it would relieve the anxiety she felt building in her stomach. She was concentrating on suppressing the churning in the pit of her stomach when she noticed the considerable increase in black SUVs surrounding their car as they made their way to the coliseum. Jacob and Philip had again significantly beefed up security, which led Lucia to think about how Jack had made his way onto the Convent's grounds one afternoon after the shooting to see her. Security had identified him as a threat when he climbed with his cane over the black iron fence surrounding the

Convent and tackled him to the ground. Lucia had heard Jack calling her name so she ran outside to rescue him. Thank God Jacob was there and helped Jack off the ground, then proceeded to haul him over the coals for breaking protocol, especially, after the attack on Sister Lucia's life.

Jack cast his eyes down and looked properly rebuked, that is until Lucia ran out and scolded him for his actions, but then gave him a big hug. She escorted him into the building where they could talk without the angry looks from the Security team. Jack apologized to the other men but explained he could not get an answer from any of the team at the coliseum; he wanted to know that Sister Lucia was okay.

Staring out the car window, Lucia felt blessed to have such wonderful loyal men and women around to help her on her holy mission. She had been praying all day in preparation for this event. Looking down at her hands, she noticed how smooth and white they were, almost translucent. She hardly recognized them from the wrinkled and reddened hands she earned from working in the cafeteria. Sensing Lucia's trepidation, Sister Louisa squeezed Sister Lucia's hand as a sign of support and solidarity.

The limo came to a stop outside the back door of the building and many men with big guns made a secure path for all of them to walk inside. At the doorway to meet her were Jack, Robert, Matthew and Vincent. They all hugged her and questioned whether she was okay. The men then turned from Sister Lucia to Sister Louisa and they all hugged her, too, thanking her for her bravery and sacrifice. She tsked them away but Lucia saw the glimmer in her eyes and the smile on her face. Lucia noticed Dr. David practically running up the hallway. She had not seen him since the meeting two days ago and he took his place by her side.

And so they went, Sister Louisa on her right and David on her left, with the four soldiers around the three of them. Lucia was directed to walk at a brisk pace and go straight to the make shift altar where more men in uniform waited. She kept her eyes on the path before her, trying hard not to notice the big guns the men had at the ready. They passed Mary Ellen at the doorway to the Rosary room and Sister Louisa made them stop for a few minutes to quell Mary Ellen's concern for the Mother Superior. The nurse had called frequently since the shooting, but this is the first time she would see Sister Louisa in person. They had become good friends sharing similar stories, though choosing different paths.

They had gotten close to the altar and Lucia could see the line of people waiting for her. Many were waving and competing for her attention, even though the guards were reminding those in the makeshift pews to pray quietly. Lucia could hear the choir singing in the background. It was beautiful to her ears and started to hum the tune in her head as she prayed. Lucia felt good and her confidence was finally intact. This was her calling and she was ready -- or so she thought.

Even with the noise of the choir, the people praying and calling to her, a single sound made its way to her ears. "Mom, Mom, it's me. Please, Mom, I need you," someone called from the pews.

Lucia's eyes shot up and opened wide. She immediately began scanning the large room filled with hope and excitement.

Lucia began, screaming, "Becky, Becky, where are you, baby? Where are you?"

David and Sister Louisa stared anxiously at Lucia who was bouncing all over the floor by the stage. The guards were at full alert with their guns drawn, not understanding what was happening. Jack came closer to Lucia and the other three soldiers followed suit, literally boxing her in, but Lucia fought them frantically, still screaming, "Becky, Becky."

Finally, Sister Louisa took charge and in a loud authoritative voice yelled for silence and the entire hall became quiet. There mid-way down the aisle in front of the altar stood a young woman with a small baby in her arms. As soon as Lucia saw her, she ran to her daughter with her entourage trailing behind. Only Sister Louisa stood still, making the sign of the cross and looking up to heaven.

"It's about time she came to see her mother," the elderly nun said to anyone listening.

Lucia and Becky were locked tight in a circle of security. Tears cascading down Becky's face as her mother held her tight.

Lucia reassured her over and over, "I got you, baby girl. I got you. Don't worry."

It was David who finally led mother, daughter and granddaughter to the front of the arena. Lucia was already holding the baby and kissing her up and down. Sister Louisa gave her five minutes, then, reminded her of why they were there. Dr. David assured Lucia that he would take care of them and stay with Becky until the end. So, Lucia surrendered her granddaughter reluctantly, kissed her daughter and marched to the altar with Sister Louisa by her side.

"Let's do this," she informed them.

The guards all sighed and rolled their eyes.

Lucia was well into the second hour before they called for a break. She was escorted to a room to the side of the altar to find Becky and the baby resting comfortably in a large recliner, sleeping. Lucia did not wake her, but her heart was filled with happiness to finally have her daughter in her sights again. The baby looked no more than two or three months old. David came up behind her and explained that Becky was afraid to tell her that she was pregnant and had been living with her brother until she had a fight with the sister-in-law. Becky felt Lucia would be very disappointed in her, but after being abandoned by her boyfriend and rejected by her father, she had nowhere else to go.

Lucia grabbed a cup of coffee, some cookies and sat down. She noticed a boy sitting across from her. He was staring at her so she smiled and asked his name. Before he could answer, John Anderson came up behind him and informed her that this was his son, Joshua; he was deaf and mute. Lucia nodded and offered the son one of her cookies, but he turned and signed to the father.
The father looked at Lucia and said, "He wants to know if you can heal him, too. We've been watching you work."

Lucia smiled and asked John to sign to the son as she spoke. Lucia explained that she was gifted in order to return the flock to the Shepherd. She was chosen to show people that God loved them and had mercy for those that were sick and suffering. Her power to heal came from God; it was not hers to give; that was God's decision. So although she couldn't guarantee that he would be healed, she only asked that his father teach him about the Lord.

The son signed back to the father for a long time, after which John looked taken back and his expression became incredulous. The son nudged John to give Lucia his response. John slowly turned to her and relayed his message.

"Apparently, my son was visited by a large man in a white sheet several nights ago. He had large eyes and a gold cord around his waist. This man told my son to find the Healer; she would help him and me find our way home."

Lucia motioned the boy over to sit in the chair next to her. He was taller and older than Lucia had originally thought. He also had a sereneness about him that drew Lucia to him. It was the same feeling she had felt with David. Lucia closed her eyes and held her hands over his ears and began to pray. Unbeknownst to Lucia, the boy before her also closed his eyes and intertwined his fingers as if in prayer. The father watched as the white healing energy flowed from Lucia's fingertips into his ears and mouth. Everyone in the room fell silent as they witnessed what was happening.

When the stream ended, Lucia stood and announced it was time to go back. John Anderson had no words to what he had just seen but he nodded and turned to his son, who wrapped his arms around Lucia and whispered in her ear. "Thank you."

Lucia nodded and looked up to see tears flowing down John's face having heard his son speak for the first time.

"Go to Church, John," the Healer told him.

Chapter XXXII

Lucia was back in the limo holding her granddaughter as they made their way back to the Convent. Becky was seated beside her with her head on Lucia's shoulder and holding her arm tightly. Sister Louisa had already called Sister Theresa to let the sisters know that they had a baby coming in and to prepare accordingly. Lucia sat back more content than she had been in a long, long time. It seems that since the angel's first visit, she had received many surprises, some good, some really bad, but seeing her daughter was by far the best.

They drove through the tall black iron gates and parked in front of the large wooden doors. The Archbishop helped Sister Louisa out but stepped aside when David sprinted over from the SUV he was in to help Becky and Lucia. Again, Lucia noticed the number of black SUVs and group of armed men emerging from each one and fanning around the Convent. Lucia was a little concerned, as she no longer worried only about herself.

She stared at the baby in her arms and whispered, "I got you Claire Elizabeth. I got both you and your mother. Don't you worry!"

Once the doors opened, the nuns rushed out to see the baby and pried the little one out of Lucia's arms. Lucia was laughing and assured Becky that little Claire was in no better hands. Lucia recaptured the baby as her and Becky made their way to Lucia's suite. The room was temporarily set up to accommodate Becky and the baby, which made Lucia deliriously happy. Her daughter had been away from her for so long, she promised the Lord to spend extra time in the Chapel in gratitude. Becky had a small duffle bag with her and the baby's belongings. Not much, but

Lucia still had a small savings that she would give to Becky to buy whatever she needed.

Sister Louisa had the nuns also prepare a late dinner for them all, which included the Archbishop, David, Mary Ellen, Jack, Jacob Bronson and Philip Sorrin, so they could discuss the success of tonight's affair. Once everyone had finished the meal, Jacob reported they had found the shooter's accomplice boarding a plane to a country without an extradition agreement with the United States. Lucia felt relieved, more so, when she was informed that the threat level had significantly lessened since their capture; however, it was still unknown if they belonged to a larger group. In addition, Philip shared that four more Healers had been identified and security teams from the Vatican were being sent to them for protection.

Jacob and Philip assured the group that the new security measures were effective and the recheck on all the staff had not raised any red flags. Then, with a great deal of irritation and restraint, they addressed the problem of Lucia breaking the security line for the second time and requested that if anyone else popped up, they would appreciate a heads up to make the appropriate security changes. Lucia sheepishly nodded, hoping there would not be a third time.

Father Lucas informed them that Cardinal Moreno had met with Vatican staff, however he admitted that he was unable to change their position. He believed the healings had to be witnessed to be believed. He needed to convince the Pope to come to the United States and meet Lucia, but unfortunately, the Vatican staff continued with their skepticism and was hesitant to put their stamp of approval, so to speak, on the Healers popping up around the globe.

Lucia wondered how many Healers were included in God's Divine Plan. There were so many sick people and each Healer brought such hope to the people in their country. Currently, the Healers were located in Brazil, Spain, France, Japan, Russia and China. The governments of those countries were surprisingly cooperative, especially the difficult governments of China and Russia.

It seemed that as in Lucia's case, the other Healers were surrounded by people who had had angelic visits or visions in their lifetime. Apparently, this Heavenly Plan had been designed a long time ago. All the angelic visits had matching descriptions of the same large man in a white toga with a gold cord wrapped around his waist. All of the people who were visited reported that the angel had the bluest eyes and curly black hair. The Archangel Gabriel has been one busy messenger with the ability to speak to each person in his or her own language, but would you expect anything less from Heaven.

After the initial rush, Lucia was able to recapture little Claire and gently rock her in her arms, barely listening as the conversation flowed around the table. She noted that Dr. David was sitting next to Becky and their conversation had not stopped since they sat down. Interesting. Lucia also noticed that Jacob had sat next to Mary Ellen and they too had not stopped talking since they sat down. Double Interesting. As Lucia was watching the two "couples" she glanced over at Jack who looked at Jacob then back to Lucia and winked. Since Jack had made his daring break in, Jacob seemed to include him in our group rather than have to take him down again.

Soon, the party was over with plans made for another event in five days with Jacob and Philip confirming they would begin making preparations immediately. Tonight's event was an overwhelming success with over three hundred people healed. Avoiding the press was becoming a very difficult task as they were interviewing anyone and everyone who knew Lucia. This was to be expected and Lucia thought the time was coming that it could no longer be avoided. She was anxious to tell her story and reinforce the importance of faith and love of the Lord.

She remembered the angel's message to her. "You will be an instrument of his peace and love to help those lost sheep find their way back home to their loving Shepherd. You will heal their bodies and their souls with God's abundant grace so that they may find everlasting life in Heaven. Find those that are sick and lost and show them God is loving and merciful. Our Lord will guide you in this quest." The Archbishop told her he would think her request over.

That night, she cuddled with Becky on the bed, her daughter revealed what Lucia had suspected. Her boyfriend was bad news. As soon as he found out Becky was pregnant, he left her for someone else. She felt that she was a huge disappointment to her mother and was ashamed to return to her. Her brother had taken her in, but his new wife was a selfish bitch and complained about everything Becky did. Once the baby came, the wife became even more critical and complained constantly to her husband. The wife even had her children complaining. Whenever the husband was home, the wife would start yelling and slamming doors whenever the baby cried. In order to appease his wife, Becky's brother conceded and forced his sister and her baby to move out even though that would make her homeless. Becky heard about the woman healing the sick and had felt a strong thread pulling her to the coliseum, even though she was not sick, she hoped for a miracle. She had no money, no home and her mother wasn't answering her phone. She had gone to her mom's apartment but no one was there. When Becky asked the neighbor, she was told that several big men came and took everything.

Becky had nowhere else to go, so she made her way to the coliseum. She had waited for hours to get in and thankfully got a seat. Becky did not know why but she just had a feeling she would get some kind of message tonight. When Becky saw her mother walking into the arena, she was shocked, confused and didn't really understand why her mother was surrounded by so many men, some with guns. Regardless, Becky screamed for all she was worth trying to get her mother's attention. She knew she had to be loud enough to be heard over the people chanting and the large choir singing off to the side. Becky kept screaming over and over, tears running down her cheeks, until finally, she saw her mother turn her head towards her. Becky was waving one arm over her head and holding little Claire with the other. Once Lucia saw her, she began to run to her precious daughter with her entourage close behind. Tearful and exhausted, Becky fell into her mother's arms and realized God had led her here to be reunited with her mother.

  Now it was Lucia's turn to tell Becky what had happened to her. She told her of the angel's visit in the night, the black shawl and how she went to the hospitals to heal the children first, then several nights later, to the VA Hospital. Lucia shared how she met Dr. Woods and how he had helped her in the beginning and continues to be at her side. Becky listened in awe, her mother, who had suffered so much at the hands of her father, was chosen by God to heal people. She hung her head down and began to cry again. Becky knew her mother's faith and love for the Lord was strong as she always tried to instill the same devotion in her children, sending them to religious school and attending Mass every Sunday. Becky had turned away from her mother because of it, especially when her father and brother berated her whenever she spoke well of her Mother. She was not worthy to be Lucia's daughter and had certainly shamed her in front of the Archbishop and Mother Superior, yet, here she was, wrapped in her mother's arms and Becky had never felt so safe and loved.

Becky decided there and then she would do everything she could to make her mother proud of her, again. She had lost her way but she would stick close with her mother. She would be one of the sheep that would return to the Shepherd that she heard her mother reference. Becky looked at her mother and said, "Mom, can we pray together. I need to thank God because I am sure He brought me to you." Lucia nodded and smiled; how she loved this girl.

Several days later, David had told Lucia how the hospital staff knew that he was close with her so he was stopped frequently with requests for Sister Lucia to see a particular patient who could not come to the arena. The Archbishop continued to reject the hospital visits, but Lucia stoically insisted that it was her duty. Father Lucas finally relented with the caveat that she only sees ten patients' maximum and be escorted by security. In and out, one, two three. No deviations. Lucia agreed.

So, in the middle of the night, four large and armed security officers accompanied Sisters Lucia and Louisa (who would not let her go alone), to visit the patients. Dr. David always met them at the hospital and walked her to the rooms. She had done this several times over the past several weeks; it didn't even take two hours and she was back in bed. All involved were informed of the sensitivity and secrecy required of these visits, including the hospital staff. If any breech were identified, the visits would be terminated; the Archbishop made that very clear.

Chapter XXXIII

Becky settled in comfortably at the Convent. Lucia was surprised that she attended Chapel daily with her and seemed relieved when one of the sisters would quickly take a crying Claire outside. The baby received so much attention. The sisters took turns feeding and changing her, and Claire seemed to thrive in the love and peace here at the Convent. In fact, Claire, who Becky always thought was colicky, spent most of her days smiling and cooing in two of many arms.

Becky spent her days working wherever she was needed, sometimes with Lucia weeding in the garden or helping Mother Superior with technical assistance on her computer. She also helped organize the elderly nun's files and color-coded them which Mother Superior found to be significantly helpful. Sister Louisa was not prepared to like the girl, but Becky's efforts to be helpful and useful, changed the nun's opinion. In fact, over the next few days, Becky fell into the habit of spending mornings at Chapel and in the garden, and afternoons in Mother Superior's office while Lucia and the other nuns took care of Claire.

Lucia could not be happier with the arrival of her daughter and the wonderful surprise of her granddaughter. Dr. David visited everyday but Lucia wondered if it was to see her or her daughter. He certainly seemed smitten and Becky had a glow about her. Things could not be going better. Thankfully, the Archbishop continued to allow Lucia to make her midnight runs to the hospital to heal the sick children, men and women who had failed conventional treatment, and as usual, Sister Louisa accompanied her.

The next healing at the coliseum was postponed for four days since the Pope himself announced that he would finally come to the United States to bear witness to the Healer's God given gift. Jacob Bronson and Philip Sorrin discussed the Pope's arrival at the last meeting and had notified them that they were taking additional measures to ensure extra security was in place for the Papal visit. Lucia could not imagine more security than there already was, but she stayed out of that discussion. It seems that more Healers were being identified throughout the world and each one reported similar stories to Lucia's. The Pope could no longer deny the army the Lord had activated to spread His message of love and abundant mercy. These women would bring his flock back to give thanks and praise to God.

The Catholic Churches were bursting and had added more masses to accommodate the influx of believers. In addition, the Archbishop had reported that many churches that had been closed were now being reopened to accommodate all the faithful returning. The Diocese had to recruit priests from around the country to assist with the increased masses and parishioners seeking absolution through reconciliation. Men were entering the priesthood at record numbers; the same being seen with young woman seeking entry into the various religious communities throughout the country. The singular message given by Lucia and all associated with the movement to everyone was to return to the Lord and Lucia was assured that this was reinforced throughout the process of entry to the coliseum. Non-believers were encouraged to join the faithful, although in truth, the Lord provided healing to almost everyone but not always in the way the person expected.

Lucia thought about the rare person that had come to her for healing that clearly had rejected the Lord and had no intention of connecting with Him. When she laid her hands on them, Lucia felt the cold emptiness of their soul and wondered why they came to her. It was made clear to them by the time they reached her that this was a gift to the faithful. So, she prayed over them in hopes they would change their mind and accept the love of the Lord. She knew by the absence of white energy flowing from her fingertips that these souls were hopeless; however, she would not give up so easily and sent them to one of the religious counselors available.

The religious communities had been very supportive of Lucia and had committed to her mission to save those who had lost their way. The organizers had put together make shift counseling rooms and had set up confessionals in the back of the arena for those seeking redemption. After the first few events, more gaps in services were identified and every effort was made to provide a variety of services to all those who came. Although, Lucia was discouraged from providing counseling; she had worked with Mary Ellen to set up an extensive referral network. She felt many individuals would benefit from the support services already available through the church and the city. Lucia would provide the healing and then make the referral she felt would help the person most. Mary Ellen was always standing by and seemed to read her mind in these instances. God bless her.

In order to provide visual validation of her work to the outside world, the Archbishop with the help of Jacob Bronson had set up an outdoor shrine to the Holy Mother where the wheel chairs, canes and crutches left by the healed were accumulating. The Archbishop had also recommended a large bulletin board be placed by the Shrine where people could write notes to the Lord or special Saints, giving thanks and praise for restoring their health.

    Lucia had strongly discouraged any marketing or selling of items; however, Rosary beads were still being distributed for free. Sister Louisa had guilted the Archbishop into paying for them. The only notification of an upcoming Healing was placed in the weekly bulletin distributed after each Mass with the date and time of the event. The Media was hounding the Archbishop to meet with Lucia, but Father Lucas was adamant that no interviews would be granted; however, he directed them to contact those who were healed.

    He declared, "They will tell a much better story." The Security Team had ensured that no one got close to Lucia, although, she knew several attempts had been made to breach the Convent walls or become part of the arena staff to get to her. Besides Jack, two other men had tried to break through the iron gates of the Convent, but both did not receive the welcome of Lucia's friend, and were arrested for trespassing.

    Lucia had learned at the last meeting that the reporters were attempting to interview everyone who knew her. Dr. Woods and Bea were frequently approached and offered a lot of money, but both of them declined. It was unsurprising to Lucia that her ex-husband had been paid a lot of money for an interview on his life with the Healer. Lucia was astounded at the lies and exaggerations he spewed; even Becky could not believe the distorted fabrication he made up to paint himself in a better light.

She had even called him and yelled at him for being a pompous ass. Thankfully, she was pretty smart and technologically savvy and had blocked the caller ID so he could not give her number or location out - for money, of course.

  The growing number of the crowd outside the iron gates of the Convent was causing some concern, especially when they loudly chanted Lucia's name. Security had their hands full with keeping the crowd back; in fact, they had considered closing the road off to all but approved staff. Early on, Lucia had walked down toward the gate, but the crowd went wild when she appeared. She hurriedly ran back inside, as the vibe she got was not one of hope but rather hostility. The guards instructed those that came to the gate that healings would only be administered at the coliseum and even threatened those who continued shouting with arrest. Things were getting crazy.

  Thankfully, Sister Louisa reassured them all that the Convent was a fortress and no one was getting in unless she gave her approval. She was after all the Mother Superior and had all the faith in the world that the Lord would keep them safe. She, herself, was a fortress and gave Lucia the strength to ignore the crowds and the shouting. Also, baby Claire took Lucia's mind off of the gathering crowds and gave her immense joy, as did her daughter who frequently wrapped her arms around her and kissed her cheek, telling her how glad she was that Lucia was her mother.

  With the impending visit by the Pope, Mother Superior spent the day shouting orders and kept everyone busy preparing the Convent for the arrival of the Pope and his entourage. Every nook and cranny was cleaned and polished. A special suite was made ready for the Papal associates and rooms made available for the Archbishop and Cardinal Moreno, who would be returning to the Convent during the Pope's visit. Lucia had offered to cook but the Archbishop smiled at her offer, assuring her he had already hired a catering agency that he often used to provide the meals.

Lucia did not realize how massive the Convent was until she joined the staff to help open up the closed off sections of the building. There were many bedrooms that included a lounge and a private bathroom and she helped ready them, including polishing furniture and putting on clean sheets. It was decided that no other staff would be hired for safety reasons, so everyone was working hard and fast.

One large room had a massive stone fireplace and a long oak table that would accommodate forty people. It seems there would be a lot of entertaining while the Pope was in attendance. The Governor, the Mayor, and other important diplomats had been invited to one or more of the planned gatherings. The Pope's schedule was full over the next four days, with many officials requesting an audience with him.

Lucia was worried that they might expect her to "perform" for them. She had expressed her fears and concerns to Father Lucas and Sister Louisa who assured her that they would block any such attempts. Somewhat assured, Lucia prayed that all would go well when the Head of the Roman Catholic Church came to visit, knowing that he was skeptical of her ability. Once he came and witnessed the gift God had given her, Lucia was sure that he would change his mind. She would show him her black shawl and Sister Louisa's Medallion and explain how it had stopped the bullet. Maybe she should have Dr. David bring over his feather. These were concrete items that were given by the Archangel. Surely, the Pope could not deny this was God's work at hand.

Chapter XXXIV

It seems two of the Pope's long-tenured senior advisors at the Vatican, Cardinal Zello and Cardinal Tzakas, were extremely skeptical of Lucia's ability to heal; in fact, they thought her a charlatan and did not believe her ability came from Heaven. They doubted that the Lord would have chosen such an insignificant woman in the United States to represent Him. They hired a private investigator, highly recommended by their American contacts, who discovered that the woman was divorced for goodness sake and lived practically in squalor. Certainly the Deity would have picked someone far better than her with established religious association. The PI could find no evidence that this woman had contact with any religious affiliation; so suspicion was heavy between them that she was a fraud. Both Cardinals had the Pope's ear and whispered words of doubt and dubious design regarding the actions of this woman and advised the Pope to distance the Church from this so-called "Healer."

The two Cardinals contrived to surround the Pope with their staff delivering the same message of uncertainty in the origin of the woman's powers, and together they convinced the Pope not to give support or validation of this woman or any of the others and their "so-called ability to heal." They began rumors that the woman was possessed by evil and accentuating the suffering of men, woman and children at the hands of God. A large sect of the church had long held the belief that suffering was necessary to cleanse the soul. Both Cardinals and their staff had long contributed to this philosophy. Humans must pay for their sins through sacrifice and suffering. God was merciful but healing the suffering of sinful men, women and children without proper atonement was inconceivable to those who opposed the possibility God gave these women power to heal indiscriminately.

To his credit, the Pope tried to counter their arguments, but he was one against many in his circle of association. Although, he did override their protests to send the Swiss Guard to provide appropriate protection for the Healer, just in case the Cardinals were wrong in their assessment that she was a charlatan. He also assigned Cardinal Moreno to meet with the woman in the United States, hoping to get a full and objective report. The Pope's thoughts became clouded with indecision. As the Bishop of Rome and Head of the Roman Catholic Church, he became fearful that if he acknowledged the Healer's powers were from God and it was proven false, he would mislead the people and provide a window of opportunity for Satan to claim dominion of the relief from suffering she provided. It seemed as if he was balancing on a tight rope and unsure where to put his next foot.

Over the last several weeks, Pope Leo had received many letters from clergy attesting to the Healer's faith in God and her conviction that she was only a messenger, given the power to heal by God, Himself. Most of the correspondence he received was from Archbishop Lucas Corvino who assumed all care and protection of the Healer. Her name was Sister Lucia and the Archbishop bore witness to the miracles she performed. He pleaded in each letter for the Pope to come meet with her. Other clergy had written the same thing; they had witnessed her perfect healings in the name of the Lord. In addition, several other Healers were identified in different countries. All claiming they were sent by God. Were all the witnesses deceived and misinformed? Satan was quite proficient in promoting lies as truth. As Pope, he had to be very careful. Even after receiving a very detailed and objective assessment from Cardinal Moreno of the healings performed by "Sister Lucia", the Pope's advisors were adamant that the Holy See not get involved.

So, day after day, week after week, the Pope remained silent on the miracles occurring in the Northeastern part of the United States and those miracles now spreading across several continents. After a while, he no longer accepted dialogue from those around him spreading distrust on all that had been reported to him and retreated to his small prayer room seeking divine intervention. He spent hours praying, hoping to receive an answer. Pope Leo took his meals in solitude and met only to discuss Vatican business. The indecision was taking a toll on him and the strain showed on his face.

One evening, he retired to his chambers, with a heavy heart, exhausted by the conflict inside of him. He had been praying for days and had yet to receive clarity on how to address the Healers. He slipped off his shoes and sat in the chair by the window in his room. His assistant had left his usual cup of chamomile tea that helped him sleep. Reaching for his nightshirt on the bed, he saw something gray sticking out from under his pillow. Tossing his nightshirt to the side, he pulled on the object and fell to his knees. God had sent His answer; it was the gray feather that he had long ago tucked away in a box stored in his closet.

Jumping up and running from his chambers, he called loudly to his personal secretary. It seems he, too, was in the midst of retiring for the night.

"Arrange for travel to the United States immediately. I must see the Healer as soon as possible," the Pope exclaimed excitedly.

"Can it not wait till morning, Sir?" the secretary replied.

"No, I've already waited too long," replied the Pope.

Against the advice of his advisors and senior staff, Pope Leo boarded a private plane to the states two days later. He had invited the two dissenting Cardinals and their administrative staff, but they had refused. They all felt he was making a big mistake in meeting with the Healer. The Pope instead brought five other Cardinals who expressed a more open mind on the possibility that the woman was chosen by God. Other administrative staff seemed glad they were included in the trip and expressed curiosity and interest in the phenomenon.

Once on board the plane, the Pope heard one of the staff comment how excited he was to meet the Healer. He then complained that he and others in the office had been forbidden to speak in front of the Pope about the Healers. Learning this, the Pope realized that the two Cardinals had conspired to silence any opposing line of reasoning from the Pope's ears. He was glad the Lord heard his prayers and left the feather. The reminder was all he needed to follow his heart. A heart he had loyally committed to Christ long ago.

He spent his time on the plane reading all the letters he had received about Sister Lucia. Each letter referenced a different miracle performed at her hands. The Pope could not understand the failure of Cardinal Zello and Cardinal Tzakas to have faith and believe that our Lord chose the woman. Pope Leo had not been this excited in a very long time. He hoped she would forgive him for his delayed response in meeting her. His advisors had carried out their agenda with malice and bias, isolating him from those that would have encouraged a meeting with the Healer. He would deal with them later.

The atmosphere on the plane was conducive to discussion on the pros and cons of meeting with the Healer and the ramifications it could have on the Church as a whole. For the most part, many on the plane had family, friends or acquaintances that had shared stories relating to Sister Lucia. All were anxious to meet her and witness for themselves. Some had questioned the time delay in taking this trip and the Pope could do nothing but agree with them. He should have come sooner.

Thankfully, since he had made the decision to come, the heaviness and exhaustion he had experienced had left him completely.
"Maybe she is already performing her miracle on me," Pope Leo thought and smiled. Archbishop Corvino had assured the Pope that he had appropriate lodging for him and his entourage. They would be staying in the same Abbey as the Healer and would have the protection of the Swiss Guard at all times. Pope Leo could not contain his excitement. He joined a group of young seminarians that were enthusiastically discussing the validity of whether the Healer received her powers from God. Joining the debate invigorated him and their arguments in favor of divine intervention confirmed the Pope's decision that he had acted appropriately in coming to meet Sister Lucia.

Returning to his seat, he called his personal secretary over to make a special reminder to ask Sister Lucia about the black shawl he had heard discussed in the seminarian's debate and the medal that had miraculously appeared for the Mother Superior. A Medallion she wore proudly over her habit for all to see and which had stopped the bullet meant for Sister Lucia. Pope Leo also had something to share with the Healer. He had packed his gray feather in his suitcase. He wasn't sure she would be interested, but he would tell her of his dream long ago when he was a young man, and how the feather turned up under his pillow after his long days of prayer. He thought he was too excited to sleep, but soon he drifted off, content with the decision he made to meet with Sister Lucia and satisfied that it was the right one.

Chapter XXXV

Pope Leo XIV arrived late in the morning in a procession of nine cars. The crowd that had accumulated outside the iron gates had been cleared and the road closed to all non-essential traffic. Lucia watched the arrival from a small lounge in the front of the building, as all the SUVs pulled up. Several dozen men jumped from the cars and spread across the grounds to join the guards already posted around the Convent. Lucia saw Father Lucas and Cardinal Moreno exit one of the black SUVs and walk toward the one parked directly in front of the large entry way.

The car door opened and Lucia saw a small man dressed in a white cassock and a white mozetta (a short, hooded cape), a gold pectoral cross and red papal shoes. On his head was a white zuchettos. Lucia observed him as he stretched and studied the old structure and well-manicured grounds. Several others in black robes stood about talking and laughing.

"Well, that was encouraging," Lucia thought.

No one seemed angry or upset to be here. Lucia was in reality hiding and dreading having to meet the Pope and be interrogated by him and his staff.

Lucia heard one of the nuns calling her name but she stood quiet, continuing to watch the men outside. It was Sister Theresa who found her hiding behind the draperies. Sister was such a sweet and kind woman. Lucia loved working the garden with her. So it was unusual for her to scold the Healer for hiding when all the sisters were looking for her. Mother Superior had demanded her presence at once, Sister Theresa told her.

Still, Lucia did not move. She felt her body and mind freeze up, and unable to respond with words or action.

Sister Theresa smiled warmly and assessed the situation before her, "Ah, I see you are scared to meet the Pope."

Lucia could only nod.

"Well," the nun went on, "if you feel nervous, imagine how the poor Pope feels meeting someone who has been graced by God with a gift so precious, given a gift by St. Mary, herself and visited by the Archangel Gabriele not once, but twice. I imagine he is so scared and intimidated by someone chosen by God, Himself. And, now that special woman doesn't even show him an ounce of respect by greeting him at the door. He will certainly feel that he is not good enough for you."

Lucia quickly denied that she was better than the Pope. Sister Theresa took this opportunity to push Lucia out of the lounge and down the hall to the front door. They just managed to get there as the door was opening, receiving a scowl from the Mother Superior. The elderly nun's expression changed quickly to a gracious smile as she took the Pope's hand and kissed it. Lucia, not knowing what to do, followed suit and took the Pope's hand and bent to kiss it, but he pulled his hand away. Lucia stood with her mouth open and completely humiliated until Pope Leo softly took her hand and raised it to his lips.
"It is my honor to kiss the hand of God's chosen disciple," he said.

He then asked for a quiet room where he could meet with Lucia alone and Mother Superior guided him to the same small lounge Lucia had been hiding in. Sister Louisa squeezed her arm and smiled in a sign of support and closed the door, which seemed to make a loud thud, increasing Lucia's anxiety. Lucia just sat in the soft brown paisley printed chair and cast her eyes down to the carpet under her feet. She heard rather than saw the Pope take the seat across from her.

After several moments, the Pope cleared his throat and smiled, "I hope you are not upset with my visit. I wanted to come sooner, but my advisors felt your story had to be verified. I, on the other hand, thought that if God had you heal only one person instead of the hundreds you have affected, I should have come to you. Please forgive my delay in showing you the support of the Vatican."

Lucia looked up and recognized the same calm and soulful eyes as that of the Angel who had visited her. Pope Leo had quickly put her at ease with a warm smile and kind words. So, she readily told him her story from the beginning. She had to leave to get the black shawl from her room to show him and when he stroked the garment, he marveled at the quality of the wool and the fragrance of roses permeated into the fabric.

"It was sent by St. Mary, I'm sure," Lucia told him. She continued to share her trepidation at going to the children's ward, but then explained how the shawl gave her such a feeling of confidence and strength. She had worn the shawl the first time and had healed all but one child that night. She has since worn it at every healing and found that the more she healed, the stronger she got.

Lucia told him how she had gone to the VA Hospital and saw the men missing their arms and legs. She heard a voice in her head tell her that she could heal them but it would be painful when the limbs grew back. She had explained this to the men and still they had both consented. She told him how one soldier was blind and he received his sight back immediately after the healing and shared how four of his friends who died on the battlefield came to his hospital bed to say goodbye. She then described Vincent, who had suffered a traumatic brain injury from an explosive in Iraq, who also had been completely healed. Lucia then told him how the four soldiers escorted her to the stage at every event, able to see with two good eyes and walking on two strong legs and possessing two good arms.

      The Pope was silent, nodding as she spoke, so she continued. Lucia told him about Dr. Woods and healing the woman who was so close to death and then how the nurses made a list of their sickest patients and all of them recovered after she prayed over them. She was reluctant to tell him about the child who had died because his mother wouldn't allow her into the room the first night she went to the children's ward. However, through God's mercy, he allowed the parents to visit with their son in Heaven. Certainly, an incredible story even to Lucia, but she decided as the Pope he should know the extent of the miracles by God's hand she had witnessed. So she told him. His eyes grew large with each word Lucia spoke and then he exclaimed aloud, "God Almighty is there no end to God's mercy!"

      Lucia shared how the angel left her the Medallion with Sister Louisa's name on it and how it had protected the elderly nun when she jumped in front of the gun and took the bullet that was meant for Lucia. She continued telling the Pope how the Medallion stopped the bullet and all Sister Louisa suffered were a couple of broken ribs, which Lucia healed the next day. She shared how she thought God knew everything that was going to happen and had planned accordingly. What other explanation was there? The Pope readily stood from the chair and called Sister Louisa into the room to show him the Medallion. He inspected it carefully and exclaimed it was certainly a work of art. The Mother Superior soon excused herself to ensure the staff would have lunch prepared for their important visitors.

Finally, she shared how Dr. Woods, Sister Louisa and Mary Ellen had also received heavenly communication when they were quite young and were told about a Healer who would need their help. All of them brushed it off as vivid dream, similar to the reaction Lucia had at first, they never gave it another thought, especially since so many years had passed. So, they were all in shock when Lucia came into their lives and knew she was the Healer they were told about.

The Pope was silent throughout Lucia's story, except for his outburst when she told him about the heavenly visit to see Joey. Lucia wasn't sure if the Pope thought she was crazy or delusional. He seemed speechless and sat staring at her. Lucia became quite uncomfortable waiting for him to speak. The Pope finally took a deep breath and slowly exhaled. He shifted in his seat and leaned toward Lucia never breaking eye contact.

"Well," he said, "you can add me to that small group who received a visit from the Archangel Gabriel," and smiled.

Lucia sat back aghast.
The Pope continued, "It was right before I entered the seminary. I was asleep and woke up to see an angelic figure, tall and surrounded by a pure white light. He had

curly black hair and clear blue eyes. He wore a toga with a gold cord wrapped around his waist. I sat up speechless, but he spoke to me in almost a melodic voice, telling me that the time would come when the Lord would send Healers to bring back his flock and that I must help their efforts to reach as many people as possible. I don't remember lying back down or the angel leaving. Well, you can imagine what I was thinking when I woke up. The dream was so real, but I dismissed it and truly forgot about it until about two weeks later when I was cleaning my room at the seminary and found a large light gray feather hidden in the corner where I dreamed the angel appeared. I didn't know what to think. I have kept that feather stored for decades in a box in my closet with my other mementos."

    Taking a deep breath, the Pope continued. "My executive staff was adamant that I withhold my support from you and the other Healers, but my heart was heavy in disagreement. After many hours spent in prayer and reflection, it was to my surprise, I found that feather under my pillow as I was retiring to bed and knew I had to see you. So, as you can imagine, I immediately made arrangements to come and assist you as the Lord has commanded. Please forgive me, for I would have been here much sooner, but for the strong objections of my staff, which delayed my visit. I finally had to put my foot down and demand to be brought to you. So, Sister Lucia, how can I help you?"

Chapter XXXVI

The event was two days after the Pope's arrival. Lucia's meeting with the Pope had relieved the anxiety that she was feeling and knowing that he also received an angelic visit seemed to fuel Lucia's confidence that the strength of the Vatican was finally behind her. The Pope stayed by her side throughout lunch asking simple questions and even asking to hold little Claire. Lucia could not believe that she was so nervous to meet him as he was such a kindhearted, gentle and loving man.

Once they were in the large black automobile on the way to the coliseum, the Pope had asked her if he could possibly assist her in her healing as he had heard the Mother Superior had done. He did not want to be presumptuous, but he truly would like nothing more than to participate in the Lord's work he told her. Lucia knew that Sister Louisa had heard him but the elderly nun focused on something outside the window, holding the Medallion in both hands; her face expressionless. Lucia gracefully accepted his help, telling him he could stand on one side of her while Sister Louisa stood on the other. The nun did not take her eyes away from the landscape passing by them, but Lucia noted the corners of her mouth tilted up.

Upon arrival, Lucia introduced the Pope to Jack, Robert, Matthew and Vincent. Philip had prepped them on how to greet the Pope and Lucia noticed how easily each knelt before him. She first turned to Vincent and told the Pope how he had traumatic brain injury from an explosion. Then, Lucia explained how Robert and Jack had lost their limbs and Matthew lost his sight in the war but through God's mercy and love, all of them had made a miraculous recovery. The Pope agreed and pulled them up to shake their hands and bless them.

Lucia could hear the choir singing. The music soothed her and she enjoyed hearing the many hymns sung throughout the night. Choirs from the surrounding churches and outside groups volunteered to sing at the events. Mary Ellen worked with Jacob and his security team to schedule four different choirs to perform for one hour each during the event. The groups were located at different points in the hall so there was never a break in the music. Lucia had heard that choirs from around the country had contacted the organizers and were anxious for an opportunity to sing during the healing event. The Hallelujah Chorus was her favorite and knowing this, one of the choirs had sung it at every event.

Lucia noted that the small room that had been designated for those that wanted to pray the Rosary had been significantly expanded. A box of Rosaries, free of course, was placed at the door for anyone who wanted one. Mary Ellen also had set up a slide show so newcomers could follow easily along. She also provided booklets explaining the importance and power of the Rosary.

Their entourage made their way down the hall to the stage that had now been adorned with white and purple hanging silk cloth with a large cross in the middle as the backdrop. It was a beautiful display. A line of priests waited for them dressed in purple chasuble attire with delicate gold embroidery. The line was held up as several of the Pope's staff assisted him in donning his full papal regalia of a white cassock and stole along with the papal mitre, the ceremonial headdress. He was making a statement to the world as the Head of the Roman Catholic

Church that the Pope was standing strong beside God's chosen Healer.

As they were waiting for the Pope, Lucia heard a familiar voice calling to her.

She peeked around Jack who immediately grabbed her arms and told her, "No breaking the line."

So she scanned the crowd but with so many people, it was hard to see. Suddenly, she saw a woman climbing on a man's shoulders, waving her arms and calling out to her. Jack felt her pull but held firmly, asking her whom she saw. She said it was the woman with the blonde hair several rows back and pointed her out.

Jack called Jacob who was standing nearby watching the crowd. He rushed over and Jack asked him to get the woman on the shoulders of the man. At first, Jacob was hesitant but Lucia said she was going to see the woman with or without his help, so off he went into the crowd.

Jack looked down at her and said, "See how easy that was."

Lucia just smiled, she knew he knew she was ready to bolt.

The man and woman were surrounded by security as they were escorted to the stage. No one but David and Lucia knew who they were, and he ran to hug the woman and shook the man's hand. The Pope was fully dressed and came to see what was happening.

Lucia introduced him to Victoria and James and whispered in the Pope's ear, "They're the parents who lost their son," but even more quietly, "you know, the couple I told you God allowed to visit their son in Heaven."

The Pope smiled knowingly and took hold of their hands and told them, "You are truly blessed by a merciful and loving Lord."

Victoria and James turned towards Lucia and the excitement on both of their faces told Lucia that great news had come to them. Victoria was expecting "Rachel," the pretty little girl that Joey, their son, had introduced them to during their "heavenly visit." The pregnancy was still early, but they both couldn't wait for her birth. They also told her that they had seen their son and Victoria's parents several times since Lucia's visit.

David did not know what had happened in the room that day, but had suspected something miraculous had occurred with Victoria's sudden change of despair to happiness and acceptance of her son's death. He had asked James but the father responded that he was sworn to silence but he did tell David that there was a Heaven and God was truly omnipotent.

David responded, "I never doubted it."
The Pope blessed them and asked if they would be free the next day to meet. Victoria and James readily agreed and asked if Lucia would also be there and the Pope confirmed that yes, it would be just the four of them. Lucia nodded and Victoria was bursting at the seams and couldn't wait to talk about their heavenly visits. She hugged Lucia and then she and James were turned over to Jacob. Having met with the Healer, they had no other reason to stay and security escorted them out the back door to their car.

On the stage, Mother Superior took her rightful place at the right of Lucia while the Pope removed his mitre and stood on Lucia's left. The first child was brought up and Mother Superior provided instruction to Pope Leo to hold his hands over the child and pray. She could not confirm that a white stream of energy would come from his hands as this was his first time, but he shouldn't be surprised if it happens. Lucia stood by silently praying. She had seen the crowd and had been informed that many had come from around the country. She took a deep breath and raised her arms. Immediately, a white stream flowed from her fingertips, as well as Sister Louisa's. The Pope's eyes popped open not quite believing what he was seeing but as his prayer continued a thin thread of white energy began seeping from his hands.

Some time had passed and a number of children were brought forth with many different ailments to receive God's mercy. Lucia saw the Pope sway a little and several priests quickly responded to lead him away, but he refused to leave. So, Mary Ellen called for a time out and they retreated to the break room.

Mother Superior sat next to the Pope and told him she too had become weak and tired early during her first time with Lucia. She assured him that it would pass and advised him to have one of the priests bring a chair up for him. The both of them spoke openly on the euphoric sensation that filled them as they assisted Lucia. Sister Louisa shared that she thought it was God's pure love that filled them. The Cardinal who had accompanied the Pope from Italy, urged him to rest, but Father Leo brushed him off.

"I am filled with the Lord's love and would gladly die a thousand deaths if only to play just a small part in His Divine Plan. Should I stop now and turn from such a grace the Lord has granted me?" the Pope challenged him.

When they returned to the stage, a chair was brought for the Pope and he was able to continue to assist Lucia heal the Lord's flock.

Many of the faithful came forward and some would kiss Pope Leo's hand before they were escorted away. He would bless them and reinforce the need to seek God in the Eucharist. Though he tried to hide his feelings, the Pope was overwhelmed with an emotion that he found hard to describe even to himself. As he prayed sitting beside Lucia with his hands extended over each person brought forth, he silently expressed a humble gratitude that the Lord had allowed him to be at this place at this time. He regretted listening to his advisors and delaying this visit, for now he knew that the Lord was truly here and as the Head of the Church, he needed to speak loud and clear that the Lord had sent all the Healers to save not only the body, but the soul as well.

Finally, the crowd grew less and less, as security had closed the doors. Pope Leo was ashen and had to be helped out of the chair. One of the priests grabbed an empty wheelchair and brought it over for the Pope to sit in. He tried to resist but Sister Louisa came over and in a stern tone reprimanded him.

"It would do no good to anyone for you to drop dead after your first time helping Lucia, now get in the chair," she told him.

Pope Leo XIV fought this display of weakness, but after digesting the words Sister Louisa had said, silently acquiesced to her demands.

Chapter XXXVII

The Pope had slept late the next morning, but when he did rise, it was with renewed energy and a deep sense of peace. Mother Superior and Lucia had attended morning Mass as usual. Breakfast, however, was far from its usual quiet affair. The Convent was filled with a great deal of activity given all the Vatican staff and visitors arriving for an audience with Pope Leo. He met with them all, giving blessings and urging all to return to Mass to receive the body of Christ. He even cancelled an appointment with an important official to make time available to meet with Victoria and James. He was so excited to meet with them and hear about their heavenly visits; he found it hard to pay attention to those who came to him before the special couple's visit. His staff was taken aback when officials were dismissed earlier than their allotted time; the Pope apologized but he was anxious to spend as much time as possible with the wife and her husband.

After a short discussion with Lucia, and with her consent, Pope Leo invited Dr. Woods, the Archbishop and Mother Superior to attend the meeting with Victoria and James. His staff questioned the Pope whether they would be included, but he respectfully asked them to wait outside. The Cardinals who had accompanied the Pope seemed somewhat irritated with what they perceived to be a slight as they were in attendance with all his meetings. Philip Sorrin was very disturbed as he was unable to fully vet the couple before their arrival. He had advised a delay in the meeting but Lucia, Dr. Woods and even Mother Superior told him there was no threat from the young couple. Mother Superior did not know Victoria and James, but she felt Lucia's affirmation of their good character was good enough for her. The Pope agreed.

A car had been sent for Victoria and James to bring them to the Convent. They arrived a few minutes early and found Lucia waiting at the door for them with open arms. Lucia escorted them to where the small group was meeting and Pope Leo jumped from his seat when they entered the room. He immediately gave Victoria a hug and shook James' hand and invited them to sit. Philip stood by the door, shaking his head at the close encounter and shrugged. Then he closed the door and stood guard.

David was surprised that he was allowed in the meeting and sat quietly hoping no one would ask him to leave. He thought that he would finally find out what happened in the bedroom that day he had brought Lucia to the grieving couple. Father Lucas also sat quietly in his chair and smiled when the couple entered, however, he was unsure about the visit, as he was not privy to why they were so special to the Pope. In contrast, Mother Superior sat firm and straight, both hands on the Medallion, as the couple entered and smiled when she was introduced to them. She had faith that the Lord always put her where she belonged and she said a silent prayer in gratitude that he had put her here in this privileged group. She and Pope Leo had formed a tight bond in the last few days and he had sought her council on several occasions. She found him to be exceptionally thoughtful and considerate in his deliberations. She liked him; however, she admitted to herself that he was no Father Lucas.

The Pope began the meeting with a prayer in which they all hung their heads and joined hands. After which, he informed the group that what was discussed here could go no further. It was imperative that Victoria and James' experience not be shared. Lucia had reinforced this with the Pope earlier. He then asked Victoria to share her and her husband's experiences after the death of her son.

Victoria looked at Lucia for approval and she nodded. The young mother told them how she had been wracked with guilt after refusing Lucia's visit to her terminally ill son, and that he was the only child to die the next day. All the others had been completely healed. Dr. Woods knew this, but Mother Superior gasped knowing the guilt the mother must have felt. Victoria expressed the hate she felt for God when her son became sick and then the hate she felt for herself when acknowledging God had sent a miracle for her son and she turned Sister Lucia away. Victoria paused as tears ran down her face.

James put his arm around his wife and continued their story. He told them how Lucia came to their home and explained that she would pray with them. This time, both husband and wife held out their hands to Lucia and closed their eyes as she prayed. James said after a few minutes, he opened his eyes to see that they were totally encapsulated in a white mist so thick he could not see anything, fearful, he squeezed Lucia's hand tightly hoping that she knew what she was doing.

Once the mist began to clear, he saw to his amazement, they were sitting on a couch in a living room and Victoria's deceased parents were standing in a kitchen in front of them. Opening her eyes, Victoria jumped from her seat and hugged her mother and father. She really needed them at this time, but what was even more surprising was that two minutes later, Joey came running in. Not the sick boy that had died in the hospital, but a very healthy and happy boy excited to see us both. James paused and took a deep breath.

    The Pope reached over and squeezed James's hand, giving him a moment to compose himself. Dr. David sat speechless. He knew something spectacular had happened, but this – THIS!!! Mother Superior began rocking in her chair, holding her talisman, smiling in confirmation that the Lord is indeed great and merciful. She reached out to hold Lucia's hand, and Lucia smiled with a feeling of deep gratitude that she was able with the Lord's direction to facilitate the visit for the young couple.

    James continued to tell them about that first visit and the two subsequent journeys to see their son. They had told no one as instructed by Lucia but spent many nights conversing amongst themselves. With a light heart, he told them how Victoria was pregnant and they knew it was the girl Joey had brought to them. Their son had named her Rachel and they could not wait for her to come into this world. They had returned to the Church where they experienced a newfound inner peace and strength. James ended with their marriage has never been better.

    The Pope at some point had reached and held Victoria's hand. Even though he had heard the story from Lucia, he sat shaking his head side to side in complete awe that the Lord had given such a merciful gift to this very grateful couple. Dr. Woods cleared his throat and said, "Well, now I know why you were so excited when you came out of your bedroom." Victoria and James both smiled and looked lovingly at each other. They admitted that it was hard not telling anyone, but they would do nothing to jeopardize their visits with their son and Victoria's parents. They turned to Lucia to confirm that this exchange would not sabotage seeing Joey and Lucia verified it would not.

After a few minutes for all to process this information, Mother Superior began pouring the coffee and handing out the pastry. The conversation became much lighter with talk of the pregnancy and how the couple was preparing the nursery. Though they mourned the death of their son, they felt blessed that they could still see him on occasion. Soon, it was time for the Pope to meet with others. Pope Leo told them that no one was going to beat this meeting and laughed. So did all the others in the room. After blessing the couple again, he and Father Lucas left for the next meeting. Lucia promised to keep in touch and hugged the devoted couple. Dr. Woods stood and remarked that he would escort Victoria and James back to the car. When he opened the door, Philip Sorrin was still guarding the door and eyed the couple suspiciously, but Dr. Woods assured him everyone was still in one piece and unharmed.

The Pope was escorted to the conference room by his staff to meet with the Bishop's Council. Mother Superior hurried out to ensure the room was prepared with refreshments, leaving only Lucia in the room. Dr. David returned quickly, closing the door for privacy.

He turned to Lucia and whispered, "Thank you for including me in this meeting. I always wondered what happened that day, but I would never have imagined that."

Lucia smiled and replied, "I could not tell you then, but I prayed and meditated on who should attend this meeting with Victoria, James and the Pope, and you, Father Lucas and Sister Louisa popped up in my head. Sometimes, the Lord puts the message in my head and I have learned to listen and act on those messages. After all that has happened, I have put my complete faith in the Lord and accept that he will guide me where he wants me and carry out what he tells me to do; sometimes to my surprise, as was the case with Victoria and James."

  A tap at the door had David answering to come in, and sure enough, Becky came in with little Claire. Lucia took the baby and began rocking her. David offered Becky the coffee still on the table and they began discussing a movie they had both watched. As Lucia rocked in the chair, she saw in her minds eye the two of them at the altar saying their wedding vows and then another picture of them older with four children. She shook her head and thought how happy she would be with Dr. David as a son-in-law, but more so that Becky finally found someone worth loving.

Chapter XXXVIII

The Convent was far from its usual subdued atmosphere, but even with so many people filling it the past few days, it was relatively quiet. So it was with a jolt that Lucia heard a lot of yelling in the hallway. She quickly gave the baby back to Becky and ran out of the room to find out what was going on. Dr. David followed her. A man holding up an obviously frail woman at his side had burst through the doors of the Convent. Lucia thought he looked familiar but could not immediately place him. Philip and the rest of the security team had stopped him in the hallway. Apparently, he was the visit the Pope had cancelled and he was demanding to be seen. Upon closer observation, Lucia could see that he was heavily supporting the woman next to him and she was doing her best to calm him down.

Lucia stood outside the door of the lounge, when suddenly the man made eye contact with her and yelled in her direction, "Are you the Healer? Come and heal my wife."

Lucia did not respond, standing in shock, as the Convent was surely her safe space. Dr. David put his arm around her and began pulling her back in the room. In spite of all the men that had contained him and his wife from progressing further into the building, his voice rose loud and strong, following Lucia back into the lounge.

Philip Sorrin was reluctant to throw him to the ground to secure the threat as he could see the woman was unable to stand without his support. The man made it known that he was the CEO of a well-known financial company and demanded entrance to see the lady who could heal his wife. In fact, he insisted that she heal his wife immediately.

Father Lucas came rushing down the hall from the conference room to see what the yelling was about and when he saw the man, he exclaimed, "Benjamin, what the hell are you doing here?"

The frantic man named Benjamin replied, "Lucas, she needs to heal my wife. Eleanor is dying!"

Father Lucas had seen Dr. Woods dragging a shocked Lucia back into the lounge; then, the elderly priest led the man and his wife down the opposite direction with security herding them to another small waiting room outside of Mother Superior's office. The distraught CEO protested the whole way but Philip informed him that if he did not comply, he would have him escorted out or arrested.

Lucia was shaking so bad when she entered the room that Dr. David practically carried her to a chair. David told Becky what had happened, while Lucia sat wringing her hands on her lap and praying. Father Lucas, the Pope and Philip Sorrin had assured her that all the guests were informed that she would not be healing anyone at the Convent. Yet, this man had gained access and was extremely agitated demanding that his wife be healed.

They stayed in the lounge since Lucia could not return to her suite without passing the room the intruders were in; and after a while, Dr. David noticed that after praying, Lucia had calmed down and her eyes had taken on a more reflective gaze. Mother Superior came into the room with righteous indignation that someone could enter her Convent demanding anything. It was to everyone's surprise that Lucia asked Sister Louisa to get her shawl from her room.

The elderly nun looked at her questioning, "You're not thinking of granting his demands are you?"

Lucia responded calmly, "Maybe, I think God wants me to."

Mother Superior shook her head and mumbled about not knowing who was crazier, the man or Lucia. When she left, Father Lucas entered the room and walked over to Lucia. She had never seen him so upset and concerned. She put her hand on his arm and told him that she understood and advised him that she would be down to the room shortly. The Archbishop was relieved and gave her a grateful look and left. Becky shared her concerns with her mother, questioning if she really had to go. Lucia just looked at Dr. David and told him she had gotten one of those messages in her head. He nodded and Lucia told them she would not be long. Sister Louisa returned and handed the black shawl to her with a harrumph. Lucia knew she was upset and told her she did not have to go with her. The good Sister informed her that she would never abandon her even if she wanted to heal some lunatic that breached the walls of her Convent. After donning the fragrant shawl and clutching it close around her, Lucia and Sister Louisa walked arm in arm down the hall to the waiting room.

Entering, they found several security guards and Philip standing over the man who was sitting on a settee. He still looked frantic, but she could see his face was flushed and his eyes red and watery. Mr. Benjamin was holding his wife who was very pale and seemed quite weak. She held on to the lapel of his jacket with her head resting on his shoulder. Father Lucas sat next to them and seemed to be praying over them. Lucia's overall impression of the man was that he was used to being in charge and getting his way but had lost complete control over his wife's condition.

As they entered the room, the man jumped up, disturbing his wife who almost fell over. He began pleading with Lucia and apologizing for yelling at her. Lucia asked him what exactly he expected from her and that seemed to break him. He openly sobbed and Father Lucas passed him a glass of water. After he had calmed down some, Benjamin told her how they had gone to London to meet with Russian investors asking for a loan. After hearing their presentation to build a large housing complex with barely any of their own money, he had decided the project was too risky and denied the loan. They seemed cordial and the leader invited them to lunch in their suite. They left shortly after and flew home on their private plane.

He went on to explain that shortly after returning, his wife became very ill with nausea, vomiting and diarrhea. Over the next few days, she became progressively weakened and fatigued; so he had taken her to the hospital. She was diagnosed with radioactive poisoning and the prognosis was extremely poor. They had given her only a few weeks to live. Benjamin had watched his wife, Eleanor, become sicker and sicker each day. He remembers switching meals with her at the luncheon. It had to be then that she ate the poison meant for him. He then looked at Lucia directly and told her they had a three-year-old and six-month-old baby at home. He fell to his knees sobbing again, crying that he would give the Healer everything he had if she would just heal his wife.

Lucia and Sister Louisa now understood his frenzied entrance. Lucia was more sympathetic than Mother Superior. She was still upset with him for demanding Lucia's services as he did, but reluctantly gave him the benefit of the doubt. Lucia told Benjamin that she did not want his money. He looked worried as if he thought she would not help his wife. Lucia told him that the powers were not hers but that the Lord had chosen her as a vehicle to do his work. The worried husband looked confused by that so Lucia began negotiations.

She told him she knew that he and his wife had excluded God from their life and that of their children as well. She knew they had not been baptized. How could someone without faith ask God to heal? They did not believe in God. Her gift was for the faithful. The Lord had asked her to gather his flock. He was not one of the sheep who had wondered away. His wife, who had been silent, held her hand out for Lucia to take.

She could barely hold the Healer's hand as she weakly spoke, "I have received all the sacraments except for marriage. I am a lost sheep; please help me return to my faith. If I cannot be healed, then allow me to die in the arms of the Lord and be saved. My husband did not believe and I followed him."

She turned to Father Lucas and asked him to hear her confession before she died. Benjamin tried to interfere but she held her hand up to stop him.

"No, Benjamin, I knew better. I turned my back on God and now He has every right to turn His back on me," the wife told him.

She reiterated that she would like to give her confession and receive Communion.

Everyone in the room stood silently watching the couple. Both the husband and the wife were crying and locked in a loving embrace. Lucia's heart was melting and saw Sister Louisa was holding tightly to her Medallion, her eyes watering at what was taking place. Father Lucas stood from his position next to Eleanor. He cleared his throat and after getting a silent okay from Lucia, spoke to Benjamin. He told him he would have to commit to the teachings of the Church as well as raise his children in the faith. The Archbishop added that this should be easy after what Benjamin would witness today. The husband nodded and Lucia could see the hope in his eyes. Mother Superior nudged him out of his seat so she could sit alongside his wife and assist her to sit up. Lucia took Father Lucas's chair on the other side of the sick woman.

Lucia took a long cleansing breath and with Sister Louisa began praying. Soon, Eleanor also began praying with them, her voice a soft whisper. It wasn't long before the white stream of energy came flowing out of Lucia's fingertips and was absorbed into the trunk of Eleanor's body. Immediately, a pink glow began to show on her previously ashen cheeks. Benjamin gasped in shock. He stood in disbelief, as his wife seemed to become healthier with each passing minute. He acknowledged that a powerful and forgiving God was giving him his wife back. He always kept his word and he would do so now. How could he not, now knowing that a higher power was able to deny the death that had come for his wife?

Slowly the white stream came to an end and Lucia smiled at the woman who already demonstrated a renewed strength in her ability to sit up alone. She hugged Lucia and Sister Louisa with fresh tears in her eyes, thanking Sister Lucia. Lucia responded by telling her that God had heard her sincere request for forgiveness. Her husband fell to his knees in gratitude. He then looked at Father Lucas and asked if that was it? Father Lucas, in a stern and firm voice, told him no. Benjamin would be expected to join his local church and become an active member to serve his community.

Eleanor was just able to stand but still required her husband's assistance to walk. Benjamin bent his head down and apologized to them all for his outburst earlier; however, it was clear that he would do it all over again for his wife. Lucia asked Father Lucas to take Eleanor outside so she could speak with her husband alone. Security stood still until Lucia assured them that the man was no longer a threat. Philip was used to Lucia overriding his calls for safety, so with Father Lucas' urging he, too, with his men, left the room.

Sister Louisa sat firmly in a chair to the side of the sofa where Lucia guided Benjamin. After sitting, Lucia asked for his hand, which he hesitantly gave her. He couldn't understand why he was alone with the Healer, he wasn't sick. Suddenly, the CEO of an important and well-connected financial firm saw the same white energy entering his body as it did to his wife. He closed his eyes as an over powering warmth penetrated to his very soul, a soul he denied until this moment. He welcomed the peace and love that seemed to enter every cell of his body. It seemed that all the hatred and revenge for the people who had poisoned his wife and others who had betrayed him in the past was pushed out of his mind and replaced with forgiveness. It was an overwhelming and unfamiliar emotion to him that seemed to cocoon him like a cloud. Benjamin felt the heavy weight of anger and thirst for power dissolve. The emptiness in his heart and mind filled with a tranquility he had never experienced before; it was such a wonderful feeling. As the healing progressed, Benjamin had become totally absorbed in the newfound feelings inside of him, so became startled when he suddenly heard Lucia speak in his ear.

    In a clear and commanding voice, he heard the Healer speak, "The Lord wants you, Benjamin, body and soul; do not forsake him as you have done in the past."

Chapter XXXIX

There was a lot of chatter going on in the Convent. The Pope was leaving and his entourage had carried their luggage to the entryway. There were many priests there to say goodbye to new and old acquaintances. The Pope had spent his morning meeting with Lucia, Sister Louisa and the Archbishop. He had asked again to feel the black shawl sent by St. Mary and the Medallion given to Sister Louisa. He repeatedly used the term miracle, holding both objects close to his chest.

When it was time to leave, Pope Leo returned the gifts and blessed the three of them. He had told them that he wanted to stay, but he also was receiving "messages" in his head to visit the other Healers and give them his support. The Pope's valet escorted him to the car and four black SUVs drove away to a private airfield where the plane awaited them. Pope Leo was determined to meet with all the Healers and hear about their heavenly encounters.

Lucia thought she would be able to take a breather; however, Father Lucas informed her that there was a meeting in one hour to plan the next healing event. The past several weeks had been very busy. Even with the Pope's visit, Lucia, with Sister Louisa in attendance, had gone to several hospitals throughout the state. The hospital administrators had contacted the Archbishop's office to schedule the visits. Patients from around the country were being transferred to local hospitals where Lucia could see them. As before, they were always late into the night and staff was sworn to secrecy until after she left the building. On several occasions, they had Mary Ellen accompany them. She was good at handling the nursing staff and answering their questions while Lucia tended to the patients.

Lucia even had made a quick visit to Jack's support group during the Pope's visit. Jacob had accompanied her, along with several of his trusted security team. Again, Philip Sorrin was the naysayer, but Jacob assured him he would protect the Healer at all costs.

A smiling Jack, who said aloud, "I knew you would come," greeted her!

Lucia recognized some of the men who had come to the coliseum to be healed by her over the past several weeks. Jack pulled two seats into the circle for Lucia and Sister Louisa. The men talked about how they had recovered; some received their sight, some regrew a limb or two and one man regrew three. They relayed how their lives had changed, all for the better. Several had gotten married; others reported that they were able to obtain great employment opportunities. All of them confirmed that they were active members in their local Parishes.

Lucia responded, "You don't think God just healed your physical ailments, do you?"
Their mouths dropped as they realized that their depression and PTSD had vanished when they were healed. All of them thought it was because their disabilities had been repaired. Jack told her she shouldn't have told them that because they won't come to his support group any more. The men all laughed. This group had a strong camaraderie; they weren't going anywhere.

On her way out of the Community Center where the support group was held, Lucia felt herself be pulled down the hall to where an AA meeting was going on. Jacob tried to stop her, but she assured him that it would be okay and he could stay by her side.

"I have to reach the lost sheep, Jacob," Lucia told him.

She walked into the room and sat in the nearest metal seat; Sister Louisa stood by the doorway, not quite sure why they were there. Lucia saw that there were about twenty people sitting while a middle age man gave his testimony to the others. She watched the broken man speak; at times he would stop, so overcome with emotion. He had lost everything, his wife, his children and his job. He was currently staying in a shelter to rebuild his life. He was thirty days sober. The crowd clapped, showing their support.

Once he sat down, the organizer came over to Jacob, telling him that this was a private meeting. Jacob responded by asking if he knew who the small woman sitting in front of him was. The man shook his head and asked if he should? Lucia put the black shawl over her head and several of the attendees gasped in acknowledgement of who she was. The organizer stood in shock finally realizing that this was the Healer everyone was talking about.

Lucia stood and walked over to the front of the group.

"My name is Lucia," she told them.

Then, asked if she could pray with them. One by one they all came to kneel before her. She tried to stop them, but they would not listen. She explained to them that she received her healing powers from the one True God, Jesus Christ, and that he was the only one they should kneel before. Sister Louisa had come to stand by her side and told the group to close their eyes and pray. When they did not stand, Lucia also got on her knees and led them in several prayers.

After a few moments, Jacob noticed that the area around all the kneelers had gotten foggy. He looked at his men standing strategically around the room. They, too, noticed that a white mist was filling the room and a cloud was encapsulating the small kneeling crowd.

"Could she really heal a large group?" Jacob thought silently as he watched Lucia stretch her arms wide and pray.

She continued to amaze him each time he saw her work. He thought how this was probably just the beginning of her adding more outings to reach more of those "sheep" she always talked about.

Jacob could hear the group buzzing when they also realized they were encompassed by a white foggy mist.

One of the woman called out, "She is healing all of us, Oh dear God!"

Through the transparent mist, Jacob could see the tears start falling down some of the faces of the men and women. Some hugged each other, not daring to interrupt the Healer as she worked her miracles in the name of the Lord.

Finally, Lucia opened her eyes and reached up for Sister Louisa to help her stand. The group tried to get close to thank her, but Jacob stepped in and told them that they had to keep their distance. Some had taken out their phones to take pictures, but Sister Louisa then threatened them in her sternest voice that no one was to snap any pictures or reveal their visit until after they left.

The man who had given testimony when Lucia had first entered the room, came as close as Jacob would allow. He asked if his life would go back to what it had been. Lucia gave him a saddened look.

"I can only tell you that if you come back to Church and serve the Lord, you will receive His peace and love," she responded.

He replied that he already could feel the anxiety leave his body and a new sense of purpose fill his heart; with a bow of his head and holding his hand over his heart, he thanked Lucia for coming.

Jacob guided her quickly out the door and toward the exit, keeping his hand on her back in an effort to deter any more diversions. Sister Louisa was grumbling that maybe Lucia would want them to check all the rooms to see if there were any more meetings going on.

"Maybe there's an eating disorder group or maybe a book club that we could pop into," the Mother Superior sarcastically told Lucia.

Lucia just smiled at the elderly nun as she was sure Sister and Jacob both knew that AA meetings would be added to the list of their nightly excursions.

They had almost made it to the car, when a young man was running trying to catch up with them calling Lucia's name.

"Please Sister Lucia, please don't leave me. I was late for the meeting," he called out to her.

Jacob was apologizing to him and advised him that Lucia would catch him at the next meeting. Lucia looked at the boy, and he was a boy. No more than twenty with the weight of the world on his shoulders. His face was dirty and his hair a mess over his eyes. She noticed that his clothes were too big and he carried a duffel bag over his shoulder.

Lucia held her hand up to Jacob and asked the boy who was now several feet in front of them surrounded by the security team.

"What's your name, son?" Lucia asked him.

"They call me PJ, Sister," he answered. "Peter John."

Lucia could see the troubled anxiety that surrounded the boy and told him that she could sense he was under a lot of stress, but he did not need healing. The boy tried to get closer but security held him back. Looking at Lucia, he begged for her help. He told her he had no one else. His mother had thrown him out after he had a fight with her new boyfriend who accused him falsely of taking his drugs. He attended AA meetings to get off the streets. He was sleeping in alleys and had been targeted by a gang that he would have to join or they would kill him. They expected him to be their enforcer.

He then cried out, "I don't want to kill anyone, Sister. I have been praying and praying for a miracle, and here you are tonight. I know God sent you to me. Please, Sister."

The longer Lucia looked at the boy, the younger he looked. His face was dirty, but his eyes were clear and bright, absent of drugs or alcohol.

Sister Louisa had already gotten into the car and as if she could read Lucia's mind, she commented, "Well, tell him, Lucia, so we can get going already."

Lucia turned to Jacob and smiled. Confusion flashed across his face and slowly she could see the light come on.

Lucia finally spoke the words, "I cannot help this boy, Jacob, but I am sure that God would be so grateful to you for helping PJ here. Don't you have barracks for your men to sleep? PJ needs a safe place to stay and what is safer than being surrounded by your security team. He could be your helper. Right, PJ?"

Jacob bit his tongue for a long time. He and Lucia had a staring contest for several minutes until he directed one of his men to take "PJ" into the second SUV and take him to home base. There was an empty cot and some spare clothes that might fit him. Lucia joined Sister Louisa in the back seat and Jacob got in the front passenger seat.

As the men and the boy were getting into the other car, Jacob rolled down his window and yelled, "Make sure he takes a shower and somebody gives him a haircut."

Chapter XL

It was the night of the event and as they drove to the Coliseum, Lucia thought about what she had heard regarding the other Healers at the last meeting. The women were traveling to Christian Churches and other venues throughout their country to heal the people. Lucia was the only one staying at the same place; however, she also was the only one to have an attempt on her life. It was logical that Philip and Jacob handled her differently. The Coliseum was a controlled environment and cameras were everywhere. Also, she did go to different hospitals to attend the sick and more recently to AA meetings to help attendees successfully achieve sobriety. Churches were bursting at the seams and more were opening everyday. Record numbers of men and woman continued to join the religious orders. It was clear to Lucia that God's plan to recapture his flock was working.

Finally, their large fortified SUV pulled up to the back entrance of the Coliseum to an army of security. Again, Jack, Vincent, Robert and Matthew met them at the door.

"Full house again, Sister Lucia," Jack told her. Lucia took a deep breath and nodded, "Well, let's not keep them waiting."

She was determined to use her gift to heal as many as she could. She knew that some who came still did not believe in a higher power, and she also knew not everyone was healed. For some, death could not be avoided. Those that she knew could not be healed were referred to Mary Ellen. She was a Godsend, literally. Lucia did not know what to say to those she could not help, but Mary Ellen seemed fluent, especially with the families, offering them support and counseling; and even hospice services as needed.

Walking towards the stage, Lucia could hear the choir and took immense comfort in the words sung. The black shawl was over her head and the fragrance of roses drifted to her nose and reminded her of St. Mary's support. Sister Louisa walked next to her grasping her Medallion in both hands whispering a prayer, she looked a little short of breath after the walk to the stage, but the elderly nun responded that she was fine. A row of priests stood on the stage, ready to give support as needed. Jack helped Lucia take a step up and then winked at her.

"I wanted to thank you again for coming to the support group. The men really appreciated your time," he told her.

Lucia smiled and squeezed his hand, "I will come again, don't worry."

She stood on the stage and overlooked the line, which seemed endless. Out of the corner of her eye, Lucia saw a tall figure in white walking through the crowd staring at the altar. He seemed to concentrate on the Medallion around Sister Louisa's neck. When he saw that he had garnered Lucia's attention, he gave her a sad smile. She looked around at security, but no one seemed to notice him. When she looked back again, he was gone. For a second, she thought it was the angel who had come to her. Then, she got nervous thinking that maybe he had a message for her, but why did he give her a sad smile. Sister Louisa saw Lucia looking frantically left and right, and asked her what was wrong. Looking over the crowd again and not seeing him, Lucia told her it was nothing and asked security to bring the sick children forward.

After some time, Mary Ellen called for a break. Lucia was ready. Her nerves over the angel's appearance here had her on edge and on full alert. In the break room, she found Dr. David and Bea waiting for her. A warm hug from her best friend was just what she needed. Becky brought over coffee and some cookies; Bea had baked Lucia's favorite. Lucia noticed Sister Louisa sitting on the far side of the table, whispering with Mary Ellen. The elderly nun looked tired. Neither was smiling, but when Lucia called over and asked what they were talking about, Mary Ellen told her the weather.

"Rain tomorrow," she said. Sister Louisa gave a weak smile.

Lucia felt like she was an observer to the events around her. She just felt off and guarded. She wondered if she should tell Philip, but then she scolded herself, everything is fine and he would probably shut the event down. So she engaged in conversation with Dr. David, who shared that he would be away for a few weeks on a visit to his parents. They lived several states away and Lucia told him to have fun, but let him know that she would miss him. Dr. David was always around now that Becky was staying with her and in fact, they had gone to the movies several nights ago. Lucia was happy about that.

Against Philip's orders, Lucia engaged with several of the men and woman who came to her. They were nice and made her feel human to hold a conversation, even the short one that security allowed her before leading the people away. It seemed like they had touched her soul, they were such good people with bad illnesses. None of them thanked her, but rather told her they were attending Mass and giving thanks to God which filled Lucia with satisfaction. After all, He was the power; she was just the pass through. She could see Philip and Jacob shaking their heads when she engaged in small conversation, but she ignored them.

Every so often, Lucia would look up to see the crowd before her and most times she was overwhelmed to see the size of the line. In addition, she was still feeling a little off kilter after seeing the Angel in the crowd. She had just turned to speak to one of the priests to come forward as she needed a boost in her energy supply and when she turned back to heal the next person, she stood in shock and disbelief of the two people standing in front of her.

Her ex-husband and his wife stood with their heads bowed before her. Lucia did not know how to respond. She hadn't spoken to him since the divorce and most times he had his lawyer relay information to her. Standing there with her mouth open, everyone around her sprung into action. Two guards grabbed her ex and his wife ready to escort them out, but Lucia held up her hand and asked Jacob to find her a quiet room where she could speak to the man who literally destroyed her by his betrayal. David offered to go with her, but instead she requested Father Lucas to accompany them.

Once they were seated, Lucia asked him why he was there? Her ex-husband replied that he had recently been diagnosed with pancreatic cancer and came to beg her to heal him. She noticed his weight loss and pallor, and then replied that he had a lot of nerve coming to her after the vicious and evil things he had done to her. He even had the audacity to tell the reporters lies about their marriage.

"I loved you with all my heart," Lucia said to him. "How could you do that to me? How could you turn my children away from me?"

Fortunately, Lucia was not the weak and pathetic woman he had left. She had been chosen by Christ to be a Healer and she was strong and full of confidence. With tears in his eyes, he knelt before her and begged for her forgiveness. Lucia was taken back by sincerity and contrition, and admitted to herself that he no longer had any power to hurt her. She told him that she forgave him, but he would still have to give Penance and left him with Father Lucas. Lucia instructed him to return to her after he was done with Father Lucas; she would heal him then. She was comforted by the belief that Father Lucas would serve her ex and his wife a proper and well-deserved rebuke for all their treacherous deception and infidelity.

The next several hours went by quickly, and Lucia was tired by the time the doors were closed and the last of the people were seen. Dealing with her ex-husband had taken a lot out of her but she was glad that she felt no loathing or hostility for him. In fact, she had high hopes that he would turn his life around and return to the Lord. She looked over at Sister Louisa, who also looked rather peaked. Mary Ellen came and assisted Sister Louisa off the stage. Arm in arm, they walked to the car and surprisingly the nurse got in the car with the elderly nun. Those two were as thick as thieves.

"Sister Louisa invited me over for a late night cup of tea," Mary Ellen told them.

Sister Louisa just got in the car without speaking. Lucia said her good-byes to the soldiers who escorted her, and then she and Becky got into the other SUV waiting at the back door. The nervous feeling was still there but she pushed it aside. It was a good night. Everything went well and she even saw that Jacob had put Peter John, or PJ as he preferred to be called, to work running errands throughout the night. He cleaned up nicely with clean clothes and a short style haircut. She saw him reporting to Jacob, anxious to please. Lucia sighed and leaned her head back on the seat. She couldn't wait to get home.

The SUV Lucia was in got home first and she quickly exited the vehicle and walked directly to her bedroom. She carefully hung up the black scarf and went right to bed. She was exhausted. As tired as she was, Lucia had a restless sleep, tossing and turning. She was glad when she saw the sun coming up and got ready for Chapel. Mother Superior was usually in her room by now hurrying her along. Lucia smiled thinking that she would be the one hurrying the elderly nun. She quickly left her room and to her surprise, heard the sound of weeping. A heaviness filled Lucia's chest. She ran to the sounds of the Archbishop talking in Mother Superior's bedroom.

There in the nun's room stood Father Lucas, Dr. David, Mary Ellen and Sister Theresa. Sister Louisa was lying in bed, both hands wrapped around the Rosary. Her skin was mottled and her long white hair was in a braid lying on the side of the pillow. Her lips were dark purple. If not for the coloring of death, Mother Superior looked as if she was truly at peace. She even had a rare soft smile on her face. Father Lucas was wiping his eyes as he prayed over the body lying before him. Sister Theresa was kneeling next to the bed and openly weeping for the loss of her good friend and mentor. Mary Ellen, silently crying, clung to Dr. David's arm. Lucia could not deny the painful truth she was witnessing and her heart seemed to break into small pieces. No one had seen her enter the room until she gave a loud moan. "No, dear Lord, please no," then Lucia fell to her knees before David could catch her. Lucia's sobbing woke up Becky who ran into the room, still in her pajamas. Becky took in the scene before her and helped David carry Lucia out to the lounge.

Shortly after, the Archbishop and Mary Ellen entered the small waiting room. The elderly priest went to Lucia and told her that our good friend entered the gates of Heaven.

Lucia could barely speak, but she whispered as she sobbed, "I knew something was off last night. I saw the angel looking at her from the crowd."

Father Lucas exclaimed, "An angel was at the Coliseum last night?"

"Yes," answered Lucia. She explained that she just thought he was checking on her. "If I knew he was coming for Mother Superior, I could have done something. God gave me this gift. I could have healed her."

The sympathetic Archbishop responded, "I, too, have lost my best friend and colleague, but I am envious that she will reap the rewards awaiting her in Heaven. We should mourn our loss but celebrate her everlasting life." Lucia just nodded. She silently wept; she was still in disbelief.

The Archbishop had already called the undertaker and left to make arrangements. Mary Ellen stayed with Lucia while David went to help the Archbishop. The nurse pulled out a letter and told Lucia that Sister Louisa had given this to her last night and told her to give it to Lucia in the morning. The nurse was astute enough that she felt something was off with Mother Superior, which is why she stayed close to her all night and came back to the Convent with her. She noticed the elderly nun struggling to stand yet refused the chair when it was suggested. Mary Ellen told Lucia she had a feeling the nun was hiding her true state of health.

Lucia opened the envelope and with tears in eyes, took the letter out to read it. Mother Superior wrote:

My dearest Sister Lucia,

I have not felt well for some time and I know death is knocking at my door. I had a dream several nights ago that the Archangel Gabriel had come to escort me back to my true home. I never really thanked you for allowing me to share with you this special and incredible journey. You gave me a wonderful opportunity to help so many people. I was a witness to the many miracles granted by God. So, thank you from the bottom of my heart. I hope I was able to give you the support you needed which the Lord had directed me to do so many years ago. I have given this support with Love and joy.

Do not mourn me, as I am where I have always strived to go – into the arms of the Lord.

Until we meet again

Your friend and protector

Louisa

Lucia handed the letter to Mary Ellen who also read it with tears in her eyes.

"She was really something," Mary Ellen said softly. "I bet she's giving them hell up there."

Lucia in the middle of a sob, managed to get a small laugh out. It was true. Mother Superior never missed a chance to give her opinion or a quick sarcastic remark. They all would miss her terribly. Mary Ellen looked at Lucia and told her that when Sister Theresa found Mother Superior, the Medallion was gone.

"Do you think the Archangel Gabriel took it back?" Mary Ellen asked incredulously.

Lucia thought about that question and answered honestly, "I think when Gabriel came for Mother Superior she refused to go with him unless she could take the Medallion."

It was strange that in this sorrowful time, Lucia found the humor that consoled her.

Lucia could hear the nuns chanting in the Chapel. She took Mary Ellen's arm and walked down the hall to join them. This was her family now and they needed her more than ever. Entering the Chapel, Lucia took her place in the first row where she usually sat with Mother Superior. Mary Ellen sat next to her. They joined the chorus of nuns and gave praise to the Lord for taking Sister Louisa into his fold. As they prayed and sang, Lucia's eyes were drawn to the right side of the Altar. There she saw the Archangel Gabriel standing tall with his white toga and gold cord around his waist. A second apparition was forming and Lucia could see it was Sister Louisa standing by his side. She was radiant and her skin was translucent. Her white hair hung in waves over her shoulders. She was no longer in her habit but wore a long white toga with a blue cord wrapped around her waist; around her neck hung the silver Medallion with a hole in the middle. The angel was staring down at the Medallion and wore an annoyed frown on his face. Sister Louisa, with both hands holding the Medallion, gave Lucia a satisfied smirk.

"I knew it," thought Lucia shaking her head, "she took the Medallion with her."

Chapter XLI

Father Lucas gave Mother Superior a funeral fit for a queen. Lucia knew he was suffering so she had urged Mary Ellen, who was now a frequent guest of the Convent, to needle him gently whenever they were talking. The spicy nurse had even elicited a laugh from him at some sarcastic remark she had made. Mary Ellen and Dr. David were concerned that Lucia was suppressing her grief. She had not cried since the morning they had found the elderly nun in her bed. She finally told her close friends what she had seen in the Chapel that morning, especially the fact that Mother Superior still had the Medallion proudly around her neck and Gabriel's clear irritation with her. Lucia admitted that she missed the nun but at those times she remembered Sister Louisa's letter and the smirk on her lips as she held her Medallion tightly in her hands with Gabriel by her side.

Father Lucas was not surprised when Lucia shared her vision with him. In fact, he asked if Gabriel wore a pained expression when he was standing next to his longtime friend. Lucia laughed and admitted that he did look a little frustrated. He hoped his good friend was not challenging the Archangel as she had so many times done with Father Lucas.

Then laughing gently, he said, "Gabriel would probably send the old battle ax back."

Lucia acted shocked, but she smiled, too. He also wasn't surprised that she had taken the Medallion with her, as he had the nuns search her room, but the pendant could not be found.

Pope Leo contacted Lucia from Japan when he heard about the passing of Mother Superior and gave his condolences. He expressed his regret at being unable to attend the funeral.

"What a terrible loss for us all," he exclaimed, "although heaven has gained a valuable asset in the fight against evil. Maybe she will be able to help you more from Heaven than from this earthly plane."

Lucia thanked him for his call and for all his support. The Pope also told her that he was jealous that Sister Louisa had made it to Heaven before him.

"I'm glad I didn't take her bet when she said she would get their first. We both knew our days were numbered," he told her.

Lucia reprimanded him and told him he was still needed here on earth to ensure God's Divine Plan would be carried out without any obstruction. She reminded him to take good care of himself and hoped to see him soon.

The Archbishop informed Sister Lucia that he had started the search for Sister Louisa's replacement. He had several considerations to fill her post but wanted to meet with the prospective candidates again before he made a final decision. He also wanted to reassign more nuns to this Convent. He felt there was plenty of room to house at least another fifteen women, but had held that opinion while Mother Superior was alive. He knew she liked the small cloister and had honored her wishes. He also wanted to engage the Order into several religious initiatives that he had already discussed with Mary Ellen. She was helping him with the planning. Lucia hoped that these new plans would keep both the Archbishop and Mary Ellen busy. Mother Superior's death had left a huge void in all their hearts and in their everyday lives.

All the nuns had stepped up to ensure the smooth operation of the Convent. Becky worked with Sister Theresa, who as the senior nun, took on the role of Administrator temporarily. Lucia had found the Sister one late evening in the Chapel and saw that she was crying. The Healer knew that she had worked the longest with Mother Superior and had looked upon her as a mother figure. Trying to ease her pain, Lucia told the nun about seeing her in the Chapel the morning of her death, wearing the Medallion proudly around her neck. This seemed to ease the woman's grief and she gave a soft smile. Lucia then encouraged Sister to share her experiences, and sat quietly while Sister Theresa reminisced.

Before Sister Louisa had become Mother Superior, she had taken the young novitiate that had come to the Convent feeling confused and unsure of her calling under her wing. Mother Superior sat with her many nights in prayer until she made peace with her choice. Sister Theresa admitted to Lucia that she never second-guessed her commitment to the Order after that. She then told many funny stories involving the recently deceased Mother Superior. She could be cantankerous but her quick wit and sharp tongue often caused the sisters on many occasions to cover their mouths and bite the inside of their cheeks to suppress their laughter. She told Lucia that the elderly nun always had a mischievous spark in her eyes. Some would think that living at the Convent was boring, but she refuted that assumption. Although Sister Louisa had advocated a quiet Convent is a happy Convent; she never punished or criticized the sisters if they gave a funny reply or comment. The sisters found love, laughter and peace with Sister Louisa in charge.

Sister Theresa did share that she was nervous with the arrival of a new Mother Superior. She hoped the new recruit would contribute to the serene and loving atmosphere found at the Convent. Lucia admitted that she knew the Archbishop had several candidates and she could not imagine him bringing someone in who would not fit with the current residents. Lucia hoped the new Mother Superior would not make Becky leave, but if she did, Lucia would also leave with her. Thinking this over, she concluded that the Archbishop would not assign someone who would upset Lucia. No, she was sure of it and if anything did go wrong, she had the Pope's number on speed dial.

Sister Theresa seemed in a better mood after their talk and left to ensure tasks were done before lights out. Lucia went to find Becky and Claire, mostly Claire. She so loved rocking her to sleep and the baby was growing so fast; it took next to nothing to make her laugh. The baby jumped into Lucia's arms and Lucia sat in the wooden rocker, as her daughter got ready to go out. Becky was going on another date with Dr. David. She knew that they talked on the phone until late into the night. She didn't tell Becky, but she could hear her laughing through the walls between their rooms. Besides the constant smile on her face, Becky seemed to glow as she performed her chores throughout the day; this glow became even more profound when David came to visit. Lucia considered this coupling a personal gift from God.

Soon, daily life returned to a normal pace, including another team meeting for the upcoming event at the Coliseum. More and more people were coming to the city from around the country to see the Healer. Hotels, motels and air B & B's were full to capacity. Most of the people waited patiently, some not so much. The hospitals had to increase security as people were demanding to be admitted when they found out Lucia made nightly visits to the sick there. AA meetings were inundated with men and women hoping Lucia would show up. Things were getting chaotic and the mayor was requesting that we come up with solutions to deal with the crowds forming at the places Lucia had visited.

Philip opened the meeting by informing the group that the Coliseum was no longer a viable venue. They had barely been able to handle the crowds who had come to the last healing. Jacob agreed. A discussion was held on buildings that could hold the masses that were expected at the next event. The Archbishop suggested going to one of the big stadiums, security would be difficult but not impossible.

They all looked at Lucia and asked, "How many people can you heal in one night?"

Lucia was confused by their question. She was healing hundreds a night at the arena. Did they really think she could heal thousands in one night? She didn't know what to say. She missed Sister Louisa at this moment because she knew the elderly nun would have already given a sarcastic remark to counter that ridiculous question. Thankfully, Dr. David interjected and told them that he and Sister Louisa had provided Lucia with extra energy when she grew tired. Maybe with some backup, Lucia would be able to heal large groups instead of one at a time.

"I saw her do it at the AA meetings. The whole room fills with white healing energy. She manages to reach everyone in the room at once," Dr. David told them. Jacob confirmed that he had also witnessed Lucia do this.

The Archbishop questioned Dr. Woods, "How many were in the largest group?"

David replied, "Forty-five men and women were at the meeting. I stood on one side of her and Sister Louisa on the other. The healing energy filled the room and was absorbed into all the people."

The room was silent. Finally, John Anderson, the security expert, spoke up. "What if priests, very strong in the faith, stood on the stage with her, allowing Lucia to tap into their energy? She could use them to regenerate and heal large groups that can be waiting for her. A large venue would be needed with large rooms. We could station ten priests in each room to help her. If she could handle forty-five, maybe we try one hundred."

Now, everyone was really silent, especially Lucia. Could she heal one hundred people at one time? Her thoughts were going crazy. She looked around the room to see most of the men shaking their heads. John Anderson was the only one nodding. It was at this point that Lucia would be holding Sister Louisa's hand, but she was gone. So, she looked at Dr. David for strength and as always he gave it. He reassured her that they could try it and if it didn't work, they could reduce the number of people in the room. Everyone nodded at his suggestion. John smiled. He had a new found faith because of Lucia and this thought had just come into his head. He thought God put it there; he would tell Lucia that after the meeting. He just felt it in his gut that it would work. She had healed his son and he wanted everyone to feel the joyousness he felt at that.

Jacob even suggested that they attach a copper wire from the priests to Lucia to see if they could amp up her energy output level. Then they started talking about electronics and how it would be based on the same technology as the wires bringing electricity into everyone's home.

Lucia listened as they brainstormed how to make her stronger. She liked the idea of reaching large groups as she had done at the AA meetings, but she wasn't sure how it would work on someone with a terminal illness. She decided that she would not get nervous but rather sit back and drink her coffee while the men sprouted their ideas.

    Philip and Jacob would work on finding a large venue and they would determine if a section could hold up to one hundred people. John suggested they contact Disney as they had a great system for crowd control. He knew someone on the team and would contact him in the morning. The Archbishop added that he would contact the Bishop to get a list of his most faithful priests. He would advise them to fast and meditate before the event. Dr. Woods recommended that they schedule a test run. He would get Mary Ellen to have the clinics identify a hundred patients and ask them if they would participate in the trial. Lucia looked at them all, their faces lit up with excitement and she thought to herself, "These guys are crazy!"

Chapter XLII

Lucia had excused herself from the event planning. She still thought they were all crazy but she was determined not to make herself that way. She returned to her daily routine of Chapel, Breakfast and Garden. She would watch little Claire in the afternoons while Becky worked with Sister Theresa on administrative duties. This was her favorite time. Playing with Claire seemed to dissolve her anxiety and fear. The baby was so innocent and Lucia realized that the only aura she could feel radiating from her was one of light and love.

On one such afternoon, Becky came back early and informed her that the Archbishop had arrived at the Convent with a visitor.

"I think it is the new Mother Superior and I think you're going to really like her, Mom," Becky added.

Lucia did not give her an opportunity to divulge any more information about the woman. She handed over the baby and quickly made her way to Mother Superior's office. She arrived to find the Archbishop sitting behind Mother Superior's desk with a middle-aged woman sitting in one of the visitor chairs, her back to Lucia. Father Lucas welcomed Lucia with a warm smile and before he could introduce the visitor, the woman turned around and cried, "Lulu, it is so good to see you."

It took Lucia a few seconds to connect the voice and the face, then, she ran into the woman's arms and hugged her tightly.

"Maggie, I mean, Sister Magdalena, is it really you?"

Lucia could not believe her good luck. Sister Magdalena or Maggie as Lucia had come to know her, had been the principal of the school her children had attended.

Lucia had often volunteered and worked many fairs and events with Maggie. She had been a great friend until the business with Lucia's deceitful husband. Lucia was forced to work all the hours she could get at her job and no longer had time to volunteer with the school. She and Maggie had often shared lunch and coffee together. Until this moment, Lucia had not realized how much she had missed her and was overwhelmed with a feeling like coming home after a long journey.

Father Lucas finally spoke up and said, "Well, I think the two of you will get along just fine." Looking at Sister Magdalena, he told her that he would leave her in the capable hands of Lucia to get her oriented to the Convent and upcoming events.

Turning to Lucia, he said, "I hope you are happy with my selection for the replacement of Mother Superior." Lucia smiled in response. Grabbing his coat, the Archbishop walked to the door, turning to Lucia, he told her, "Call if you need me."

The two women held hands like teenagers, giggling and chatting about old times. Maggie asked if that young woman who was in the office was Lucia's daughter Rebecca and Lucia nodded. The new Mother Superior commented that she remembered her with frizzy hair and braces. She certainly had grown into a beautiful young lady. When she asked about her son, Lucia's face saddened. She lamented how her son truly disliked his mother and in spite of his coordinated attacks with his father, they could not get Becky to turn against her, too. Lucia also told her how her ex-husband had turned up at the Coliseum to be healed. She confessed that in spite of the magnitude of his betrayal, Lucia had forgiven him.

Sister Magdalena reached for Lucia's hand and told her they would pray every night to change their hearts to love. Lucia thought to herself, same old Maggie, always seeking resolution through prayer. The Healer had adapted that same strategy and with the return of her daughter, she was confident in its effectiveness. Lucia gave her friend a tour of the Convent, introducing her to the other nuns as they walked through the building. The sisters received Sister Magdalena, who did not have a cruel bone in her body, graciously. The new Mother Superior told them how happy she was to be there and so anxious to work with Sister Lucia again.

When she was alone with the new Mother Superior, she told her that she did not go by Sister Lucia since she never took her vows and was not officially part of the Order. Mother Superior responded that Father Lucas had updated her on what had been going on and all the people involved in Lucia's work. She informed Lucia that although she did not take her vows, she felt that the vows Lucia had taken with the Lord were sufficient to give her the title of Sister and that is what she will inform everyone to call her from now on.

Maggie added, "Who are we to question the path we are given by the Lord. Did not Lucas tell me that the Archangel Gabriel called you Sister Lucia?" Lucia smiled; life was black and white for Sister Magdalena, no gray areas for her.

Over the next few days, the newly installed Mother Superior met with each sister individually and reviewed the new direction the Archbishop had requested of her to implement at the Convent. So far, all feedback from the sisters about the new leader was good. They liked her warmth and honesty. She was forthright about the upcoming changes and asked for their support as well as their ideas to make things better. It wasn't long before the staff was preparing for the arrival of fifteen new nuns that would take residence at the Convent. Maggie, or Mother Superior as Sister Lucia tried to remember to call her, never questioned Becky having a small suite next to Lucia at the Convent. She even took time each day to play with little Claire, although never asked where the father was. The new Mother Superior seemed to glide easily into her role and intertwined in the lives of the other sisters.

In addition, Sister Magdalena was much more computer literate than Becky or any of the other Sisters who had not touched a computer in many years. She promptly enlisted IT staff recommended by the Archbishop to install a server and Internet connectivity throughout the Convent. She also ordered laptops for all the staff. The nuns had already been informed that they would be adapting work processes available to them in the twentieth century. Becky would begin giving classes on how to use the software and teach them how to access the common schedule so everyone would be aware of meetings, visits and events taking place at the Convent. Many of the sisters were younger and were relieved to be able to access the Internet again.

"I mean it is the information age," one of the sisters was heard saying aloud.

The Convent was a buzz of activity and the nuns were too busy to complain about the fast changing environment around them. Sister Magdalena knew that change was difficult so she still maintained the quiet times in the morning during Chapel and breakfast, but soon after, the hum of activity grew louder as the IT staff worked throughout the building, installing computers and internet wires. The arrival of the new sisters also increased the noise level and confusion, as they were trying to adjust to their new residence and also a schedule full of classes and projects put forth by the Mother Superior. The existing sisters were welcoming, but they too were overwhelmed by the changes occurring. Throughout it all, Mother Superior walked around with a warm smile asking each and every sister how it was going and actively listening to her when they were frustrated; giving them just the right amount of support to elicit their compliance.

As for Lucia, she continued her midnight hospital rounds and was transported every two nights to one of the hospitals in the state, and several times to a neighboring state, to heal the sick. Since the venue was being changed, and there would be a significant delay in holding another event, Father Lucas agreed to an unlimited number of patients Lucia was allowed to see during these visits. All the local hospitals collaborated with an assigned administrator to coordinate Lucia's schedule in order to maximize the number of patients seen. In fact, most of the hospitals dedicated a wing just for the patients scheduled for the Healer because the turnover was so fast.

Dr. Woods and Jacob had arranged for Lucia to be brought to a warehouse so that the extent of her range of healing could be assessed scientifically. Philip, Jacob, John and Dr. Woods had agreed to initially start with ten people diagnosed with various illnesses. Five priests were positioned closely around her and all meditated in prayer with their hands held outward toward the Healer while Lucia, with her black shawl over her head, held her hands over patients in the room. The four men watched as the white healing energy flowed around the room and was absorbed into the bodies of the ten men and women. The next day, the ten people were evaluated on the success of the healing by various doctors, of which one of them was Dr. Woods. The findings, which included an examination and blood work, confirmed that all of them were healed of their ailments.

Two days later, twenty-five people were brought in and this time, seven priests were in the room with a cloaked Lucia. Again, the four men watched the Healer's energy flow through the attendees. Evaluation the next day yielded the same results as the first test. Two days later, the number of ill men and women was raised to forty; again, all with a variety of ailments. The four men happily watched as the same result that had occurred the previous trial transpired; the energy flowed throughout the room healing all the participants. The next day, Dr. David came to her with the news that all were successfully healed. David informed her that John wanted to jump to one hundred for the next trial. Lucia agreed. She had no idea of the extent of the healing power given to her by the Lord, but Sister Lucia wanted to reach as many of the sick as possible. However, she still thought they were all crazy.

  Two days later, she returned to the warehouse to find one hundred men and women diagnosed with an incurable illness. Ten priests were now closely positioned in a half moon around her. Sister Lucia could see them deep in prayer, some of their mouths softly moving with their hands extended over her. Lucia adjusted the black shawl around her head and over her shoulder, closed her eyes and began praying. The people before her were sitting in metal chairs or wheel chairs in rows of ten across and ten down. The four men watched as the white mist flowed from her hands and flowed through the chairs over the first five rows. After a few minutes, Lucia opened her eyes and knew she had met her limit by the defeated look in Philip, Jacob and Dr. David's eyes.

John stepped forward and yelled to the priests to hook up the wire. Lucia looked over and noticed a copper wire lying on the floor behind the priests. She looked back at John in confusion.

John reassured her, "Don't worry Sister, we tried going wireless, now we are going to try to amp up your energy supply with connectivity." Lucia watched as the priests wrapped the copper battery around their hands and the priest closest to her brought what looked like a copper bracelet to place around each of her hands.

Again, the priests closed their eyes and began praying. Lucia had great difficulty concentrating because all she could think about was getting fried by the copper wire. After seeing her discomfort, Dr. David came over and reassured her that she would not explode or overload. He stood next to her with his hand over hers in solidarity. With Dr. David touching her, Lucia grew calm and was able to concentrate on her prayer. Soon a white mist began flowing from her fingertips, the stream growing larger and stronger with each passing minute. David opened one eye to see the mist filling all rows completely; in fact, it went over the heads of some of the participants. He squeezed Sister Lucia's shoulder to let her know it was going well. When the stream stopped flowing, Lucia opened her eyes to see John's eyes filled with excitement and laughed to herself.

"I guess his crazy idea worked."

Lucia felt a little woozy, but David helped her to a chair and someone rushed over with a bottle of water. Dr. David accompanied her in the ride home, and handed her over to Becky. Lucia, exhausted over the past week's activities, fell into bed and a deep sleep. David was somewhat concerned and stayed at the Convent until Lucia she woke up; at which time, Lucia reassured him she was fine. It was a busy week she told him. Somewhat placated, David left but instructed her to call him if she felt unwell no matter the time. Lucia agreed and left him to go to the dining hall. Waking up from a four-hour nap, Lucia was so hungry, she asked for extra portions. Healing one hundred people sure made her work up an appetite.

Chapter XLIII

The next executive meeting with the event team was overwhelming for Sister Lucia. The men had been making plans to accommodate thousands of people instead of the hundreds Lucia had healed at the previous events. They had contracted the Major League Baseball stadium fifteen miles away and had begun expanding their security team exponentially. Several members of Disney's crowd control team had flown in and expressed hope that they would be able to meet the Healer, however, Philip informed them that unless they attended the event, he didn't think it was possible. The Disney team told him they would be there; then began the task of working with Philip, Jacob and John to determine the best way to efficiently and effectively move the people through the stadium while providing the highest level of security. They reviewed the options available and everyone agreed that it would be best to fill up each section of the stadium with a hundred sick men, woman and children and allow one guest to accompany them. Ten priests would be assigned to each area, too. Sister Lucia would be transported to each section by golf cart accompanied by security along with two experienced licensed electrical contractors. They would be tasked with bringing the copper cable wire to the priests in the section and retrieving it to bring to the next section with Sister Lucia. They were hoping to reach at least two thousand people, but Dr. Woods said anything over five hundred was a win.

Lucia stayed silent; she was scared that she would not be able to restore the health of so many. The Archbishop noticed her lack of participation in the conversation and held up his hand to quiet the others.

When everyone went silent, he asked her, "Sister Lucia, what do you think about the plan?"

The Healer bit her lip and told them that she felt their expectations were too high. Everyone but John Anderson looked down at the table. John was adamant that she could do it. He looked at Lucia directly and told her that she was right, she could not do it, but she wasn't doing it, God was. He told her he had faith. He reminded her how he was an atheist until she had healed his son. Now, he told her he had all the faith in the world that the Lord would provide her with the strength she needed.

Lucia was amazed in the transformation of John Anderson. His son was very well and had already joined several sports teams. John was always sharing pictures and stories of his son's ability to make a basketball or hit a homerun. As promised, John, his wife and son were at church every Sunday and in the small amount of spare time he had, he and his family worked at the local soup kitchen. He shared his story with whoever would listen and always gave thanks and praise to God. Lucia had met his wife, a former model who was raised Catholic, but had grown away from her faith. She said the healing of her son was like a kick in the butt. She forgot the peace and love she had always experienced after receiving Communion. Then she thanked Lucia for taking on God's mission as John always told her the Healer was just a pass through for God's work.

Philip sat at the head of the table, shaking his head. He then directed his words to Sister Lucia. "If you don't think this will work, then it will not. There are hundreds of men and women working around the clock to pull this off. Thousands of people are praying that God will hear their cries. Sister Lucia, you have given them all hope that they will no longer be abandoned and left to suffer. I believe in you, Jacob believes in you, the Archbishop believes in you; we all need you to believe in yourself. I have instructed everyone involved in this effort to pray that you are able to heal the masses. I have absolute faith in the power of the Lord. Can you please have that same faith?" Lucia took a few moments to let his words sink in and then nodded.

The date was set in three days' time. The next time she would see the men would be at the stadium. They were working night and day to prepare. Cities within a sixty-minute ride of the Convent were bursting with the sick, waiting for the next healing event. Hospitals, clinics and hotels were overwhelmed with the number of people coming to be seen. In addition, the churches were filled to capacity, with the overflow standing outside. Speakers were set up so that everyone could at least hear the Mass. Priests had been transferred from around the country to the area to assist in serving the faithful. Money was pouring in from everywhere. The Church had increased access to Mass and confession to almost around the clock. Mary Ellen had worked with the Archbishop to identify venues where penance could be allocated and community volunteer opportunities could be recommended.

Lucia was still visiting hospitals while waiting for the big event, however, Jacob thought the streets were getting too dangerous for her to travel, but Lucia insisted. In fact, the roads around every hospital in the area were packed with people hoping to catch sight of the Healer. When she voiced her concerns to the Archbishop, he told her he would work on it. Father Lucas contacted Lucia several hours later and told her that transportation had been arranged and would arrive the following night.

Lucia waited patiently in the front lobby for a car to come for her, but was surprised to hear a really loud noise outside in the back of the Convent. All the sisters, including Mother Superior had run outside, some in their nightgowns and slippers, to see what was going on. There in the large field behind the Convent, they watched as Lucia was being escorted to a helicopter that would transport her to the hospital.

Lucia could hear Maggie yell above the noise of the blades, "Wait till I get my hands on Father Lucas. He could have at least given us a warning."
The hospital administrators had instructed guards to lock and guard all the doors to the building, and only true emergencies be allowed in the emergency room. Under duress, the Archbishop, Jacob and Philip consented to one hour each at two of the local hospitals. That was the agreement Lucia had made with Philip to ensure her safety; for once the crowds outside knew she was there, he was afraid they would storm the doors.

Dr. Woods and Mary Ellen were at the hospital roof waiting for her. They quickly guided her to the rooms of those not responding to treatment. The parents in the children's ward all welcomed her and most of them prayed with her for the healing of their sons and daughters. Several of the children made drawings for Sister Lucia and she accepted them gladly. This was the best part of her work. She only wished that she could be there in the morning when they woke up with pink cheeks and an enormous appetite. She was going to have Becky text Bea to make sure that she would have plenty of chocolate chip pancakes to send up to Pediatrics in the morning.

When she was taken to the adult floors, the elderly asked for her blessing, and then shushed her away. They now had confirmation that God had not forgotten them and they were anxious to be taken home to Heaven. They assured Lucia that the priest had come and taken their confession, then given them Communion. They were ready; unfortunately, their families did not feel the same. Lucia was glad Mary Ellen was there to provide much-needed family counseling.

Of course, there were others who feared death. They had not repented their sins yet expected redemption. Lucia did the only thing left for her to do; she would pray for their souls.

The helicopter was quite an efficient mode of transportation between the two hospitals. Dr. Woods was keeping a close watch of the time. A small team of doctors and nurses guided her throughout the hospital to those deemed incurable by modern medicine. Everyone was sworn to secrecy. They knew what was at stake. Philip explained to the team that he would immediately stop the visits if even a whisper of her appearance was leaked before her departure. Everything went well, but Lucia being who she was, asked Dr. David to make a small detour on the last floor they were on. Dr. Woods and two security men walked behind her as she made her way to a small conference room.

Without knocking, Lucia opened the door and then stood still with eyes closed, as if waiting for instruction. Several moments later, Lucia opened her eyes to see two women sitting at the table and four hospital security personnel standing around them. One of the woman had her back turned to Lucia and did not see that the Healer had come into the room. The older woman sitting toward Lucia was surprised when the Healer walked in, unexpectedly. The other nurse turned and Lucia could see she was much younger and obviously upset. Lucia sighed.

"Yes," she said to Dr. David, "This is where I was supposed to come."

Sitting in the lap of the younger nurse was a little girl being held tightly to her chest. The girl, no more than five or six, was obviously ill as her pale face was sunken in and her lips had a blue tinge to them. Her big brown eyes were dull and listless. Lucia noticed similarities between the child and the nurse holding her. They were obviously related and Lucia rushed over to them. She was in a time crunch and she did not want to waste a minute. The woman holding the child had tears in her eyes and Lucia could see the child was afraid and holding the nurse tightly.

The older woman stood quickly and apologized to Sister Lucia, "I am the charge nurse, and I am so sorry, Sister. This nurse was informed of the importance of secrecy, yet she broke established protocol and snuck her niece onto the ward. She will be terminated and escorted out of the building when you are well off the premises."

Lucia leaned over and asked the aunt if she could hold her niece. The aunt, whose face was still tear stained, assured her niece that this was the woman she told her about that would make her all better. She then handed her over into Lucia's waiting arms. The aunt then tearfully pleaded with the Healer, telling her that her sister begged her to bring her if the Healer came to the floor.

"How could I refuse, Sister, she is dying," the young woman pleaded.

Lucia asked the little girl her name and in a weak whisper replied, "Charlie". Lucia then asked her if she would pray with her and again in barely a whisper that took her breath away, the little girl prayed in Lucia's arms. Everyone gasped as the white stream of energy encircled the little girl. Dr. Woods could hear the child's voice getting stronger and stronger as the healing light was absorbed into her body. She then handed the little girl back to her aunt. Already there was a noticeable difference in her appearance. Her lips were no longer blue and her coloring was improving. Lucia looked up at the charge nurse and in a stern and firm voice told them that this woman's niece was identified by God to be healed. She further informed her that the aunt was not to be fired but escorted to her car so she could bring her child home to her mother. Lucia hugged the aunt and then she, Dr. Woods and Mary Ellen along with security rushed to the helicopter to return home.

Sister Lucia always spent the days prior to an event eating well and gardening, which put her mind at ease. She thought of John Anderson's words over and over. She even asked Mother Superior to pray with her in preparation of the upcoming event. Maggie had not yet seen Lulu in action, but told the Healer that she agreed with John Anderson.

"If God brought you to it; He will bring you through it," she told Lucia. Lucia just had to trust the Lord and what ever happened was His will.

"Well," said Sister Lucia, "If He can stop a bullet from two feet away, this should not be that big of a challenge for Him."

She then reminded herself that she was only a medium to channel the Lord's energy. It wasn't her healing anyone, anyway. With that thought, she sighed and continued to pray that she be given the strength to do God's work.

The night before the event, Lucia had difficulty going to sleep. She tossed and turned trying to get comfortable without success. She got out of bed and settled in the big comfortable chair in the corner of her room by the window. She picked up a book she had been reading on the life of St. Mary. Suddenly, a blinding ball of light appeared which seemed to grow larger and larger before Sister Lucia's eyes. Expecting Archangel Gabriel, she was startled to see a woman appear. Her head was covered with a pure white linen cloth with wisps of her light brown hair escaping, framing her face. A blue gown fell softly around her feet, which were barefoot. A white aura with purple and silver sparkles surrounded her as she held her hands towards Lucia. Lucia could see that only kindness and love emanated from her soul. At first, Lucia thought that the woman was here to take her to Heaven, and she became sad as she had just gotten Becky back and she could not imagine not holding little Claire anymore. A tear rolled down Lucia's cheek at this thought.

After a few minutes, the woman spoke to Lucia in a voice the Healer could only describe as angelic. Lucia was mesmerized by it. The Heavenly vision introduced herself as St. Mary, Mother of Divine Grace and told Lucia that this visit was not done to make her cry. St. Mary confessed that it was she who gave Gabriel the black shawl for Lucia to wear. She had hoped it would give the Healer comfort and strength to carry out her son's request. She had been watching Lucia as she carried out the Lord's work on Earth. All of Heaven was exalted with her progress. Sister Lucia finally found her voice and shyly admitted to St. Mary that Lucia was expected to heal people on a grand scale. She was afraid she would fail.

    St. Mary reached for her hand and Lucia could feel the loving warmth of her firm grasp fill her heart. Then, she replied' "My son is sending His Angels with you tomorrow. There is no need to fear for you will not fail. A lot will be asked from you, for sure, more than what has passed, but know the strength of the Heavens above will surround you as you complete your task. I wish I could be by your side, but that is not to be. Sister Lucia, you have been a good and faithful servant of the Lord. I am here to tell you that you will be given the power you need to heal all those who come before you and not to fret."

    Lucia felt her eyes grow heavy and slipped into a deep dreamless sleep. When she awoke, she saw the sun starting to rise over the horizon. Lucia now had a blanket over her and the aroma of roses filled the air. The book was closed and carefully placed on the table beside her. Lucia looked left to right to see if St. Mary was still there. Her immediate thought was that it had to be a dream, but given the history of her visions, Lucia knew it was real. She tried to recall the entire conversation with St. Mary. Her thoughts were wildly flying through her mind. She had to tell Maggie. She rose from the chair and was folding the blanket when she saw it. On the third finger of her left hand was a thin gold band with what looked like hieroglyphics on it. She fell back into the chair in shock. She tried to remove the ring but it would not budge. She couldn't turn it or move it at all. It seemed bonded to her hand yet it did not cause her any pain or discomfort. "Wait till the team sees this."

CHAPTER XLIV

The Archbishop rushed to the Convent after hearing of Sister Lucia's new gift. He didn't even wait for someone to open his car door; nor did he wait for someone to open the door to the Convent for him. He just burst into the hallway and rushed down the hall to Mother Superior's office. Sister Magdalena and Sister Lucia were standing under a lamp studying the ring.

Father Lucas interrupted them and exclaimed, "Let me see it."

Like Lucia did earlier, the priest tried to pull it off her finger, but it wouldn't budge. Then, he tried to turn it but he could not do that either. "This is incredible; it is a miracle. Sister Lucia, tell me everything, no, wait, let's get Pope Leo on the phone. He will want to be included in this conversation."

It took a few minutes before the Pope came to the phone, but once he learned of Sister Lucia's new ring, he, too, became very excited.

"Please good Sister, tell us what happened," he begged her.

So, Lucia told them how she was having trouble sleeping, given the next event was the following day. She then shared her conversation with St. Mary, telling them every detail she remembered, including how she woke up in the chair with a blanket covering her, and finding the gold band on her finger. No one spoke for quite some time. The Archbishop was still holding her hand and studying the ring. He tried to explain the hieroglyphics on the ring to the Pope who grew more and more frustrated with the Archbishop's slow and poor description.

Pope Leo then yelled to his staff, "Will you stop standing around and make yourselves useful. Someone please hook me up to that FaceTime thing."

Once FaceTime was connected, Lucia held the ring close to the phone's camera and allowed the Pope to study the ring. He told them that he had never seen that specific pattern, but would contact a friend of his who was familiar with many languages that used hieroglyphics.
Pope Leo then had Sister Lucia repeat her story again. The Archbishop had shared how the ring could not be removed or turned at all. Both men and Sister Magdalena were speechless. None of the other Healers had received this gift yet, only the black shawl from St Mary. The Pope shared that no one else had received the Medallion either, so the Lord must have anticipated an attempt on Lucia's life. When Pope Leo asked who had the Medallion now after Sister Louisa passed, the Archbishop chuckled and told him how the stubborn mule took it with her. That comment had all of them snickering, but the Pope gave a full-hearted laugh.

They completed the phone call after promising Pope Leo that they would contact him immediately if anything else occurred. The Archbishop then contacted Philip and Jacob and told them about the new development. The two heads of security called for an emergency team meeting, but Lucia assumed they just wanted to see the ring. Lucia had realized while they were looking at the band that it appeared to be a type of gold, however, it seemed to wave around her finger. The pictures on it did not move but the gold seemed fluid; even Mother Superior noticed it and they watched it for several minutes. It was truly bizarre how the gold seemed to shift in waves yet Lucia could not move it around her finger at all.

Word traveled fast around the Convent and soon all the nuns congregated outside of Mother Superior's office. Sister Theresa asked if the sisters could see the ring from St. Mary, so Sister Lucia invited them to examine the ring under the light. Lucia was taken back, when unexpectedly each nun studied the band for a few moments and then bent and kissed the ring. Lucia tried to stop them but Maggie told her this ring had touched the Virgin Mother and deserved all the love and respect given by the women. Sister Theresa approached Sister Lucia and exclaimed that they were blessed to know a saint chosen by the Lord and His Mother.

Lucia didn't know what to say, but in a soft whisper, she told them, "I'm just Lucia."

Philip and Jacob must have been working together, planning today's event, because they both stormed in similar to how the Archbishop made his entrance. Their eyes went directly to Sister Lucia's hand and could see the band shining brightly.

Philip asked the Healer, "Do you feel different? Did you try to heal anyone since you got the ring?"
Lucia shook her head and answered him honestly, "No, I feel the same, except I am really hungry. St. Mary told me not to fear tonight. She said she was sending many angels for support. I think she knows that we are trying to heal a lot more people this time. I think it is going to work out just fine."

Both of the men came closer to Lucia and studied the ring for quite some time. Philip took pictures and both men tried to turn the ring but again it wouldn't budge an inch.

Philip announced he was holding an emergency meeting with the Planning Committee.

Sister Magdalena took Sister Lucia's arm and informed the three men standing in her office that she was taking Lulu to eat.

"I'm sure you don't want her passing out before the event. How can you expect her to heal thousands of people on an empty stomach?" Mother Superior told them.

They left the office and a crowd of nuns, IT staff and members of the Event Team parted the way like the Red Sea. They all stared at her like she was a freak and Lucia grew uncomfortable.

"Please" she said tearfully, "you all know me, please don't treat me differently now."

Sister Theresa broke the silence in a reprimanding tone, "Okay, we will not treat you differently, but I am here to tell you that you were not excused from Chapel this morning. Make sure you are there on time tomorrow morning; and I expect you in the garden in an hour."

Then, she shushed all the shocked nuns to their chores and the IT staff to complete their wiring. She loved how Sister Theresa acted like Sister Louisa. She was such a good and kind soul.

Lucia was starved and ate double portions. She knew she would need her strength tonight and after St. Mary's visit, was feeling rather confident that tonight would be a success. Maggie sat quietly by her side while she ate.

Finally, she spoke up and shared with Lucia that she had not expected such miracles to occur so soon after taking her post. "Lulu, I want you to know that when the Archbishop told me all that was going on with you, I thought he had exaggerated. Now I see that he did not express the real depth of the miracles that are happening here. I am truly blessed to have you as my friend and I want you to know that the Lord could not have chosen anyone better for this mission. Now, let me look at that ring, again."

Sister Lucia never made it to the garden, as the meeting was held soon after Jacob and Philip arrived and notified the Planning team. So many priests and administrative staff showed up for the impromptu meeting; all asking to see the band on her hand. They had crowded around her and finally, Jacob asked everyone to take a seat. While everyone was getting settled, John Anderson burst into the room.

"What happened? Why was an emergency meeting called?" John exclaimed wildly. Lucia noticed that his son, Joshua, was with him and he walked calmly over to Lucia and gave her a hug, which Lucia returned lovingly. Philip was filling John in, while the boy was telling Lucia all about his team and how he caught a pop fly and won the game. The boy then noticed the ring on Lucia's finger and reached out to touch it.

"Wow," he said, "I can see so many colors when I touch it?"

The room grew eerily silent.

John walked over and said, "What colors do you see, son?"

"All of them, Dad. I see a river of different colors. It's beautiful," he responded in wonder.

John reached over to touch the ring, but no such vision appeared to him, however, he did feel a pulsating sensation. He studied the ring, especially the small pictures engraved around it. He noticed the ring was imbedded in her finger and asked Lucia if it hurt. She shook her head and told him it gave off a soothing warmth. John Anderson knelt before her and kissed the ring reverently. When he stood up, he took a deep breath and reassured everyone that this was a great sign that tonight would be successful. John informed the group that the crowds had been lining up since yesterday and the flow was anticipated to go smoothly. Maggie quietly reached over to touch the ring. She looked at Lulu and shook her head.

The boy was still standing next to Sister Lucia and wondered if he had said something wrong. John, sensing his son's confusion, told him, it was all right, and only special boys got to see the power of the ring.

The boy then spoke out loud to Sister Lucia, "I bet that white stuff that comes out of your hands is gonna come out in color now. That is going to be so cool. Dad, can I go watch tonight?"

Lucia laughed and thought how "cool" it would be to see each section filled with people surrounded by a mist of psychedelic colors.

Unfortunately, this new development became quite concerning to Philip and Jacob. If the mist was colored, would they be able to see if anyone was attempting an attack.

Jacob asked if Sister Lucia would consent to a test run on one person, "Just so we could see if the white mist changes colors that will impede our observation."

Lucia agreed and before they could continue, one of the female attendees asked if she could be the person. Lucia was so focused on the ring that she had forgotten to study the people in the room. She had become adept at reading everyone's aura during the meetings, but today the ring distracted her. It seems she missed the woman who had spoken up, and there it was -- a huge gap of energy over her neck.

The woman asked again if she could be the test subject. Jacob was shaking his head at first, but when Lucia stood and went over to the woman and held her hand out to her, he remained silent.

"What's your name?" Sister Lucia asked her.

The woman was standing still, her listless eyes filled with hope. She wasn't very old, maybe forty, Lucia surmised. There were dark bags under her eyes and she noticed that her clothes, though expensive, hung limply around her.

"Darlene," she answered, "but they call me Dolly."

Philip interjected and asked why she was here; she wasn't on the team list. She explained that her coworker was not feeling well so she asked me to attend the meeting for her.

Philip asked everyone to leave the room while they conducted the experiment. Once the room was clear, he returned to the woman and asked her, "Did she send you here to be healed?"

The woman dropped her eyes to the floor, and quickly apologized. "I was recently diagnosed with late stage thyroid cancer and my coworker told me to come and beg Sister Lucia for healing." Turning to Lucia, she continued, "She said you had a good heart and were a kind woman. Please, Sister Lucia, I'm sorry for lying, but I don't know what else to do. My supervisor wouldn't give me the day off to stand in line, even when I told him why."

Lucia smiled, "No worries, Dolly, let's get started, shall we? Maggie, could you call Becky and tell her to bring my black shawl please?"

Becky arrived with the shawl and looked at Lucia with questioning eyes. Lucia gave her a hug and told her she would see her shortly. Becky's eyes fell to the ring on her mother's hand and her mouth dropped open. Lucia nudged her out the door, and then directed the woman to sit in the chair next to the Healer. Lucia donned the shawl and closed her eyes in prayer. Then, she raised her arms to the woman's neck and as expected a strong stream of white energy surrounded by different pastel colors shot from her fingertips. It was a river of color just like John's son had told them. Both, Jacob and Philip gasped at the phenomenon. Yes, there were many colors but they were localized around the white mist and very transparent.

Once the stream stopped, Lucia dropped her hands and sighed. This healing was like none in the past. She could feel the energy force build up and shoot out of her fingertips. It was powerful. Dolly turned and dropped to her knees in front of Sister Lucia.

She tearfully told the Healer, "Thank you, I can actually feel a warm tingling where the tumor is. Already, I can swallow more easily. Thank you, Sister. God Bless You. I can never thank you enough."

Lucia shook the hand she extended to her and answered her with a smile. "Your faith has saved you, that and the fact that you have a great friend at work." Turning to Philip and Jacob, Lucia said, "Her supervisor seems to lack faith and compassion. I think someone needs to have a talk with him so that this does not happen again."

Lucia walked back to her room clearly upset by the people obstructing the Lord's work. First the Head Nurse almost prevented her from healing the small little girl and now this supervisor blocking the woman from attending the healing at the stadium. Then, she thought about the man who had tried to kill her, but shot Sister Louisa instead. How many reporters and newscasters vilified Lucia's name, doubting her abilities and purpose; those that called her a charlatan or worse? The Archbishop had told her that many were inciting violence against her. Even the Vatican staff cast doubt on her and delayed the Pope's visit by weeks. How many others without faith have promoted the devil's work? These intentions were the manipulations of evil and wicked spirits that have corrupted the population.

"Tonight," she thought, "Tonight she would silence the nonbelievers and naysayers. Tonight, she would be the Lord's handmaiden and heal the masses. St. Mary's words gave her strength and confidence that she would not fail."

Chapter XLV

The Archbishop arranged another helicopter to transport them to the stadium. He felt the ninety minutes to get there was too long and he had received a report that traffic around the stadium was at a standstill. Even though they were all given CEP or Communications Earplugs as the pilot explained at Lucia's previous ride, it was difficult to speak in the chopper, so Sister Lucia and Maggie could not engage in their usual reminiscent and chatty conversation. Sister Magdalena did ask Lucia if she thought everyone would be able to see the angels St. Mary said would be there. Everyone's ears perked up to hear Lucia's answer. Lucia responded saying if she saw any angels she would identify them by time. So if an angel was directly to the right side of her, she would say three o'clock and if they were above her she would say midnight. Sister Magdalena laughed and said if she saw them she would scream and point so everyone could see them. Lucia laughed; Philip and Jacob sat stone-faced to the joke.

Lucia could tell they were getting closer when she saw hundreds of cars and crowds of people walking or being wheeled to the stadium. This was nothing like the arena. She could see the people coming from all directions. At every intersection, Lucia could see the flashing lights of a police car and two or three policemen trying to direct traffic. Jacob informed them that there was a drop off lane that was supposed to be kept moving so the sick did not have to go far to get to the stadium.

Philip responded, "Well, the line isn't moving; you better call someone."

As the helicopter approached, Lucia could see the people waving and cheering. The scene was something out of a movie.

A security team helped Lucia and Sister Magdalena exit the helicopter and surrounded them as they walked to the building entrance. Lucia took a deep breath to keep calm; she could feel the static energy all around them. Suddenly, the security team parted and to her delight stood four handsome soldiers waiting to greet her.

Jack, always first, gave her a big smile and hugged her. "It seems you made it to the big time, Sister."

Lucia asked Robert how Diana was doing with the pregnancy and he could not have been more proud in his answer. "He's the son of a marine, ma'am; he's causing hell, of course."

After hugging Matthew and Vincent, Lucia invited them to visit her next week at the Convent. Matthew informed her that he was currently dating the nurse from the hospital and asked if it was okay if he brought her?

Philip showed up by her side and added, "They will have to get clearance first, Sister Lucia."
Lucia, after a long pause, reluctantly agreed and Philip sighed. Jacob laughed, as did the soldiers, then he shouted "Showtime."

Lucia could hear a large choir singing Gospel songs over the noise of the crowd. She was escorted onto a stage that was decorated similarly to the arena, with the exception that there were now thirty chairs lined up across the stage instead of the usual ten and saw there was a priest sitting in each chair with their head bowed in prayer. Lucia looked more closely at the clergy and recognized most were Cardinals as they were wearing red caps on their heads.

The Archbishop introduced Sister Lucia to each one, however the only priest she recognized was Cardinal Moreno, a supportive friend of the group. Thankfully, Lucia found all of them received her with a smile and kind word. Some made the sign of the cross toward her and others bent to kiss the ring on her left hand. She was sure Pope Leo sent them and welcomed his support. The Archbishop stood at the podium and opened the event with a series of prayers, followed by Cardinal Moreno who gave the homily. Philip Sorrin was next reminding everyone of the guidelines that must be followed to ensure that Sister Lucia was able to reach each section in a timely manner.

    The plan remained for Lucia to be transported section to section by golf cart as security surrounded her. Sister Magdalena and Dr. Woods would accompany her, but the doctor was late. Jacob finally reached him to learn the doctor was stuck in the gridlock around the stadium but he left his car on the side of the road and was only at that moment walking in the entrance. Jacob sent a team to go get him and they waited patiently for him to arrive. Ten minutes later, Dr. Woods jumped on the golf cart and the driver brought them to their destination.

    Lucia entered the first section and all the people were instructed to remain sitting, although she could see some of them kneeling. Several of the priests brought over the copper wire, but Lucia asked them to wait and see how she did first. The two priests looked down at the ring and nodded; everyone involved in the Church knew of St. Mary's visit and the gift she left on Lucia's hand. She smiled and looked over the little faces before her, staring back at her with such faith and hope in their eyes. Lucia could feel the energy building up inside her and even noticed small sparks coming off of her fingertips. Lucia already had the black shawl around her head and when she spread her arms in prayer. She was truly a heavenly spectacle. The Healer generated a soft lavender aura that could be seen by all around her. When she began to pray, the people gasped in wonder as streams of energy emanated from her hands and over the crowd.

The warm healing energy exploded from her hands. The usual all white stream now had different pastel colors running through the flow. It was a beautiful testament of God's love and mercy. Even Philip, Jacob and the security team kneeled in reverence. Sister Magdalena stood at the doorway with Dr. Woods, her hand covering her mouth at the miracle she was witnessing.

Lucia opened her eyes to see what was happening, and could not believe the amount of healing energy flowing from her hands. She saw balls of different colors floating around the children as she healed them. Some of the younger children were trying to catch the balls that floated next to them. After a few minutes, the stream waned and finally stopped. The entire section speechless, dumbfounded by what they had just witnessed.

The stadium was filled to capacity, in addition to the sick, many had come just to bear witness to the miracles performed. Lucia noticed the crowd was almost silent after the first healing. They too were mesmerized by what they had just witnessed. She hoped it would stay like that as she really enjoyed hearing the choir as she healed. She observed that many of the first sections were filled with children. There were a lot of wheelchairs and some of the children were being held or supported by their parents. She thanked God for healing them. No one deserved the pain and suffering of illnesses that ravaged the body, but even more so her heart ached for the children and she had demanded that at all functions they be given priority.

Lucia chose to walk to each section and repeated the healing with no sign of fatigue or weakness. Sister Magdalena and Dr. David doted on her as they walked, providing Lucia with water and David giving her cookies baked special by Bea for her friend. So far, the copper wire was not needed, the energy mist had penetrated all spaces between the children and the priests confirmed they saw all of the children absorb the multi colored mist into their small fragile bodies. When the parents tried to approach Lucia, they were held back, but every so often a child would run forward and Lucia would lift them up for a hug. Each hug seemed to fill her with more and more spirit. After all, this was what it was all about: gathering the lost sheep and returning them to the flock with love, mercy and grace.

After a time, Sister Magdalena who accompanied Lucia silently spoke and asked her if she noticed what was happening to the ring on her finger. Lucia immediately looked down and saw that the ring was glowing with a beam of light surrounding the band. It seems Maggie was the first to notice it, because once Lucia held it up, the entire team working with her came over to observe the phenomenon. Dr. David tried to touch it but the beam seemed to repel any touch.

"Does it hurt or burn?" David asked her, but the Healer shook her head.

"It just feels warm and comfortable, protective," Lucia told him. "Let's keep going or we'll be here all night."

It took one hour for Lucia to heal five sections and there was at least fifteen more. Philip and Jacob were worried that Sister Lucia would not be able to continue for three more hours. They had tried to rush her but given the occasional child who broke through, there was no other time saver available to them. No one was allowed to talk except to pray. Everyone was already sitting or kneeling waiting for her to come and she only came five feet into each section. In fact, her walking saved minutes of her getting in and out of the cart. Lucia could see the two men conferring and shaking their head.

She heard them declare quietly, "She isn't going to make it."

Lucia sighed and asked the Lord what she should do. She agreed that three hours of healing two thousand people would definitely take its toll on her. As she raised her eyes, the answer was before her.

She grabbed Sister Magdalena and yelled, "One o'clock, two o'clock, three o'clock, four o'clock, five o'clock; oh, dear, the angels are everywhere."

Maggie, David, Jacob, Philip and the rest of the security team saw the angelic figures descending all over the stadium. There were hundreds of them coming from the sky. The sounds of the crowds and the choir had stopped. Everyone was looking at the angels floating throughout the stadium. The men fell to their knees and began praying.

Sister Magdalena held Lucia tightly, "Is it the end of the world, Lulu?"

Lucia didn't know what to think, some of the people began running out of the stadium, afraid of what was happening. Others, the true believers, stayed where they were praying to God. Lucia thought a few angels would be around, but this was spectacular. They were beautiful and all of them were looking at Lucia with expectation, but for what she did not know. Then, she saw him, the Archangel Gabriel floating to her in his entire splendor, his wings flapping as he floated to where Lucia was standing. Lucia saw Maggie, who was standing right next to the Healer holding her hand, close her eyes tightly and her mouth was murmuring words of prayer.

      The Archangel smiled and in his melodic voice proclaimed, "Sister Lucia, Heaven is celebrating the success of God's Divine Plan of which you have played no small part. There is no need to go section by section to heal all these people; St Mary gave you the ring. As a result of your obedience to God's will, you have been given great power. Go to the clearing in the middle of the stadium. Come, the Angels of Heaven have come to bear witness to the love and mercy of the Lord."

      With that, he extended his hand, and Lucia took it; however, she did drag a frightened Sister Magdalena with her. David, Philip and Jacob also jumped up to follow as the angel guided Lucia to the clearing in the center of the stadium.

      Many of the observers had fled, but those that were sick were steadfast and remained in their sections, more determined and hopeful to be healed than afraid of the arrival of the angels. Lucia could see that those able were on their knees and everyone was chanting in prayer being led by the Cardinals on stage; who were also on their knees.

      At some point, the choir started up again.
Philip and Jacob were on their phones responding to the pandemonium happening outside the stadium.

Apparently, there were thousands of sick men and women who were turned away from the event because capacity had been reached. They were now storming the doors and rushing to occupy any available space throughout the stadium. Lucia could hear Jacob yelling to lock the doors and post at least ten guards at every entrance. David was helping Mother Superior, who was still in shock and struggling to keep up with Sister Lucia and the Archangel.

Dr. David took this opportunity to study Gabriel.

"Yes," he thought to himself, "he was the one who came to me back when I was eighteen years old."

As if reading his mind, Gabriel looked over at him and winked. "Do you still have the feather I left, David?" Gabriel asked him. Too shocked to answer, the Archangel just laughed at David and continued walking with Lucia. David hurried along behind them in a state of disbelief.

Once they reached the clearing, Gabriel assured them he would keep the Healer safe from the crowd. Then, he advised all those around the Healer to step back, that she would need plenty of room. He stood next to Lucia, then, nodded for her to continue her work. Lucia looked at Dr. David who was hesitant to leave her and whispered that he would not be far, and remained closer to her than the others.

Sister Lucia looked up at all the faces staring back at her, noting all the people now filling the stairwells and every open space in the stadium and closed her eyes. She raised her hands wide and far apart. Sparks were flying out of her hands and her arms literally glowed. The ring on her finger gave off a bright sparkling aura and suddenly a wide swathe of white energy filled with colorful balls flowing through the stream, shot across the stadium up to the rows of people. Lucia moved her arms slowly left to right and then back again, over and over, the stream of light never waning in intensity or strength. The white fog enveloped all those in the stands, as well as those who had rushed the doors and filled the stairwells and the edges of the clearing. The energy could be seen being absorbed as needed. Over and over, Lucia moved her arms until she had completely covered everyone in the stadium.

Security was stationed throughout the sections watching the crowd for any danger, but none were prepared for this magnificent showcase of angels with their large wings flapping in the sky, and a whole stadium of people being healed at one time. No one even coughed while Lucia made good on God's promise. Lucia, so wrapped up in the moment as the healing energy left her body, finally noticed that it was not the choir singing but rather the angels in a beautiful harmonious rhapsody.

Lucia felt like she no longer had control of her body although she was very aware of the overwhelming electric energy pulsating within her. Time was irrelevant. Lucia could feel the Holy Spirit fill her whole body as she was used to heal the sick in attendance, she felt light as a feather and in union with the Trilogy. It was an amazing feeling and Lucia almost forgot why she was there. The healing energy coming out of her seemed never ending, making sure that each and every faithful person who stayed behind was healed by the will of God.

After what seemed like ages, Lucia was in shock when suddenly she felt like a switch had been pulled and the energy being generated stopped cold; the flow of energy coming from her fingertips abruptly ended. She no longer felt light as a feather. The energy she had put forth left her empty; her body felt heavy and void. She could feel her arms and legs shaking and growing weaker and weaker. Gabriel was still standing at her side watching her but he did not seem concerned about Lucia's deteriorating condition. Lucia could see the angels had stopped singing and were floating back up to the Heavens; their bodies dissipating like smoke the farther away they got. Gabriel stood next to her murmuring in her ear, then, followed the others wordlessly.

Lucia knew she was going down but could do nothing about it. She looked at the ring on her hand and saw that the white glow that it held earlier was gone. Lucia called out weakly, "David," as she lost consciousness. David managed to catch her right before she hit the ground, screaming for a medic and an ambulance. Security was running around trying to prevent people from coming to where Lucia lay in David's arms. The priests in each section were trying their best to guide the people to the exits, but chaos was everywhere. All the attendees were shouting about what they had seen. The pandemonium outside was now occurring inside the stadium.

CHAPTER XLVI

Lucia's eyes fluttered open. She could see the sun shining brightly through the window and she could hear the birds chirping in the tree. She tried to lift herself up but her arms and legs felt like lead. She could turn her head and when she did, she saw that Dr. David had dragged her big chair by the window next to the bed. He was sitting there reading. Always well groomed, Dr. David's hair was sticking out in all directions and he had almost a full beard covering his face. His clothes were crumpled and even from here she could smell him. Lucia could also see the worry lines around his eyes and forehead. "How long was I out?" she thought to herself. She knew she was the cause of David's worry, especially when she remembered how she fainted after the healing.

David looked up and threw his book on the floor. "Sister Lucia, you are finally awake. Let me get Becky and Mother Superior."
He ran out of the room before she could ask him to help her sit up. Now, she had to wait till he returned. While waiting, she tried to move her arms, then her legs. She wouldn't be dancing anytime soon but she could move them with a great deal of effort. She checked out the gold band on her finger and could see that it was still there but without the supernatural glow it had given off at the stadium. Her mouth was so dry; she wished Dr. David had given her a sip of water before running out

Sister Lucia heard a commotion outside her room and Becky burst through the door and threw herself on the bed. Mother Superior and the nuns followed; thankfully they did not throw themselves on the bed and just surrounded it. She could feel and hear Becky's tears and her cries of how worried everyone was; it had been five days since the event. She held her daughter for a few minutes to reassure her that she was okay, but then had her and Maggie help her into a sitting position. Becky brought over a glass of water and sat on the edge of the bed. Lucia sipped the cool fresh water slowly, savoring the relief of her dry desert mouth. When she gave Becky back the glass, Lucia looked at all the anxious faces and asked, "So, how is everyone?"

Mother Superior was the first to respond and if Lucia closed her eyes, she would swear it was Sister Louisa. "Well, you have given most of us a heart attack as a result of you being in a coma for five whole days. We have been worried sick. Dr. Woods hasn't left your side and I get phone calls throughout the day and night, inquiring about your status. The Archbishop is in and out of the Convent checking on you and John Anderson is beside himself. He has taken it upon himself to assume all the guilt for your comatose state. In addition, I believe Pope Leo has canceled his travel plans to return to the Convent on your behalf. Oh, and Mary Ellen took a leave of absence to take care of you. Other than that, everything is hunky dory."

Lucia cast her eyes down, staring at her hands. Then the irritated Mother Superior threw her arms around her, saying, "For all that, we are just happy that you have finally woke up. We have been praying nonstop."
The other sisters confirmed her statement. Lucia smiled and thought, "How she loved these women." Sister Theresa left to get Lucia breakfast and the other sisters were helping Lucia to the washroom. Sister Lucia was weak but her ability to support herself improved with each step.

Lifting her head, she saw Dr. David standing by the doorway watching.

"I'm fine, Dr. David, go home and take a shower. We can talk when you return," Lucia reassured him.

He was ready to shake his head but Mary Ellen appeared and told him to go. "I will stay with her, don't worry," she told him.

After a quick shower and breakfast, Sister Lucia felt a whole lot better. She got comfortable in the other big chair by the window, watching the nuns work in the garden. They saw her and waved. Returning to her favorite chore would have to wait a few days, she thought, stretching her legs. Mother Superior sat with her making small talk while they waited for Dr. Woods to return. Sister Lucia asked her to check to make sure her black shawl was hung up in the closet and the nun confirmed that she had hung it up herself, although she admitted she did try it on for a brief moment and had the same overwhelming feeling of comfort and love Lucia told her about. Lucia just smiled.

Dr. David finally came, smelling so much better; and he shaved. He asked if Lucia thought she could make it to the conference room, as it would be easier to give her an update on all that had occurred while she was unconscious. With Dr. David on one side and Maggie on the other, they slowly walked her to the conference room where Father Lucas, Philip, Jacob, Jack and John were waiting and anxious to see her for themselves that she was okay. John ran to her as soon as she entered the room, apologizing for causing such suffering after all she had done for him by healing his son. Sister Lucia assured him she was fine and with or without him, the Lord had planned the event and the outcome. He had sent St. Mary with the ring and his angels to ensure Lucia would heal the massive crowd.

Philip started the meeting by announcing that all two thousand five hundred people in the stadium were healed, however that was not including the thousands that were not registered but had stormed the stadium with hope that they somehow would be healed, too. The miracle was documented by the press and was announced throughout the world. In fact, each of the other Healers also received a ring and plans were being made for a mass-healing event in their own country. Philip thought that Sister Lucia was the Lord's guinea pig, testing her healing abilities. Lucia laughed and told Philip, the Lord knew exactly what was going to happen. Even Gabriel showed no concern and floated away when she fainted, which is probably why he allowed David to be so close. Philip continued sharing that some of the guards received minor injuries when the crowd rushed the clearing, but for some mystical reason, not one person could get within fifty feet of where Sister Lucia was lying.

"It seems the Lord will always protect you, Sister Lucia. I need not have been so worried about you," Philip told her.

Jacob then informed her that once the angels appeared, many of the observers fled the stadium and it took hours to clear the cars and stragglers. Reporters had flooded the outside of the stadium and were interviewing anyone who attended the event. Jacob was just glad that his security team did not leave their post in spite of angels floating all over the stadium and he thanked God that the heavy metal doors around the outside held fast, however thousands had already entered the stadium before they were able to close them.

Dr. David squeezed Lucia's hand and informed her that as she was healing the crowd, he inched closer and closer to her until he was within a foot and the angel Gabriel finally held his hand up to stop. It was as if he knew Sister Lucia was going to collapse and needed the doctor close by. David had carried the unconscious woman out the back entrance to a waiting helicopter. He informed Lucia and the group that before flying off, he assessed that her vital signs were textbook perfect. Her heart rate was completely normal and she did respond to pain. So making a split second decision, which he thought was heavenly inserted in his head, he redirected the helicopter to the Convent. Lucia was arousable on the second day but never stayed awake long enough to answer questions. Lucia did not remember any of it, and she was glad that Dr. David brought her home. Yes, she admitted to herself that the Convent was her home and the nuns, her family of which Dr. David, Becky and Claire were a main part.

Now, it was Lucia's turn to tell them what happened to her. She explained how her body filled with an extraordinary energy, like a super power she told them. The ring was buzzing on her hand and it felt like energy was being created in the center of her body and traveled out her fingertips. She felt like the Trilogy was inside her, the Father, the Son and the Holy Ghost and that is was them directing the healing energy throughout each section of the stadium. Through it all, Lucia had felt lighter than air, almost like she was floating as she directed her arms back and forth over the crowd. The energy just kept flowing without waning or weakening.

Lucia remained quiet for a moment. It was hard for her to continue because she could remember how it felt when the energy stopped. She crashed and burned as they say. At first, she could no longer feel filled with the Spirit of the Holy Trinity; it was a loss like no other. She felt the abrupt cessation of energy being created. It wasn't like the energy flow slowed down; it just stopped. Lucia continued and described how her arms and legs began shaking uncontrollably. Her whole body then went numb and everything went black.

"I remember calling for Dr. David, but that's about it." Lucia finished. "Thank you for catching me, Dr. David. I didn't know you were that close and I thought I was going to hit the ground."

The small group was quiet, taking in what Lucia had told them.
After a few minutes, Lucia added another very important detail. "Oh, and I am pretty sure my healing ability is over. Gabriel had whispered in my ear before I went down. He said I had done well. The Lord was well pleased and since I and my team had completed our part of the Lord's Divine Plan, He no longer needed me to serve as his healing vessel; but know this Sister Lucia, there is a place in Heaven when your time on this earthly plane is over."

Growing tired, Lucia had Mother Superior assist her back to her room. She was completely drained and needed more rest. It would take a few more days before she was back on her feet. The Archbishop had reassured Sister Lucia that the Convent was her forever home and Becky was welcome for as long as she wanted to stay. Lucia was relieved that she was not being thrown out; she had nowhere else she wanted to be. Mary Ellen met them half way to her room and worked with Maggie to get the former Healer back to bed.

    Alone and lying in bed, Lucia thought about the miraculous journey the Lord had chosen for her. It was long and demanding, at times, she doubted herself and her ability to carry out the Lord's Plan, but she persisted in spite of her doubt, and not only had she been used to heal so many men, women and children; she had met so many wonderful and loving new friends. She silently thanked the Lord for choosing her to be a Healer and give so many people back their health. Lucia thought on the many miracles God had performed through her. She thought back to her tiny little apartment where she cried every night alone and prayed to the Lord for the return of her family and friends. The Lord did not disappoint. Although, she would always lament the loss of her son, she had her daughter and granddaughter. And Dr. David was like a son to her. She had great friends such as the Archbishop, Pope Leo, Mary Ellen, Bea, John, Maggie and all the sisters at the Convent. And how could she forget Jack, Robert, Vincent and Matthew. She then remembered they were coming to visit her next week. Yes, the Lord had answered her prayers and truly blessed her. She was no longer alone in this world and certainly never lonely.

Epilogue
Five years later ……

Sister Lucia was working in the garden. Today, the sun above was beating down on her, so she took a small rest on the bench under a nearby tree. There Sister Lucia sat, a sun hat on her head and her gardening gloves on her hands, hands that were no longer ethereal as in the past, but calloused and worn. She loved working in the garden and weeding brought her peace and calmness in her soul. Her thoughts went over all that had happened over the past five years. She was no longer known as the Healer, but settled comfortably for the title of Sister Lucia.
The Archbishop and Maggie had brought significant change to the Convent, and had the nuns extensively involved in community projects. Many of these projects involved programs to strengthen family units and others to promote deep seeded religious programs for youth in order to combat the influence of gangs, drugs and other outside influences. The churches were still overwhelmingly full, especially on Sunday, since there were many who bore witness and still remembered the power the Lord had demonstrated through a small but mighty woman.
 Mary Ellen was still coming by several nights a week for dinner and always accompanied by Jacob Bronson. They made a charming couple and remained great friends of Sister Lucia's. Jacob had told her that the last of the Healers had lost the ability. All of them had retired to religious orders around the globe. Their work was done. The Roman Catholic Church had been reinstated as the strongest and most populated across the world; even the

Communist countries could not deny there was a God anymore.

    David and Becky married three years ago and Becky was now expecting a son in two months. Lucia was thrilled as she loved Dr. David like a son and she would often go and visit them in the new home they had purchased not far from the Convent. The first time Lucia went to visit, she noticed that Becky had hung up family pictures all over the walls. They really made the place a home, one, which David rushed back to each day to spend time with his family. David asked Becky if they could name their son Joseph, and Becky knowing the reason, readily consented. Sister Lucia had shared that with Victoria, who although shed a few tears, was happy that he chose to name his son after theirs.

    Sister Lucia had recently received an invitation to the Ordination of Father Simon Murkowski. The Archbishop had asked that he be assigned to his diocese, especially when Father Lucas was told that Lucia healed his mother. Father Lucas informed Sister Lucia when Simon had joined the seminary and she was thrilled to hear it. She couldn't wait to see Janet and Gerald again. Lucia always delighted in seeing those whose lives she had changed to see how they were doing. Simon had written Sister Lucia every Christmas, still thanking her for saving his mother. Next to Dr. David, Simon was the sweetest boy she had ever met. A gift from God she would tell Janet.

    Bobby and Diana visited at least once a month and usually brought the kids with them. There were two boys and as predicted, they were as stubborn as Bobby, but so loving. Sometimes, Bobby brought his mother who was forever grateful for Lucia's ability to get through to her son.

"How different things would have been for us if you had not interceded, Sister Lucia," the mother would always tell her.

James and Victoria could only stop by once a year since James accepted a better position four states away. Thank God for Facetime, because Victoria called often and sent pictures of little Rachel. The little girl was the spitting image of Victoria, and the apple of James's eye. In almost every picture, Sister Lucia could see her hugging her pink teddy bear. Fortunately, both husband and wife kept their secret and the visits to Joey had not stopped. At least once a month, the two of them were transported to Heaven to visit with their son and Victoria's parents, for which they were eternally thankful.

Pope Leo passed recently. Sister Lucia and the Archbishop were invited to attend the funeral and were given seats up front to the amazement of everyone. Sister Lucia finally had the opportunity to meet all the other Healers who were invited and attended. It was amazing to finally be together with them and although not all spoke English, love was a universal language that they all were fluent in, plus translators had been provided so they could share their stories with each other. They all seemed to look up to Sister Lucia since she was the first and the oldest. Each of them brought their black shawl and wore the ring given by St. Mary, which still could not be removed from their finger. The Archbishop had insisted the group take a picture together and Sister Lucia treasured it.

The ceremony was long and filled with traditions honoring the well-liked Pope who served his people faithfully. All during the ceremony, the Archbishop made comments about how the Pope and Mother Superior have probably taken over in Heaven making Lucia struggle to hold in her laugh. She could still see Mother Superior grasping the Medallion tightly on her chest. Lucia was sure that Sister Louisa gave Gabriel and the other angels a run for their money. Father Lucas told Sister Lucia he was jealous of their passing, but the Sister told him there was still work to do and he was needed here.

Then, she reminded him, "Whom would Maggie and Mary Ellen complain about if you left us?" and that got him laughing.

Jack spent most Sundays with Sister Lucia after he attended Mass. He had even taught her how to play poker and they used Monopoly money for betting. She had grown to like the game and especially loved it when she would beat him. It wasn't often, but even the few times she did, she relished the victory and the sour puss on Jack's face. His support group had grown and even though Lucia could no longer heal, she would visit the men and pray with them. Jack still used his cane, which now he used to hit people who got in his way. Some people never change.

The Convent was a busy bustling hive of activity. The nuns could be found surfing the Internet for new projects or ideas for community improvement as well as networking with other religious orders, some in other countries. Maggie, as Sister Lucia comfortably called her, kept everyone busy and involved. She believed with every fiber of her body in the power of prayer, and prayed with Lucia every day for the healing of her relationship with her son. After all the time that had passed, Sister Lucia believed this was surely a lost cause.

So it was with great surprise and shock that on one special Sunday, David, holding five-year-old Claire, and a very pregnant Becky walked in to the Convent asking if they could bring a friend and his children to dinner. She went on to tell her mother that his wife, who had taken all his money and possessions, had recently abandoned her "friend" and his two kids. Becky told her mother that she thought her mother would be especially considerate of his circumstances and offer him much-needed consolation. Sister Lucia agreed at once, knowing from past experience how any kindness and support was greatly needed and appreciated during this tragic time. Her eyes watered just remembering how isolated and depressed she had felt after her husband's deception. She may not be able to heal but she could definitely offer some help and compassion at this man's time of need.

Becky left to go get the man and his two children from the car where they were waiting. In the meantime, Lucia added three more place settings at the table. She let the sisters know that three more guests were coming and they assured her there was enough food. Lucia brought Claire into the kitchen where she received unlimited love and affection from all the sisters. The nuns always spoiled her with gifts and candy whenever she came to visit. Some things never change she thought.

Lucia returned to the dining room to find Becky and the small family standing in the doorway. The man was around thirtyish and sported a short beard and glasses. His dark brown hair was neatly trimmed and Sister Lucia noticed flecks of gray giving him a distinguished air. The two children, a boy and a girl, stood on either side of him and looked frightened to be here. They both had his dark hair and dark eyes. Lucia's heart broke. Returning her eyes to the man, she was about to welcome him and tell him she was glad he and his family could join them for dinner, when her eyes met his, Lucia was suddenly overcome with a feeling of familiarity. Her mouth opened but no words came out. The man just stood there staring at her. His eyes, so much like her own, watering and his lips were trembling.

Lucia, so afraid to ask, whispered the words she had prayed for so long, "Ryan, is that you?" Lucia opened her arms and without thinking Ryan ran into them, holding his mother so tight, she could barely breathe, but she did not complain. Her son was home in her arms. God had given her everything; there was not a thing on this earth Lucia could ask for.

After the long, warm welcoming embrace of his mother, Ryan introduced his two children. Like his father, Ryan's wife had disappeared after cleaning out the bank accounts and mortgaging the house to the limit. She had taken it all and Ryan had nothing but two kids; leaving him virtually homeless. His father and his wife had relocated to Tennessee and although they offered him a place to stay, Ryan could not leave his job. That and his children were all he had. His father encouraged him to reconnect with his mother, but Ryan felt guilty for how he had treated her. In desperation, he sought out his sister for help and asked her to help him find their mother so he could repair their relationship. He wanted to beg his mother for her forgiveness, but Lucia told him he never had to beg. There was not a day that went by that Lucia did not send him her love, even when he turned his back on her.

Lucia held her two new grandchildren and walked them around the Convent introducing them to everyone she saw. Similar to Claire, the sisters spoiled them with gifts and candy and tons of affection. Soon they were running around the room laughing and playing with the nuns.

Ryan had told her that he had found a cheap rent in the inner city but was having difficulty with day care. Lucia assured him that she would watch them for him, but told him she would prefer he be closer to the Convent so his travel was not so far.

Lucia had recently found out that Father Lucas had been contributing to an account for Lucia since her arrival to the Convent. The Archbishop thought she knew about it and had recently asked her why she never took money from her savings. She was happy she hadn't because she now offered it to Ryan as a down payment on a small house in the area and when he refused, Lucia put her foot down. She spoke in her sternest voice and told him that as his mother, she was entitled to do what she wanted with her money. Becky agreed. Ryan fell back in her arms and couldn't say I'm sorry enough and how much he missed her but was afraid she would turn her back on him.

"Never," she told him, "Never, not in a thousand years," his mother told him.

Sister Lucia looked up to see Maggie standing at the doorway giving her a thumbs up sign.

Then she raised her hands in prayer, "Works every time. Sometimes it just takes a while."

Made in United States
North Haven, CT
27 September 2023